BLOOD & MIDNIGHT

THE WITCH'S MONSTERS BOOK 1

Blood and Midnight
The Witch's Monsters, Book One
Copyright © 2021 by Sarah Piper
SarahPiperBooks.com

Published by Two Gnomes Media

Cover design by Luminescence Covers

This book is a work of fiction. Names, characters, places, businesses, organizations, brands, media, and incidents are either products of the author's imagination or are used fictitiously. Any resemblance to actual events, locations, or persons, living or dead, is entirely coincidental.

v3

E-book ISBN: 978-1-948455-57-2
Paperback ISBN: 978-1-948455-28-2
Audiobook ISBN: 978-1-948455-64-0

BOOK SERIES BY SARAH PIPER

M/F Romance Series

Monstrous Obsessions

Vampire Royals of New York

Reverse Harem Romance Series

Claimed by Gargoyles

The Witch's Monsters

Tarot Academy

The Witch's Rebels

GET CONNECTED!

I love connecting with readers! There are a few different ways you can keep in touch:

Email: sarah@sarahpiperbooks.com

TikTok: @sarahpiperbooks

Facebook group: Sarah Piper's Sassy Witches

Twitter: @sarahpiperbooks

Newsletter: Never miss a new release or a sale! Sign up for the VIP Readers Club:
sarahpiperbooks.com/readers-club

DEDICATION

To the woman who missed someone so much,
it hollowed out her fucking insides.

To the woman who saved up her tears for the shower,
where no one could hear her cry.

To the woman who fell to her knees
over a song, a scent, a photograph.

To the woman who stood alone at the witching hour,
forehead pressed to the window,
wondering how the fuck it'd even happened.

To the woman who didn't know
if she could drag herself up off the floor
to face another day.

I see you, you fucking goddess.
I've always seen you.
You were never alone.

Just because you fell apart
doesn't mean you're broken.

So, scream if you have to.
Cry.
Shatter.
Fucking feel it.

You're still the baddest bitch.

This story is for you.

PROLOGUE
HALEY

There's an old adage about the difference between falling in love with a hero and falling in love with a villain. Go for the latter, it says, because a hero would ultimately sacrifice you to save the world, but a villain? He'd burn down the world just to save *you*.

Sounds pretty epic, right? And let's be honest—who doesn't love a bad boy?

The thing about villains, though... Ultimately, they're just the heroes of their own stories. Still fighting for a cause. Still trying to prove something to the world.

Trust me, I've fallen for both. And those assholes? They broke my heart every damn time.

So now I've got a new saying:

Screw the heroes and villains.

I want the *monsters*.

Dark. Vicious. Depraved. The men who slide into your

heart like a surgical blade, so sharp you don't even feel it until you're on your knees, trembling and soaked in blood.

A monster won't try to woo you with roses and chocolates, with sweet promises whispered across satin pillowcases. He'll kick down a fucking door to get to you, though. Snap a man's neck just for leering. One threat against you, and he'll tear out the guy's throat with his teeth, then kiss you with a mouth full of blood, no apologies.

A monster's got nothing to prove and nothing left to lose.

And in bed?

Damn.

He'll *own* you, pushing until he finds the very edge of your limits, then smashing right through them. And oh, how you'll *beg* him for it—beg him to break you, again and again and again. To absolutely ruin you for anything less than a life of obsession and fire.

And while the hero slays his dragons and the villain burns down the world for the woman he loves, the monster will simply hand you the matches and gasoline, step aside, and smile as you burn it down yourself.

Because all along, the monster always knew you could.

He just had to make sure you knew it, too.

The blood on my boots was still wet when I stepped inside.

My weapons needed a good cleaning too, but the novitiate asked me to leave the daggers and stakes at the entrance, and I obliged.

The Temple of the Dark Moon, she reminded me, was a holy place.

Right.

Appropriately chastised, I nodded and followed the swish of her long black robes across the threshold, my eyes widening as the interior came into view.

The temple had probably been beautiful once, but now it lay in ruins. Half the ceiling had caved in, and broken pillars of onyx and moonstone flanked the inner sanctuary, several of them reduced to rubble. Deep, angry gouges scored the masonry as if some feral god-beast had been locked up inside.

Everything smelled like rot and death.

What the hell happened here?

Hoping whatever it was had already been dealt with, I lowered my eyes and quickened the pace.

"Yours?" the novitiate asked from beneath her dark hood, and I knew she meant the blood I'd tracked across the chipped marble floor. I wondered if she'd be the one mopping it up later or if that would be my job now—one of the many menial tasks the Goddess surely had in store for me.

"No." I scraped the toe of my boot along the floor and left another smear, which was about all the acknowledgment the previous owner of the blood deserved. "Listen, I'm sorry about the mess, but I was summoned here kind of last-minute and I didn't really have time to... I mean... Should I bathe before I meet her?" I dragged the back of my hand across my forehead, skin gritty with dirt and sweat and probably more blood. "Maybe do a purifying juice cleanse or... something?"

With a serene smile, the novitiate lowered her hood and said, "The Goddess Melantha does not require purity of body. Only purity of intent."

She looked younger than I expected—only a teenager—and she wasn't a witch. Just a regular human girl. I wondered what she'd done to end up a servant in the realm of the Dark Goddess, a place you couldn't even access without being summoned by the deity herself, then portaled in by her magick. Ruined or not, this temple was more than just a holy place—it existed in a liminal space all its own, nothing but stars and darkness as far as the eye could see.

Didn't the girl have parents? Friends? *Someone* missing her on the other side?

A sharp pain lanced my heart, but I breathed through it. I had no idea how long the girl had been here, but this was merely day one for me, and I had a long road ahead. I needed to stay grounded. Committed.

"How will she know my intentions are pure?" I asked. "Is there a test?"

"Fear not, Daughter of Darkwinter. I'm certain Her Holiness will be quite impressed with your offering."

Ignoring the Darkwinter bit, I forced a smile and scratched the back of my neck, sneaking a covert whiff of my armpit.

Let's hope her Holiness is impressed with Eau de Urban Warfare, because that's about all I'm offering at the moment...

"Come. She's expecting you." Still wearing a look of pure serenity, she continued on through a doorway at the back of the temple sanctuary, gesturing for me to follow.

The antechamber was small and intimate, much less imposing than the main temple. The warm glow of hundreds of candles flickered across plain mud walls and a low ceiling, the ground nothing but bare earth. My boots sank into it with every step, and as the scents of candle wax and dirt washed over me, I let out a sigh of relief.

This room, at least, had remained untouched by whatever monster had gone batshit crazy in the sanctuary.

My eyes adjusted to the candlelight, my gaze drifting to the stone altar in the center of the room—a large slab covered in fresh flowers and bowls of fruit, ringed by votive candles in red glass orbs.

Offerings, I assumed. For the...

Oh, shit.

I gasped as I finally spotted the boy, no more than ten or eleven, lying in repose on the altar. His skin was milk white, the robe they'd dressed him in much too large, as if it was borrowed in haste from someone much older.

Someone much closer to death than this child should've been.

"How did he pass?" I whispered.

"He didn't." The novitiate frowned. "Melantha's son is very much alive."

"Her *son*?" I couldn't hide my shock. The Dark Goddess was tens of thousands of years old—probably older. Lots of witches prayed to her, worshipped her, wrote volumes about her history and magick. I'd never once heard of a child. "How long has he been like this?"

"Six months." She sighed, running her fingers through the sweep of dark hair across his forehead. "He was cursed by a dark fae warlord called Keradoc. A vicious monster who punishes children for the sins of their parents."

An icy shiver ran down my spine. Dark fae were powerful, but Melantha was a dark *goddess*. *The* dark goddess. How could a fae warlord have gotten anywhere *near* her child? And what sin could she have committed to provoke such terrible retribution?

"He's alive," the novitiate continued, "but his soul is trapped in moonglass." She retrieved a small wooden chest from the offerings at his side, opening it to reveal a glass-like sphere as delicate as a soap bubble. At her gentle touch, it glowed with a bright, pearlescent sheen. "It's made from pure moonlight, cast with dark fae magick that's been banned for thousands of years."

"Because it's a prison," I said, disgust churning inside. It wasn't the first time I'd encountered moonglass. According to legend, the very first fae created it by deceiving the moon into lending the fae her light, then forging the magickal globes to trap the souls of their enemies. Eventually, they'd release those souls into the most hostile fae realms, sentencing them to an eternity of torment. "How did this happen?"

She met my eyes, but her serene smile was gone, replaced now with a look of grim determination. "What matters, Daughter of Darkwinter, is that you alone can free him."

"Me? But... how?"

"Breaking the curse requires the blood of the one who cast it."

"Keradoc. Of course." I blew out a breath, the tightness in my muscles loosening as the pieces clicked into place. I was a blood witch—a damned good one at that. Melantha needed me to do some sort of spell to help the child. "So, when do we start?"

"You will travel to his realm as soon as possible," she replied. "Once you've extracted the blood, you'll return to the Temple of the Dark Moon to perform the spell with Melantha, breaking the curse and—"

"Wait. Did you just..." I blinked at her, my mind racing to keep up. "You don't have his blood? Then how can I do the spell?"

"As I said, once you return to the Temple—"

"Her Holiness expects me to hunt this guy down? Some psychotic warlord from a realm I've never been to?"

She arched an eyebrow, as if in warning. "Her Holiness granted you untold strength and power in your time of need, for which you so eagerly pledged your service."

Tension simmered in the air as she glared at me, making my skin hot and itchy.

"I know. It's just..." I took a breath, trying to regroup. Who *was* this girl, anyway? Where were the other novitiates? Melantha's soldiers? "Forgive me, but when Her Holiness summoned me, I was under the impression I'd be meeting with her elite guard."

"Elite? Hardly." A bitter laugh rang out through the small chamber. "No honor among them. No fortitude. I'm sorry, but the Guard of the Dark Moon is no more."

A prickle of unease tingled at the back of my mind. What the hell did "no more" mean?

Fired? Furloughed? Executed?

Crushed to death by falling pillars?

None of this made any sense.

I paced before the altar, my sudden movement snuffing out a few of the votives. "The guards are gone, so now it's on *me* to assassinate some creepy warlord?"

"Not assassinate, no. If Keradoc dies before we perform the spell, the blood will be useless." She grabbed a taper candle and touched it to one of the votives, reigniting the flame. "You must retrieve the blood without harming him —without so much as *alerting* him—or all will be for naught."

"Are you serious? You just said he's a warlord!"

"And you're a formidable blood witch, are you not? One with access to spells and magick you're only just beginning to tap into."

"I'm good at what I do, sure. But dark fae warlords? I'm not... Look, you seem... knowledgeable. Clearly, you're fond of the boy." I smiled, fighting to keep the desperation from my voice. "Maybe you should go instead? I'll stay here and keep an eye on things until you get back." I took the taper from her hand and lit the remaining votives. "See? Already getting the hang of it."

She pinched one of the flames between her thumb and forefinger, the frustration in her eyes finally boiling over. "One candle remains unlit to honor the darkness that exists in all of us, without which we can never know the light."

"Right." I raised my hands in surrender. "I should've known that, but I didn't. That's what I'm trying to tell you. I'm not the witch for the job. I'll do anything else she asks of me, but—"

"*This* is the quest the Goddess has set out for you," she snapped. The girl was unraveling, her eyes blazing, her voice nearly trembling. "Are you reneging on your sacred vow?"

"No, of course not. I just think we should look at all the options. I'm sure if we put our heads together, we can—"

"How *dare* you question the will of the Goddess!" she bellowed, the force of it making the ground rumble. Her eyes turned a fiery red, two hot embers smoldering in a shadow-dark face. Flames crackled suddenly at her feet, the inferno rising higher and higher until she was completely engulfed.

The mud walls cracked and bubbled around us, and I watched in mute horror as her robes burned away to reveal a body as black as the night sky, pale white serpents slithering around her thighs and torso. Her limbs elongated before my eyes, twisting like those of an ancient tree, hands and feet curling into monstrous talons. Two massive black wings burst from her back and smashed through the walls of the antechamber, each feather dripping with blood.

The altar remained untouched, the boy undisturbed.

I stumbled backward, my heart slamming against my ribs.

The novitiate.

All along, it was her. Melantha.

And this was her true form. Dark and magnificent. Hideous and terrifying.

I dropped to my knees, half-tripping, half awed, and bowed my head. "Forgive me, Your Holiness. I was wrong to question you."

Sharp claws pierced the underside of my chin, forcing me to look up and meet her fearsome gaze. I blinked through the pain, ignoring the warm blood trickling down my neck.

"Daughter of Darkwinter," she said, her voice echoing across the night like a death knell. "If you value the lives of the sisters you fought so bravely to protect in Blackmoon Bay, you *will* achieve this task. By blood and by blade, as you have promised."

By blood and by blade.

The words of my spell echoed as clearly as they had the night I'd first spoken them.

Blood of hell, blood of night
I call on the darkness to show us the light
May evil and malice and violence intended
Return to its hosts uprooted, upended
Dark Goddess I bend, Dark Goddess I bow
Hear my petition, and thusly I vow
My service is yours, by blood and by blade
Until my last breath shall deem it unmade.

That night, my allies and I—my sisters among them—had been trapped in a prison compound hidden in the Olympic National Forest. We'd managed to free the prisoners—dozens of witches and other supernaturals captured by human hunters and the corrupt fae they were working for—but soon our enemies surrounded us, outgunning us four to one. They were hybrids—nearly unstoppable beasts with the combined powers of vampires, shifters, and genetically altered super-monsters we couldn't even identify.

Even with our own formidable team of supernatural heavy-hitters, there was no way we could've survived their relentless attack.

In a last, desperate move, I petitioned Melantha for the strength and magick to turn the tides. She answered my call at once, and thanks to her, we earned our victory—first retaking the compound, then finishing the job last night at the Battle of Blackmoon Bay.

The battle for our lives and our home. For everything we held dear.

I glanced down at my boots, the last of the blood soaking into the dirt, along with any hope I had of avoiding this disastrous mission.

If I refused her, everything I was able to accomplish through the spell would be undone. The city of Blackmoon Bay would fall. My sisters—the family I'd only just discovered—would die. And everything we'd fought so hard to save would just...

It would end.

A surge of renewed strength shot through my limbs, my blood simmering with magick. *My* magick.

"My service is yours," I said now, repeating the vow I'd made that night. "By blood and by blade. Until my last breath shall deem it unmade."

"Rise, Daughter of Darkwinter."

I got to my feet and met her gaze once more, hoping like hell we were done with the Big Goddess Energy show. I'd seen enough of her scary magnificence to fill my nightmares for the next decade, thanks.

Her dark wings fluttered in the breeze, and the same rot and ruin I'd smelled in the sanctuary assaulted my senses. I tried not to recoil.

"Are you prepared to accept this task?" she asked. "To see it through by any means necessary?"

"I am," I said firmly. I was in it to win it now, no going

back. With what I hoped was a confident smile, I asked, "What must I do?"

Melantha extended her arms. One claw held my weapons. The other clutched a glass vial about the size of a tube of lipstick.

After re-securing my stakes and blades, I took the vial and peered inside. Magick swirled beneath the glass, red smoke shot through with threads of black and gold. It was oddly mesmerizing.

"Keradoc dwells in the dark fae realm of Midnight," she said. "This portal spell will take you there, but you won't survive it alone. There's a man in your home realm— also fae—one rumored to have escaped Midnight alive. You must ask for his assistance."

My heart stalled. All the confidence I'd conjured up evaporated in an instant.

The ground spun out from beneath my feet, and I fell back to my knees, my lungs struggling to suck in air.

Deep inside, beneath all the magick and fire, behind all the parts of myself I'd sharpened into weapons and hardened into shields, a tiny box lay hidden, bolted with iron chains and encased in cement. That box held my darkest, most private pain. All the ghosts that had the power to eat through my very soul.

I'd sealed them away years ago, vowing to never open that box again, no matter how often it called to me. And though it still rattled inside on occasion, for the most part, I'd kept it on strict lockdown.

Until now.

The dark fae realm of Midnight... One rumored to have escaped... Ask for his assistance...

Her words were the bolt-cutters on those iron chains, unleashing all the pain I'd so diligently buried. It seeped into my heart, burning it like hot acid, taunting me from across the long years as if no time had passed at all.

Midnight. The most treacherous realm in the universe, controlled by the darkest of the dark fae. A place where the sun never rose and so much blood had been spilled upon its war-torn lands, the lakes and rivers ran red. Melantha was right—there was no way I'd survive it alone.

And the fae who had?

There was no way I'd survive *him*, either.

Not again.

"I will return you to the mortal plane," the Goddess continued, as if I wasn't falling apart before her eyes. "To the city of—"

"New Orleans," I whispered, and she nodded, sealing my fate.

A tear slipped down my cheek.

New Orleans. The one place I swore I'd never, ever go. A place that terrified me even more than Midnight.

No, not because of the ghosts that haunted the city's many cemeteries and historic landmarks.

Because of the ghosts that haunted my heart. The ones she'd just set loose.

"And this... this *fae*," I said, still unable to speak his name out loud, even after all these years. "If he refuses to help me?"

Her black lips twisted into a cruel grin, her wings spreading to their full, terrifying span. The ground rumbled beneath her feet, but instead of flames, skulls rose from the dirt, a dead army blooming at her command.

Behind me, a portal opened, ready to ferry me to New Orleans.

To him.

"Convince him, Darkwinter," Melantha hissed. "Or the ones you claim to love will suffer the consequences of your failure."

I nodded and took a deep breath.

Fought off an onslaught of memories—strong hands sliding into my hair. Eyes the color of molten silver. Promises whispered, promises broken. The salty taste of tears and the dull ache of wounds that never fully healed.

I took a step backward, then another.

Closed my eyes.

And tumbled, ass over teakettle, into my own private hell.

2

———

HALEY

*T*wo years.

That's how long I'd spent convincing myself this place didn't exist. Convincing myself that Elian's return from captivity in Midnight and the subsequent launching of a whole new life in New Orleans—one that *didn't* include me—was just a rumor.

Now, standing before the entrance to his exclusive French Quarter club, I could no longer deny the truth.

Saints and Sinners, the sign read. To humans, it was just another abandoned cathedral with blown-out windows and crumbling spires, complete with a hulking gargoyle perched above the main archway.

But for those of us who could see past the illusion of the fae glamour, a set of glowing silver doors awaited—an invitation I still couldn't bring myself to answer.

There were no bouncers or velvet ropes, no demands

17

for the secret password. Just the ancient gargoyle and the doors and a small plaque reminding me this was hallowed ground, so could I please check my weapons at the armory inside the narthex?

I practically snorted.

Fat fucking chance.

This was no Temple of the Dark Moon. Just because Elian's den of supernatural sin was housed in an old church, that didn't make it hallowed ground any more than it made him a priest.

No one showed up in a place like this looking for redemption, anyway.

They showed up looking for an escape.

Or in my case—to beg.

Damn it. The thought of even *facing* that prick again— let alone asking him for help—tied me up in knots. But what choice did I have? My sisters' lives depended on me seeing this all the way through, and Elian truly was my best shot at surviving the horrors of Midnight.

Probably my *only* shot.

So, decked out in a new lace dress the color of the stars and thigh-high leather boots I'd picked out just to make him suffer, strapped from hip to ankle with weapons that would finish the job if the outfit failed, I pushed open the doors and stepped inside.

And immediately fell under its spell.

Everything about the place was designed to hypnotize, from the rich, blood-red walls to the restored stained-glass windows that pulsed with magick. Suspended in gilded cages from the ceiling, painted fae couples performed dances so erotic, I was already wishing for a cold shower. Semi-private candlelit alcoves lined both sides of the former cathedral, and the pews had been removed from the nave, the flooring replaced with black marble that glittered with tiny silver points.

It looked as if the club's many revelers were dancing across the night sky.

I was relieved not to spot Elian among them. Despite the fever-inducing performances of the fae dancers, five years' worth of resentment and abandonment issues still simmered inside, and one look into his entrancing silver eyes would set it all ablaze.

Not a fire I wanted to face while sober.

Chin raised, shoulders squared, I beelined for the bar and slid onto an empty barstool at the end, trying to spot any potential threats. Hunters were always my first concern, but we'd taken a pretty big bite out of their organization during the Battle at Blackmoon Bay. Those who remained loyal to their fucked-up cause would likely be licking their wounds for a good long while.

Here at Saints and Sinners, vampires and fae made up the majority of the clientele, all of them rich, well-dressed, and predatory. The fae were even more refined than the bloodsuckers, their otherworldly beauty as mesmerizing as it was dangerous.

The bartender, though... He didn't fit the profile. Demon. Rough around the edges. A head of messy, jet-black hair and a mouth so sultry it was almost a crime to look at. He wore a white dress shirt and dark slacks but no tie, his sleeves rolled up to reveal muscular forearms mapped with scars.

My own scars practically tingled in response.

As he finished up with one of his vampire customers, I studied him. Another sexy scar ran the full length of his face, slicing through his eyebrow and ending in the dark stubble along his jaw. A black patch covered the injured eye.

When he finally made his way over to me, he nodded and set a coaster on the bar, but didn't smile or say hello. Just waited, arms crossed over his broad chest, one blue eye glowering at me like he was daring me to ask about the missing one.

What I *really* wanted to ask was what time he got off work and how soon he'd like to get started on becoming my next ex-boyfriend, but...

"Drinking or leaving, new girl?" he asked, smooth and cold as ice. "You're holding up the line."

I took a deep breath, trying to re-focus on the mission.

Midnight.

Begging.

Elian.

"Drinking. Definitely drinking. I'll have... I don't know." I offered a flirty smile. "Whatever you think I'll like."

He leaned in close, his demonic scent enveloping me. It reminded me of the smoke that lingered in your hair when you spent too much time by the fire, a hint of lemon simmering beneath it, and holy *hell* did I want to jump across the bar and—

"I need a bit more to go on," he said, then shot me an icy grin to match his voice. "If it's not too much trouble for you."

"Fine. Let's do something with a kick, but nothing boring or predictable. That rules out whisky, vodka, and tequila. I'm not a huge fan of bubbles either, and I don't like anything too milky. Sweet's good, but not *too* sweet, and a little fruit is fine, but nothing *super* fruity, unless it's—"

"Sorry I asked." Without waiting for me to finish, he wiped his hands on the towel draped over his shoulder, selected a martini glass from the rack overhead, and turned toward the multi-colored bottles lined up behind him.

Before I could offer any more helpful pointers, a wave of vertigo hit, alerting me to the presence of a vampire. One getting way too close and personal.

"Did it hurt?" A husky voice breathed in my ear.

I turned to meet his gaze, resting bitch face locked and loaded. "Excuse me?"

"When you fell from Heaven?" He spread his arms and grinned as if I might find the whole package so charming I'd leap into his embrace, wrap my thighs around him, and ride him all the way home.

"Not as much as it did when they cut off my horns and tail," I said. "Anyway, I'm all set here, so... Have a good night."

"Can I at least buy you a drink, beautiful?"

"No, thank you. I'm not interested."

His face fell, then twisted into a scowl. "You don't have to be such a bitch."

"Actually, I do. Because otherwise bloodsuckers like you assume a smile or a kind word is a full-on invitation to Pussytown, and I promise you, friend. *That's* an exclusive ticket."

"Check the guest list again." He reached over and touched my hair, bringing a lock to his lips before dropping his hand to my thigh and giving it a possessive squeeze. "Pretty sure I'm on it."

Pretty sure you're going to regret touching me, but ooh-kay...

"Well, since you're so persistent," I cooed, "maybe I *should* check." With a faux-seductive smile, I slid my fingers into the top of my boot, seeking that cold, comforting piece of wood I never left home without.

One minute, the hawthorn stake was minding its own business in the boot holster. The next, it was jammed into the back of the fucker's hand.

Such was the beauty of my sharp and pointy friend.

He jerked back with a howl, the hawthorn poison already paralyzing his fingers. I yanked the stake free, spun it in my palm, and shoved it against his crotch, stopping just short of inflicting a more serious injury.

"Touch me again, bloodsucker," I hissed, "and your hand won't be the only thing going limp."

"Go... go fuck yourself, bitch."

"I'd return the sentiment, but I'm pretty sure that hand won't be up for the job any time soon." I laughed. "Get it? Hand? Job?"

He bared his fangs, then stumbled away like a wounded, dejected bird.

"First drink is on me," the bartender said. "That was the best thing I've seen in months."

I reached forward and yanked the towel off his shoulder, then wiped the blood from my stake. "Thanks for the assist, demon."

"You had it handled. Be grateful I don't toss your ass out for smuggling in that stake."

"This teeny tiny little thing?" I finished cleaning it off, then slipped it back into the holster. "It's not like it was going to kill him."

Wooden stakes could poison the fuckers—hawthorn

was especially good at interfering with their healing abilities, and a well-placed stake to the chest would knock them out for hours—but still, that was just a temporary fix. Killing vampires required decapitation or burning, and I wasn't about to ruin my new outfit with all *that* mess.

"In any case, best not to draw too much attention." The bartender set down the martini glass, now brimming with pale amber liquid. A single mint leaf floated on top.

"What is it?"

The barest hint of a smile quirked his lips. "It's called a Fallen Angel."

It was the smile that saved him. *Asshole.*

Hiding my return grin behind the rim of the glass, I took a sip, then another.

Damn, that Fallen Angel concoction was good—good enough to savor over a long conversation laced with innuendo. A conversation that on any other night might've led to a kiss and maybe even an orgasm or two.

But tonight?

I tipped back the glass and chugged it all down. Then, before I could talk myself out of it, I said, "I'm looking for Elian."

3

I blew out a breath, seriously impressed with my ability to say the bastard's name without crying and/or breaking something.

Progress!

The sexy bartender, however, was *not* impressed. Quite the opposite, actually.

"Elian," he said flatly, folding his arms over his chest again, and I swear the temperature dropped ten degrees.

It didn't feel like jealousy. Aside from a little teasing, he wasn't exactly putting out any "let's take this back to my place" vibes. So why did he clam up when I asked about Elian?

"Is he in tonight?" I pressed.

The guy sized me up with his singularly intense blue eye, which apparently found me lacking. When his gaze finally made its way back to mine, he scowled as if I'd just threatened *his* dick with the stake. "Who the *fuck* wants to know?"

"Pro-tip, buddy. Usually, when a person straight-up tells you they're looking for someone? Dead giveaway right there."

Glaring. He had it down to a science. The eye, the ticking jaw muscle, the flex of those pin-me-down forearms.

I tried to glare right back at him, but when it came to squaring off with intimidating, hot-as-hell demons, I was out of practice. "You *do* realize the size of your tip is inversely proportional to your bullshit, right?"

"What do you want with... *Elian*?" His lip curled when he said the name—a reaction I understood all too well.

"I need to speak with him. It's private and it's important. So if you could just fix me another drink for the road and point me in the right direction, I'll gladly—"

"Are you a dancer?"

A dancer? Was this demon for real?

I reached for my stake again. It wouldn't take much. I could probably put it through his good eye before another insult had time to fall out of that sexy mouth.

The thought calmed me almost as much as the booze.

"I'm more of a stabby, pokey kinda girl," I said. "With a little magick thrown in for fun."

"Well, we're all set on security detail and spell casters,

so unless you can work that stabby, pokey bit into a cage dance, we're not hiring."

"You think I'm here about a job?"

"Not sure I care enough to give it much more thought, honestly." He grinned, but I could tell he didn't mean it. Something about all this had gotten under his skin. Something about Elian.

I opened my mouth to push him on it, but before I could utter another word, he flicked his hand to shoo me away, already turning to the next customer.

"Enjoy your evening, *angel*," he said over his shoulder.

Enjoy my *evening*?

It'd taken me two years and the threats of a scary-ass goddess to work up the nerve to set foot in this city, a killer outfit to walk through those silver doors, and a good dose of booze just to say Elian's name without a string of curses attached.

And this demon thought I was *done*?

I was on a hot streak—no way was I bowing out now.

I waited until he finished up with his other customers, then tapped my empty glass. "Still needing that second drink, friend."

He watched me for a beat, then muttered something inaudible before clearing away the empty glass and reaching for another. "Shall I start a tab, then?"

"I'm not staying long enough for that." I opened up the

black hole otherwise known as my purse, emptying its contents onto the bar as I searched for my money.

Cell phone, lipstick, lip gloss, a vial of shifter blood.

Hand sanitizer, emergency tampons, emergency black tourmaline, breath mints.

Three vampire fangs, black eyeliner, a stun potion left-over from the Blackmoon Bay fight, Melantha's portal spell, a hair tie, and...

Aha! Sweet, shiny credit card of questionable remaining balance. After today's shopping spree in the Big Easy, I wasn't too sure how much farther it would get me, but hey. Hope sprang eternal.

"Let's give this one a whirl." I held out the card, but the demon didn't take it.

His gaze was on the glass vial from the goddess, utterly transfixed. The blood-red smoke roiled inside, its black and gold threads shimmering.

He glanced up at me again, and I braced for another argument. A brush-off. Anything but what flashed through that stone-cold eye.

Recognition.

The demon *knew* that particular magick. Which meant...

Holy shit. Had he been to Midnight too? Was that how he knew Elian?

He reached across the bar and covered the vial with his hand, his voice turning dark. "Put it out of sight. Now."

I did as he asked, too stunned to do anything else.

"Wait here," he said in that same deadly tone. "Do *not* leave this bar."

"Okay, but what about my—" *Damn.* He was already gone. "Drink," I said with a sigh. I was just about to hop behind the bar and make something myself when the vertigo hit me again, this wave so strong it nearly knocked me off my barstool.

I fisted my stake and palmed the stun potion, slowly turning to face the newcomers—three of them this time.

My wounded bird was flanked by two of his friends, each one more despicable than the last. Whatever supernatural genetics made most vampires hot as fuck and impossible to resist? Clearly skipped this lot.

A quick scan of my surroundings and my heart sunk. No sign of the demon, and the other patrons in the vicinity were too wrapped up in their own flirtations and petty skirmishes to pay any attention to mine.

Shit.

"Sorry, boys," I said as the vampires crowded in close. "You really *aren't* on the guest list."

"It's not pussy we're after tonight, witch," my original stalker said, ever the romantic. His hand hung limp at his side, the skin black and blistering. "We're here for—"

I shoved the stake into his chest, taking him down for the count, then hurled the stun potion at the second vamp's feet. It exploded in a bright yellow starburst, freezing him on contact, but the third one wasn't close enough to the blast to feel its effects. I tried to reach for one of my daggers, but he was too fast, too strong, and too smart.

He was on me in a heartbeat, hauling me out of the stool and locking me in a vise grip, my back against his chest.

"Got any more tricks, witch?" he growled in my ear.

I struggled against his hold, but it was no use. My arms were pinned at my sides, my feet no longer touching the ground, and I had maybe a minute before the stun potion wore off on the other vamp. "Let me go and I'll show you all *sorts* of magick."

"I don't think so, pretty girl." With a sick groan of pleasure, he clamped down hard on my neck, fangs piercing the skin. Before I could even cry out, he'd drained enough blood to make my world spin.

I fought to remain conscious, to reach the dagger in my boot, to do something other than let this asshole finish me off. The temporarily stunned vamp was already on his feet again, stumbling toward me with rage in his eyes, fangs bared, mouth practically foaming for a taste...

Someone slammed into us from behind, breaking me out of my captor's relentless hold and knocking me to the ground as another man—the bartender, I realized—staked my two attackers in quick succession.

Guess I'm not the only one good with the stabby, pokey bit...

I caught his gaze and managed a quick smile of thanks, then turned my attention to the guy who'd knocked me down.

The *fae* who'd knocked me down. Half-vampire too, I realized, dressed in a three-piece black Nehru suit that perfectly hugged his leanly muscled frame.

My mind spun.

How was this possible?

He was partially on top of me from the fall, one hand cradling the back of my head, lips muttering my name like a prayer. His long hair brushed across my face, a fall of silver waves and intricate braids I itched to run my fingers through.

Only the strongest magick could erase time, and there was no magick more powerful than scent for yanking you right back into the past. It washed over me like a dark curse—the particular mix of bergamot and rain that could only belong to him.

Butterflies danced through my insides, my heartbeat quickening.

When I finally found the courage to meet his eyes, my breath hitched, and not just because his weight was half-crushing my lungs.

Five years ago, he walked out of my life without so much as a goodbye... and crushed my fucking heart.

"Elian," I whispered.

Accidentally.

Shit.

His molten silver gaze swept down to my lips, then back to my eyes. A cocky grin curved his mouth, tugging slightly higher on the left.

It did things to me, that crooked grin. Always had. Bad things. Stupid things. And before I knew it, I was grinning right back at him.

Elian brushed his thumb across my lower lip, eyes sparkling, his touch making me shiver. "Still dreaming of me, little sparrow?"

"I am," I admitted.

Then, just to prove it, I did something I'd been *dreaming* about every day for the last five years.

I punched that sexy, silver-eyed fae-hole right in the mouth.

4

ELIAN

outh full of blood, aching jaw, and a throbbing hard-on I couldn't do a damn thing to fix?

Not exactly the made-for-tv reunion I would've scripted, but it could've been worse.

After what I'd put Haley Barnes through, I was lucky my cock was still attached to my body.

"Ouch!" she hissed, jerking away from my touch. "Careful."

"Damn it, Haley." I tipped her head to the side and got back to work. "Hold still."

Normally, I liked a woman squirming on my desk, but the bullshit with those vampires made my blood boil. Inspecting the gaping holes in Haley's neck, it was all I could do not to smash something. Vampire skulls would've been my first choice, but Jax was already dealing with those fuckers.

Now, alone in my office with the woman I'd ghosted five years ago for the first time since my big disappearing act, I was seriously regretting sending away the demon.

"How much longer?" she asked.

"Almost there." With the gentlest touch I could manage, I finished cleaning out the bite wound, then pressed a gauze pad to her neck, taping it around the edges. She wouldn't let me near the knuckles she'd split clocking me in the face, though—pretty sure she wanted to keep that particular injury as a souvenir.

Couldn't exactly blame her.

I ran my finger along the tape to secure it, and she shivered, then swatted my hand away and yanked her hair forward, covering up the evidence.

"Sorry," I said, completely out of my depth.

"For what, exactly?"

I gestured vaguely. It was a lot to encompass.

Fuck.

Half a decade of radio silence, no explanation, a broken heart she damn sure didn't deserve, and *that* was all I could say to her? Sorry for... whatever?

Jax was right. I was seriously fucked in the head.

Arms wrapped tight around her chest, one leg crossed over the other, booted foot bouncing, Haley shook her head and let out a bitter laugh, probably reconsidering the whole letting-me-keep-my-cock thing.

Five years. Five fucking years of fantasizing about the woman, and now I was ready to bash my own brains in as punishment for all the weak-ass memories it'd served up. They were *nothing* compared to the real thing, and she'd only gotten more stunning with time.

I sighed, the sound of it laced with regret. "Haley, I didn't—"

"Save it. I'm not here for the overdue explanation." She glared at me with the gorgeous green eyes that still haunted my dreams, but they were different now. Harder. Edged with a deep, dark anger trying real damn hard to mask the pain.

Then why are *you here, sparrow?* I wanted to ask. *Come to turn my life upside down? Congratulations, woman. Mission fucking accomplished.*

But I said nothing. Just nodded and waited her out. She'd get to it when she was damn good and ready, just like she always had.

Jax didn't know the story either. All he'd said before the vamp attack was that a green-eyed witch had shown up at the bar asking for me by a name I'd left behind years ago, and she was packing weapons, an attitude, and a portal spell to Midnight.

I knew right away it had to be her. Knew right away she had to be in some deep shit, too.

"Where's the hot demon?" she asked, hopping to her feet.

I tried to pretend the question didn't send a bolt of jealousy straight through my gut. "Cemetery out back."

"Smoke break?"

"The only thing smoking will be the vampires who touched you, but I'm afraid you'll have to wait until sunrise if you want to see *that* show live and uncut."

Her eyes widened a fraction, the faintest flicker of a smile touching her lips, but she turned her back on me before I could really enjoy it.

That's right, little sparrow. Don't say I never did anything nice for you.

She paced my office, checking out all the shit I'd collected in here, none of it particularly meaningful. Aside from the private bar set up behind my desk, it was mostly just dusty tomes and relics left from the original church. Still, she examined each shelf with interest, as if an old bible or wine-stained chalice might give her a clue about why I'd done what I'd done.

She'd known me as fae, but I was half-vampire now, my senses picking up more than she probably realized. The rapid-fire beat of her heart. The familiar strawberries-and-cream sweetness wafting from her skin, mingling with the intoxicating scent of her blood and—even more impossible to ignore—the scent of her arousal.

The woman might've hated my guts, but old habits died hard.

And if I didn't stop staring at her ass in that tight lace dress, I was going to die hard, too.

Damn it, Haley. You should've stayed far *the fuck away from me...*

I sat in my leather chair and steepled my hands on the desk, my gaze everywhere but on her. A blur of dark hair here, a flash of those boots there, a quick glimpse of black lace stockings... Bits and pieces. It was all I dared to take from her now, and even *that* felt selfish.

Fate had given me a choice five years ago, and I'd picked wrong. Now, there *was* no choice. Only consequences.

So, as badly as I wanted to give her the answers she was seeking from those musty shelves—as much as I *owed* her those answers—I couldn't do it. Couldn't risk her life just to ease my guilty conscience.

It was time to put those walls back up. Time to freeze her ass out, once and for all.

She'd hate me forever, sure. But I'd rather she hate me on her feet than love me from the bottom of a fucking grave, and right now, those were the only possible outcomes.

"So this is your life now, huh?" She finally turned to face me again, doing a damn good job of keeping her shit together, despite the raging heartbeat. "Serving up fae strippers and designer drugs to the supernatural elite? Impressive, Elian. Truly."

"Serving up *fantasies*," I corrected, still not meeting her gaze. "And try not to judge me too harshly. It's a lucrative endeavor."

"I'm sure it is."

I propped my hands behind my head and grinned, focusing on a spot just past her shoulder. "Stick around. Maybe you'll see something you like."

"Aside from your bartender?"

I let that one go. She deserved to take a few more jabs at me.

"And this... this vampire business." Her gaze roved over me, nearly setting me on fire. "All part of your fantasy schtick? Give the highborn fae girls a taste of the dark side? Bet they *love* that."

"Certainly doesn't hurt," I said, grin still firmly in place. "But it's no schtick. I was turned a few years back."

"By force?"

"Necessity."

In my case, there hadn't been a difference, but I wasn't about to get into all that. Pretty sure Haley hadn't come all the way to Louisiana just to hear my Midnight sob story.

"Don't feel *too* sorry for me, though," I added. "Thanks to my fae blood, I ended up with most of the perks and hardly any of the weaknesses. Super speed and strength, healing, mental influence, and no aversion to sunlight."

She flashed a cruel grin. "You're saying I could chop off your head and you'd survive?"

"That's... untested."

"Can I try?"

"No."

"Let me know if you change your mind."

Ignoring the offer, I said, "Really, the only downside is the minor inconvenience of my complete dependency on human blood, but that's... manageable."

Silence drifted between us once more, and she blew out a breath and glanced up at the ceiling. I didn't need to look at her to know she was holding back tears.

"God. What *happened* to you, Elian?"

"He goes by Saint now," Jax said suddenly. He'd just stepped into the office, his white shirt stained with vampire blood, but otherwise no worse for the wear.

"*Saint*?" Haley laughed again, and damn if the sound of it didn't stir a deep longing inside me. "And let me guess," she said to Jax. "You're Sinner. A little on the nose, no?"

"We're all sinners, angel," the demon said, no trace of irony. "Even you."

Asshole. Thirty seconds in the same room together, and I already hated the way those two were eye-fucking each other.

"*Jax*," I said, a little harsher than necessary. "You take care of our guests?"

"Tied up, staked, and awaiting the sunrise barbecue."

"Excellent."

Burning by sunlight was the most painful way to take out a full-blooded vampire, and the fact that we were making them wait for their demise, conscious but paralyzed, made it all the sweeter. As a general rule, I tried not to make a habit of murdering my clientele, but sometimes exceptions had to be made.

"Jax, huh?" Haley flashed the demon a genuine smile I wanted to steal for myself. "Okay. Much better than Sinner. Do you—"

"And what business brings you to New Orleans, Ms. Barnes?" I asked coolly, rummaging through some papers on my desk as if I had better shit to do—*anything* to do but sit here and watch the former love of my life fawn over the fucking demon I wanted to murder on the best of days.

The look she shot me made my balls shrivel, but the faster we got down to it, the faster we could both move on.

Again.

"I was hoping we could talk privately," she said.

"Whatever you need to say, you can say it in front of Jax."

Mostly because I was too chicken shit to be alone with her again.

"Fine," Haley said. "Let's just rip off the Band-Aid then,

shall we? I need to get to the realm of Midnight and then back to the Temple of the Dark Moon. Alive. And I need to do it soon, or everyone I love is going to die." Then, with a bright, heart-stopping smile, "So, what are you guys doing later? Fancy a road trip? My snack game is *killer*."

uck. I'd really hoped Jax had been wrong about that portal spell.

"Why Midnight?" I asked.

Haley sighed, her megawatt smile dimming. "For reasons I have *no* interest in sharing, I'm in debt to the Goddess Melantha. She needs a blood witch to sneak into the realm and retrieve the blood of some warlord... Kayden? Karaden?"

"Keradoc?" I asked, and she pointed at me with finger guns and winked.

Normally, I might've found the gesture adorable. But now?

My heart dropped into my stomach.

How the hell had Haley Barnes gotten mixed up with Melantha and fucking Keradoc of Midnight?

"*Saint*," Jax warned, as if he knew exactly where my mind was heading. "Don't even think about—"

I lifted a hand and cut him off. Ignoring his glare—along with every alarm blaring inside my head—I said, "Define *retrieve*, Haley."

"Retrieve," she replied. "As in steal. And I need your help getting in and out. I wouldn't mind a few pointers about this warlord douchebag either, but that's just frosting on the cake as far as I'm concerned. Escort me, and I'll handle the rest."

"Steal. You want to steal the blood of the warlord of Midnight, and you're asking for *my* help?" I laughed, forcing myself to shore up those walls around my heart. "Ask me again, sparrow. Put a little more oomph into it this time."

"Seriously?"

"*Very* seriously. In fact, for something like this... Yeah. You should probably beg." I stood up and leaned back against the bar, my gaze raking down her body, then back up. "Feel free to get on your knees—probably won't convince me, but who knows? Maybe I'll be inspired by your performance. Wouldn't be the first time."

Hurt flickered in her eyes, but I couldn't let it get to me. Couldn't give in. Couldn't deal with *any* of this shit —not now.

In a soft voice that cut deeper than the dagger strapped to her thigh, she said, "Were you always such a prick?"

Only since I walked away from the best thing in my immortal life to chase after a ghost...

"Was a time when you liked pricks," I said.

"Well now I like men, so you can sit *your* prick-ass down."

I shook my head. *The nerve of this woman...* "Is someone paying you to fuck with me, Haley, or have you just lost your damn mind?"

"The fact that I'm even here should be a pretty good indicator of my current mental state." She shoved her hands into her hair, stopping just short of tearing it out. "Let me break it down for you, okay? Basically, I'm supposed to portal on over to some deadly dark-fae realm where the sun never shines and the good guys never last, hijack the blood of a psychotic warlord without killing him, and zip back home like fucking Dorothy with the ruby slippers. Only I don't have ruby slippers, Elian. I have you. The asshole bloodsucking fae who *somehow*—even though he's a spineless amoeba who needs to crawl back into his petri dish and *ripen* for a few more decades—holds the distinguished honor of being the only guy to ever escape Midnight alive. So I'm sorry if my sudden arrival is confusing or annoying or inconvenient for you and Mr. Tall, Dark, and Demon over here, but seriously? How fucked am *I*?"

"On a scale of one to ten," Jax said, still glowering at

me, "you're fucked by a magnitude of a thousand, give or take."

He was right. Didn't matter that there were actually *three* of us who'd escaped Midnight alive; Haley was well and truly fucked. Whatever she'd gotten into with Melantha was so far beyond fixable, the best I could do for her was hand over a pile of drugs, say goodbye, and put her in a permanent coma.

"Aren't you going to call him a prick, too?" I asked.

"Jax? He's just being honest. *You're* being a prick."

"Honesty doesn't preclude prickishness. In fact—"

"You know what? I didn't come here to reminisce about my penchant for pricks, thanks." She crossed the office and stood before my desk again, staring me down. "Are you going to help me or not?"

Shit.

My cock throbbed at the proximity of her. The fall of dark brown hair over her breasts. The lace top of her dress, dipping just low enough to make my mouth water...

Fucking witch was putting me under her spell without even trying.

"I'm not an inter-realm Uber, Haley," I said. "So unless there's a fantasy I can conjure up for you, no. I can't help."

"You know what my fantasy is, *Saint*? A man who keeps his promises. A man who doesn't pledge his immortal love one night, then vanish into the mist the next." She leaned across my desk, black manicured fingertips pressed against the glossy mahogany, the scent of her red-hot blood rushing over me in a seductive wave. "You *owe* me this, asshole. So man up, help me get it done, and I'll be out of your life again before you can say 'how much for the fae lap dance.'"

Darkness swirled in her eyes. It'd always been there—the quiet rage, the simmering fury she hid so well with jokes and smiles. But still... the Haley I'd walked out on all those years ago was softer. Hopeful, despite what she'd been through. This one was hard-edged and gunning for a fight, ready to blow up her whole life over some debt to a goddess she had no business fucking with in the first place.

It broke my heart to see her like this.

Turned me on like nothing had in years, but damn.

What was her life like now? In all the time that'd passed since our last kiss, what mountains of shit had fate thrown at her?

Or were all those hard edges because of me? Because of what *I'd* thrown at her?

Fuck me. In that moment, all I wanted to do was take her into my arms, push her down on my desk, and claim her until she knew *exactly* how sorry I was. How much I'd truly missed her.

But I wasn't that man anymore.

Haley was right—I *was* a prick. Worse.

And I needed to *stay* worse. For both our sakes.

"You're welcome to hang out for another drink," I said. "Maybe that fae lap dance you mentioned. On the house, of course."

Disappointment chased the darkness from her eyes.

Never before had I so badly wanted to kick my own ass.

"Tempting offer," she said, her tone dripping with sarcasm. "Unfortunately, I think I left my kneepads back at the Temple of the Dark Moon." She stood up to her full height and headed for the exit, those sexy boots thudding across the floor, her hot little ass swishing. "I'll be sure to give Melantha your regards. Thanks again for reminding me *exactly* why I never came looking for you here. Enjoy your fantasy life, Saint. Sweet dreams."

She grabbed the door handle, and my world ground to a screeching halt.

Fuck. Five years on, and she was still as stubborn and fiery as the night she'd pushed me off a pier in Blackmoon Bay for spilling coffee on her shoes. It was the first time I'd ever seen her, standing out behind Luna's Café, her long hair blowing into her mouth, eyes flashing in the dark. I'd sworn it was an accident, but we both knew I was full of shit. I just wanted a reason to talk to her, and I panicked and pulled a dick move with the coffee.

So, into the water I went.

Then she felt bad about it and jumped in after me.

She splashed me.

I dunked her.

We'd started the night nearly drowning each other in the Salish Sea. Ended it with me drowning in the taste of her as I made her come on my tongue, again and again and again. She was wild. Insatiable. So passionate her touch set my skin on fire.

Of all the exotic drugs we served at Saints and Sinners, the fae magick, the cocktails that would've been illegal in a human bar, Haley Barnes was still my favorite fucking addiction, and I'd never stopped fantasizing about her.

Now she was here. In New Orleans. In the club I'd built for the sole purpose of giving people the very escape I could never truly find for myself.

One good tug on that door, and she'd be out of my life again—probably for the last time.

Let her walk, asshole. Just let her go...

It was the smart thing to do, sure. Cut it off, forget she'd ever set foot in my city. Forget how damn good and right she felt in my arms when I'd knocked her away from that bloodsucker tonight. Forget the way my insides twisted up when she'd looked into my eyes and whispered my real name.

Elian...

Yeah, letting her go was definitely the right call.

But no one had ever accused me of being a fucking hero, and they weren't about to start now.

"Wait," I said.

One word. Barely a whisper.

But Haley heard me. She always knew exactly what I was thinking anyway, whether I said it out loud or not.

She sighed, then turned to face me, her face etched with so much sadness it made me want to choke the life out of something with my bare hands.

"I'm not here to fuck with you, Elian," she said softly, a tear sliding down her cheek. "I'm in a jam, and I don't know where else to go. I wouldn't ask if it wasn't life-or-death."

I closed my eyes and sighed. Her pain was too close, too raw. It took everything in me not to go to her, gather her close, and promise I'd find a way to fix this without her ever having to set foot in that hellhole.

But that was a fantasy even *I* couldn't produce.

"We'll figure something out," I said instead. "Tomorrow. We'll make a plan to get you where you need to go."

Even with my eyes closed, I felt the red-hot burn of Jax's scornful gaze as deeply as I felt the hope rising in hers. But for all my protests, the demon *had* to know how this would play out.

Hell, I'd known it from the moment he stormed into my office ranting about the witch at the bar holding a one-way ticket to hell.

After two years as free men, barely outrunning the

ghosts forever nipping at our heels, it'd finally come to this.

We were going back to Midnight.

And this time, we probably *wouldn't* escape alive.

But Haley would. I'd make damn sure of that.

*I*t was an hour before sunrise when the last inebriated vampire stumbled out of the club and I finally tracked down Elian again.

Damn it. Saint, not Elian. The witch was getting in my head—definitely not a good sign.

He was holding court on one of the velvet couches in the former choir loft that overlooked the club, the VIP lounge he'd designated for our more exclusive clientele.

Two lilac-haired fae women writhed in his lap, one kissing his neck, the other moaning softly as Saint dropped little black pills onto her tongue. Two demon cocktail servers lounged beside them, thoroughly engaged with each other.

Saint's mouth shone red with blood from a fresh feed, though I had no idea who'd offered up the vein this time.

Fae blood was the most exquisite in terms of taste, but it didn't sustain him. He needed regular infusions of human blood for that, and the supply was always an issue. We usually imported it for our vampire customers from a network of blood banks down in Mexico, but the human authorities were starting to crack down on our smugglers, squeezing the supply and pushing up our costs.

Live-feeding was the best alternative, but Saint didn't allow humans in the club, and outside he kept a low profile, avoiding humans whenever possible. All of us did —most humans didn't know the supernatural world existed, and we preferred to keep it that way. Exposure was bad for business and bad for our health.

I folded my arms across my chest and leaned against the massive pipes, all that remained of the cathedral's original organ. Images of the woman—Haley—flickered through my mind.

After promising to meet Saint at his home in the Garden District the following afternoon, she'd said her goodbyes and headed back to her hotel, and he'd spent the rest of the evening making arrangements with our top advisors to keep the business running during his... unforeseen absence.

Direct quote.

Operational and profitable at all times—that was the deal. All part of the fucked-up agreement we'd made with the crooked Midnight fae who'd helped us escape. And in the two years we'd been smuggling drugs out of Midnight, we'd done everything in our power to keep things running smoothly, to keep bringing in the green for everyone involved, and—most importantly—to keep the entire hustle off Keradoc's radar.

For all Saint's bullshit, Haley was a complication I hadn't seen coming.

What was her deal, anyway? Clearly, she and Saint had been in a relationship, but I couldn't make sense of it. The woman was a little on the crazy side, sure. But she was smart. Confident. A fighter. Drop-dead beautiful.

What the hell had a witch like that *ever* seen in a grade-A fuckup like Saint?

He whispered something into the pill-popping fae's ear, no doubt weaving some vampire-influenced fantasy she'd paid for, then finally met my gaze across the dim space. "Something I can do for you, Mr. Tall, Dark, and Demon?"

"No," I ground out, and we both knew I wasn't talking about whether he could do something for me.

"No?" he asked.

"*Hell* no. Would it help if I added a fuck? Fuck no. As a matter of fact, fucking hell no. Saint, you're a crazy fuck, but this... this is next-level insanity, even for you."

His silver eyes burned into me, even as his hand roamed down to the fae's ass. He gave her a quick swat, then all four of his guests rose from the couch and exited the loft.

"You've got history with her," I said once we were alone.

"Ancient, over, and not up for discussion." He retrieved an envelope from his inside jacket pocket and tossed it to me.

I opened it up. Thumbed the thick stack of money inside. "Fuck is this?"

He rose from the couch and headed for the bar, pouring himself a bourbon. "Insane or not, Jax, I don't have a choice."

"Because you owe her?"

He didn't respond.

"Haley's calling in your debt," I said, "so you're calling in mine? That's how this works?"

"I'm paying you. It's not the same thing."

"And you know I can't take the money, which makes it *exactly* the same thing." I shoved the envelope against his chest. "Newsflash, asshole. I'm not interested in playing escort to some witch who used to suck your—"

He grabbed my wrist. Leaned in close. "Careful, hellspawn."

His pupils were so dilated they almost swallowed the silver in his eyes. The sickly sweet scent of Devil's Dream clung to his breath. I didn't need to see his tongue to know it would be covered in the drug's signature black whorls.

Apparently, the fae woman wasn't the only one popping the pills of Midnight.

Fuck.

Back in The Black, they called it. Dancing with the Devil, visiting an old friend, tripping down memory lane. There were as many terms for the addiction as there were for the drug itself—Devil's Dream, D2, Dizzy Devil, Sweet Dream, The Black, Dark Delight. It obliterated your inhibitions, erased your conscious awareness, and put you in a state of pure euphoria, leaving you wide open to the twin powers of imagination and suggestion. Combine that with vampire influence whispered in a willing ear, and you had the perfect recipe for crafting the ultimate fantasy... assuming you could pay the price.

Saint had always struggled with the stuff—in Midnight and New Orleans both. After nearly burning down the club in a drug-induced haze six months ago, he'd managed to stay clean, but an hour with his ex had sent him running right back into the Devil's arms.

I broke out of his grip and poured myself a bourbon. Saint didn't need me to enumerate all the ways in which he was slowly killing himself. I suspected he'd been hoping for that exact outcome ever since we escaped that shithole realm.

I used to resent him for it. Hell, maybe I still did.

He didn't sell Midnight's exotic drugs here in the States because he wanted to—he did it because he had to, same as I did. Taking them, though? That *was* a choice.

And when it came down to choices—no matter how many he'd been given—Saint had never managed to make the right ones.

"We're not talking about an overnight trip to the coast," I said. "There are people in Midnight—fucking *mercenaries* —still out for your blood."

He met my gaze again, his eyes glassy. The fact that he was still on his feet at all spoke volumes about the tolerance he'd built up over the years. Even after taking enough Devil's Dream to turn his eyes black, he was still nowhere near the unconscious delirium it promised.

"*Our* blood," he said. "Isn't that what you mean? You. Me. Hudson. Blood before roses, right?"

Blood before roses.

The old vow echoed, the blood oath the three of us had sworn to one another in the Hollow—the neighborhood where we'd first crossed paths inside Midnight's walled city of Amaranth. Where we'd first figured out how to turn the realm's infamous corpsevine plant into the pills that would ultimately buy our freedom... And promptly enslave us.

It felt like a lifetime ago.

Saint grinned, black eyes haunted by the ghosts of everything we'd done. Everything we were *still* doing. Memories, guilt, leverage... What did it matter? All of it bound us like the iron chains we'd left back in the Hollow.

A bitter taste filled my mouth. A lot had happened since the days of blood oaths and brotherhood.

"Fuck you." I shoved him away and turned my back, unable to look into those drugged-out eyes for another moment. "The realm is at war. Always has been, always will be. Even if I *did* want to help your witch, what makes you think we could survive another go? That we could even reach Amaranth City before some rebel faction wasted us?" I shook my head and laughed. "Maybe you should get in touch with Keradoc yourself. Negotiate a peace treaty—you'd have a better chance at *that* than making it through the realm alive."

Now it was Saint's turn to laugh. "And what would peace do to our supply chain?" He poured himself another drink, then resumed lounging on the couch. "It's a balancing act, Jax. We don't want the realm blowing itself to bits, but we still need them at war. A peaceful, law-abiding realm is no good for us."

"Tricky thing, this war profiteering."

"The Empire doesn't run itself, brother." He held up his glass in cheers, then sipped.

It was an old argument between us—one I'd never win because the bastard was right. And however repugnant it was, the Empire—the code name he'd given our operation—was what kept us alive.

Then *and* now.

"Haley needs my help," he said. "Sure. But this isn't about her at all. She brought us an opportunity. A golden fucking opportunity we'd be fools to squander."

"An opportunity for death? Great. Sign me up."

"Not ours, Jax." He stared into the amber liquid in his glass, dark eyes glinting with a malice I hadn't seen since our last days in Midnight. "*His.*"

*K*eradoc?" I asked. "Are you high? Wait—don't answer that."

"Then don't ask."

"Saint, there's no way. No fucking way. Besides, Haley said she needs to get the blood without killing him."

"Everyone needs *something*, Jax. Sometimes I can meet those needs, sometimes I can't."

"And most of the time, you just plain *won't*." I sipped my bourbon, half-wishing it was as good as Devil's Dream at obliterating my thoughts. "Why would you risk your life for a doomed assassination attempt on Keradoc?"

"For fuck's sake. He's the warlord responsible for the genocide of tens of thousands of people. Do I really need a reason?"

"He's the warlord you smuggled weapons for in the

Hollow. Your drug enterprise is probably still funding half his campaigns."

"*Our* drug enterprise. And as for the things I did and why I did them... Let's not confuse survival with loyalty, shall we?"

"Saint—"

"I've got unfinished business with the warlord of Midnight," he snapped. "Leave it."

Saint had unfinished business? I nearly snorted.

We *all* had unfinished business. Midnight wasn't exactly the kind of place that let you tie up loose ends, say your goodbyes, and fuck off to the next chapter in your happy little life.

As far as I knew, Saint, Hudson, and I were the only bastards who'd ever left at all, and the things we had to do to escape... I fought back a shiver. It wasn't just the drug smuggling. Leaving that place might've saved our lives, but it broke something inside each of us I was pretty sure we'd never be able to put back together again.

Hudson still didn't speak, not that he ever did in Midnight. But now, he disappeared into himself for days at a time, not eating, not sleeping. I kept waiting for the night he'd hop on his motorcycle, head out on the interstate, and disappear forever.

Since we got back, I hadn't been able to sleep more than an hour a night either, the nightmares too fucking close. Too real. And don't even get me started on the headaches.

And Saint... No matter how many pills he swallowed, no matter how much blood he drank, no matter how much fae pussy he chased, that poor fuck was as twisted up now as I'd ever seen him in Midnight.

Yes, the three of us had called ourselves blood brothers once. Bonded for life.

But life in Midnight turned out to be a lot shorter than we expected, and now we were here, facing an entirely different reality.

Most of the time, I still wasn't sure we'd made the right call leaving that fucking place.

"Besides," Saint said now, "taking Keradoc off the board could be a lucrative move for the entire operation."

"How do you figure?"

"Within the instability lies the opportunity." He scratched his jaw, considering. "A power vacuum would leave room to maneuver some of our people into influential political positions. Positions we could leverage to get more resources. More products—I'm talking stuff beyond D2. Midnight is a veritable blank check, Jax. One *we* could write and cash."

"Sure." I huffed out a laugh. "Less a juicy cut for the middlemen."

Aside from Keradoc and his extended family, an elite group of dark fae sorcerers and witches were all that remained of the pureblood Midnight fae. As purebloods, they could travel freely between Midnight and our realm, no portal spells or dark bargains necessary. They were easily bought, completely amoral, and notoriously honorable in that honor-among-thieves sort of way—perfect combination for drug smugglers.

Those were our so-called people. The ones who'd aided and abetted our escape. They'd been helping us move product and payment between realms ever since, and so far, it'd worked out.

But the only reason we had to move product at all was to keep those dark fae happy. As long as the drugs and money kept flowing, they'd ensure no one ever looked too hard for the three monsters who'd supposedly slipped through Midnight's cracks.

Payoffs made the world go round—it was as true in Midnight as it was here in NOLA.

"Or," I said, "we could try to buy our way out of this shit and find a legitimate way to live out the rest of our miserable immortalities."

"Go legit? A one-eyed demon, a mute shifter, and a strung-out vampire-fae mutt who can't get through a day without a stiff drink or a handful of little black pills?" Saint laughed. "Sorry, but I think our straight-and-narrow days are over."

"They don't have to be."

"Face it, brother. We're falling from grace like meteorites hurtling to earth. Might as well enjoy the spoils on the way down." Saint leaned his head back against the couch and sighed. He was motionless for so long, I wondered if the Devil's Dream had finally taken hold. But after a few long moments of silence, he sat up again and said, "I need you with me on this, Jax."

"Yes, you do."

"If you won't take the money, what the fuck do you want?"

"I *can't* take the money," I said. The asshole fucking knew it, too. He'd saved my life getting me out of that shithole, and I still owed him for it. Only reason I still worked for him—otherwise I'd be halfway around the world by now, as far away from *Saint Elian* as I could get.

Demons were notorious for making deals, and when it came to the desperate and depraved, we held all the bargaining power. But on the rare occasion a demon found himself on the receiving end of a favor? Fuck. Carrying debts of any sort—financial, emotional, physical, even just implied—chipped away at our power. The longer it took us to crawl out from under it, the weaker our ties to our physical bodies became, until one day we found ourselves smoked to oblivion, no chance of re-spawning.

I'd lost enough of my natural-born demon mojo in Midnight. I couldn't afford to lose any more just because Saint wanted to ease his conscience with a payoff.

"How about a little honesty instead?" I offered.

"Ha! That's a new one." Saint tipped his glass toward me and grinned. "I'll do my best. No promises."

I crouched down before him. Placed a hand on his knee and looked into his glassy black eyes. "Tell me this is just about Keradoc."

"I want him dead," he said firmly, and because he was half-tanked and his guard was down, he didn't have the mental fortitude to uphold the facade. To keep me out of his head.

Yes, he wanted the warlord on ice. But that wasn't the real reason he was so hell-bent on going back to Midnight. Not even close.

I got to my feet, trying to keep my annoyance in check.

Mostly, I fucking hated the burden of being a fear demon. But at times like this, I appreciated the insight it gave me. No, I couldn't read minds, but I could sense what people were most afraid of, and that was damn near the same thing.

Nothing revealed truth like fear. Dig deep enough, and I could turn that fear against a person, making them believe their darkest terror was playing out before their very eyes, much in the same way Saint could use his vampire influence.

Depending on how hard I pushed, that kind of manipulation could shatter a person's mind.

I didn't need to manipulate Saint, though. The drugs had eradicated his mental vigilance. Now, he telegraphed his fears like a child trembling over the monsters in the closet.

It all came back to the witch.

Saint really *had* loved her. *Still* loved her. And the thought of her coming to harm in Midnight fucking gutted him.

I headed to the bar. Abandoned my glass and went straight for the bottle.

"I do this for you, we're done," I said, taking a swig. "My debts are cleared. Understand? The minute we get back —*if* we get back—I'm leaving New Orleans. Leaving the Empire. Leaving this fucking country. Leaving *you*. And I never want to see you again, Saint."

He nodded as if he'd been expecting as much, though a hint of sadness flickered in his black eyes. "Promise to send me a postcard from your glamorous new life, and I won't stand in your way."

Ignoring his pathetic attempt at humor, I said, "So what's our move?"

"We need to coordinate this from the inside."

"Agreed."

"I'll send word to Gem, let her know the boys are heading back to the Hollow."

I allowed a thin smile. Of all the pureblood Midnighters, Gem was one of the good ones, just as her name implied. "You think we'll actually make it into Amaranth City?"

"With her help, we've got a shot. We'll need supplies, though—more than we can bring through Haley's portal. A place to crash. Midnight currency. Intel on Keradoc's whereabouts, and no, before you even say it, I *won't* be telling anyone about my plans—or Haley's, for that matter. That information's on a strictly need-to-know basis, and right now? You, Hudson, and I are the only ones who need to know."

"Hudson?" I groaned and scrubbed a hand over my jaw. "Don't even *think* about dragging him into this shit. Haven't you done enough damage? He's barely—"

My words fell away as the man in question landed in the loft, tucking his wings behind him.

For a massive gargoyle shifter who towered close to eight feet tall in his winged warrior form—a mix between man and winged beast, with bulging human musculature, talon-like claws, and smooth, slate-gray skin—he moved with the grace of a ballerina. Even in his human form— blond, bearded, and covered in tattoos that made him look more like a motorcycle club president than a mythical beast—he was silent and stealthy.

"Good to see you in living color again, Hudson," I said, and I meant it. By day, the sunlight turned him to stone. But after sunset, he was free to roam in his winged or human form. Lately, though, he'd been spending most of his time stoned by choice, perched on the cathedral eves or hiding out in the gardens behind Saint's place.

He nodded hello but didn't say a word, as usual.

"Hudson's the only one who can get everyone across Beggar's Moat," Saint said matter-of-factly, and from the incurious look on the gargoyle's face, it was clear he'd been listening in and was fully up to speed. "Unless you're ready to grow a pair of wings along with the balls you're still working on."

Hudson folded his arms across his massive chest and grinned, his fangs catching the light. Man or beast, it was the closest he ever got to laughing.

With a contempt I didn't bother to veil, I glanced down at the black smoke now curling off Saint's fingertips—side effect of the Devil's Dream. "Keep dancing with the Devil, Saint, and we'll see who needs new balls."

"Don't tell me you're losing your nerve." Saint lifted his hand to his mouth and blew, making the smoke dance. His grin stretched wide. "A fear demon, scared of a little trip to the dark side?"

"You know better than that."

Midnight was a brutal place, every square inch fraught with the kind of horrors that could reach into your chest and carve out your heart—the kind of horrors that would send most men to an early grave just to escape the memories of what they'd seen. What they'd endured.

But no, the prospect of going back there didn't scare me. I was largely incapable of fear, rational or otherwise—

all part of the forced indoctrination of my particular demonic breed.

Didn't mean I was completely immune to it, though. And right now, one thing had me by the fucking throat.

Haley Barnes.

After two years of walking through life like a lukewarm corpse, Saint was coming back to life.

And he could say whatever the fuck he wanted about assassinating Keradoc, but I'd seen his truth, and it wasn't the prospect of spilling the warlord's blood that'd suddenly set his cock on fire.

It was a gorgeous, green-eyed witch who'd shown up at the club with a devious smile, a portal to Midnight, and a heart full of fury for the man who'd broken her.

I'd seen *her* truth, too. Yes, she had eyes that lit up the room and a smile that could bring a man to his knees. But that pitch-black flame inside her burned so hot, it was a miracle she hadn't incinerated herself.

She wasn't just an angel.

She was an angel of darkness.

And we were about to see just how far she was willing to fall.

"What do you say, brothers?" Saint asked. "Up for a rendezvous in the old stomping grounds?"

Hudson scratched a claw behind one of his horns and nodded.

I took another hit of bourbon first, but yes, I nodded, too.

And Saint...

Well. That asshole just laughed, as if he'd known all along his brothers wouldn't let him walk into the fires alone.

"Excellent. We'll finalize the plans with Haley at my place over lunch. In the meantime, the sun's almost up." He popped another pill into his mouth, grabbed a fresh bottle of bourbon from the bar, and headed for the exit. "If anyone needs me, I'll be in the cemetery furiously jerking off to the smell of flambéed vampire."

I wanted to hate it.

The lawn was overgrown, the paint chipping, and the humidity so thick my hair needed its own zip code.

But the sight of Elian's butter-yellow mansion made my heart ache with longing.

He'd stolen it. The future we'd always planned. The dream we'd created together.

A new life in a city drenched with magick that made our skin tingle. An old home in the Garden District—an original we could restore from the ground up. Businesses in the Quarter—a club for him, a witchy café and bookstore for me. Music and revelry floating on the air at night, the song of crickets drifting through the windows, the soundtrack of a beautiful life.

Had this house always been his—some weird double

life he'd never confessed to? All the lovely pictures he'd painted in my mind... Was it all just to torment me?

Or had he bought this place after his return from Midnight, trying to torment *himself?*

Yeah, and speaking of tormenting yourself...

That's exactly what I was doing with all this pointless speculation. I'd spent *years* missing him. Now I was going to miss some pie-in-the-sky daydream about a future that'd never stood a chance? Screw that. I had a *real* life to miss—with people who actually cared about me. Sisters and friends. A coven of witches waiting for me back in the Bay.

Elian was nothing more than an escort service now—a means to an end. The sooner we wrapped up this mission, the sooner I could get back home.

No one answered the door when I rang the bell, and peering through the thick, dusty windows didn't reveal any signs of life either. So, after a quick walk to a corner café for a coffee refill, I stashed my bag on the porch and headed into the backyard to wait.

The place was something out of a fairytale. Southern live oaks and flowering dogwood trees circled a small pond, curtains of Spanish moss dripping from every limb. Bright pink azaleas bloomed at their feet, and a wooden footbridge arched across the pond like a pathway to a secret world.

A stone gargoyle sat at the water's edge, catching my

attention. It was an odd placement for a garden statue, and he reminded me of the one who'd perched on the cathedral at Saints and Sinners.

I never knew Elian had a thing for them.

As I approached the pond, a sense of calm washed over me. Removing the dagger holstered beneath my sundress, I took a seat in the grass beside the gargoyle, hoping he didn't mind the intrusion.

We hung out in companionable silence for a few minutes, but as soon as I finished my chicory coffee, I was overcome with the inexplicable urge to talk to the guy.

Yes, the gargoyle.

Further evidence of Elian's deleterious effects on my mental state, but for now, I was rolling with it.

"Tough talk, Gargs," I said. "Am I a *complete* idiot, or just three-quarters' worth? Don't get me wrong—it's not like I came here expecting him to grovel. But is it crazy to trust him with this? He really wrecked me, you know? And not in the good way."

I laughed and swatted away a mosquito, but before I could speak again, a wave of emotion rose in my throat. Memories bombarded me from all sides—memories I'd taken out and examined so many times before, all the edges should've been worn smooth by now.

No such luck. These babies were as sharp and painful today as they'd been the morning after he'd left.

Motherfucker. How was it possible I had any more tears left for the man?

I closed my eyes, letting a few of them slip down my cheeks. Prying open the door to the past was a dangerous habit—one I thought I'd kicked. Yet there I was again, cracking it open and peering inside. An inch at first. Then a foot. A little wider, and...

Boom. I was right back in Blackmoon Bay, shoving a cocky, silver-eyed fae off the edge of a pier.

"I was in a dark place when fate put Elian in my path," I told my silent friend. "Even after I invited him back to my place that night, I thought we were just heading for a one-night stand. A little horizontal adventure to take my mind off the shitshow of my life."

It *was* a shitshow, too. I was barely nineteen. The grandmother who'd raised me after my adoptive parents died in a car crash had suddenly dropped dead of a heart attack. No warning, no goodbyes. I was lost without my Nona—a complete disaster. I got mixed up in dark magick —lots of forbidden shit. Bailed on college, sold Nona's house, and wandered the country until I finally ended up in Blackmoon Bay.

Turned out I'd been born there, though I hadn't known it at the time. Somehow, the city had called me home.

I was looking for something, though. A purpose. A reason to get out of bed each day.

Instead, I found *him.*

"I know this sounds cliché," I said, "but with Elian? It really was love at first sight."

A week after our so-called one-night stand, I was moving into his apartment. A month later, we were already talking about New Orleans. About forever.

Sometimes, you just knew.

And sometimes, your intuition needed to be drop-kicked into the nearest dumpster and set on fire, but hey. Hindsight, right?

"I was with him for three years," I continued. "Three of the most intense, mind-blowing, soul-shattering years of my life. God, even our fights were hot." I gathered the hair at the nape of my neck and fanned my face, trying to convince myself the sweat trickling down my back was from the Louisiana heat and *not* the vivid memories of Elian's tongue on my nipple, his hair tickling my stomach, one hand wrapped around my throat and squeezing—oh, *fuck*… just right.

We were good together in every way. No secrets—or so I'd thought. No shame.

"But one night I just got this really bad feeling," I said. "He'd been acting strange all day, and even after he'd spent two hours in bed giving me the most intense orgasms of my life, whispering over and over how much he loved me, something still felt off. I woke up in the middle of the night feeling like someone had ripped something out of my chest. I glanced at the clock on the nightstand—three-thirty-three AM. And before I even rolled over to check on him, before I trailed a hand across the sheets to touch his shoulder, a deep sadness washed over me and I just... I *knew* he was gone. Not in the bathroom, not out for a nightcap, but *gone*."

Memories of that night tore through my heart, and I unsheathed my dagger, the familiar feel of the smooth bone handle steadying me.

"I got up and searched the place," I said. "The only things missing were a backpack, his wallet, and some clothes. He didn't even take his keys or phone. He left almost all of his possessions behind, yet I still knew he wasn't coming back. It was as if our very connection had suddenly shattered—everything we'd meant to each other, everything we'd promised." I turned the blade, catching the sunlight and reflecting it onto my face. "Losing someone you love is hard enough, but the not knowing? It makes everything so much more unbearable. You think you can handle shit, but the brain *hates* a mystery. Things need to be solved. Cases closed. If you don't have the answers? Your oh-so-helpful brain fills in all the blanks for you. And let me tell you something, Gargs—brains are mean little assholes. Be grateful you don't have one."

The breeze whispered across my shoulders, and I ran my fingers along the flat of the blade, the metal warm from the sun.

Elian *left* me that night—I wasn't stupid. He'd packed a

bag. Fucked me like he knew it'd be our last time. But I still spent months searching for him. Scouring every fae and vampire club in the vicinity, asking every connection, friend, and supernatural neighbor we'd ever encountered if they'd heard from him.

After six months of bashing my head against nothing but dead ends, I was starting to think maybe I'd imagined him. Dreamed up my fae soulmate as some kind of manifestation of all the people I'd lost in my life. All the people who—by choice or the cruel winds of fate—had left me.

The months dragged on. Everyone else seemed to forget he'd ever existed, but me? I was still waking up every single night at three-thirty-three and crawling the walls in the dark, my heart pounding so hard I swore it would kill me, mind spinning with the same pointless *why, why, whys*?

"You know what I finally figured out?" I glanced over at my new friend, silent and stately as ever. "Sometimes, things just end. They're messy and complicated and it sucks, but life doesn't owe you answers and a neat little bow to tie things off. Sometimes, all you get is a smashed heart and a choice: make friends with the pain and move forward, or curl up on the kitchen floor, fall back into the past, and fucking *drown* there. I didn't want to drown, Gargs. I wanted to fight."

I told him about my so-called rise from the depths of that dead sea—leaving Elian's apartment, joining Bay

Coven, practicing my blood magick, trying to build an actual life for myself that didn't involve looking at old pictures and waiting for them to talk to me. I made new friends, found things to smile about. I even met a new guy —a wolf shifter. I thought I could love him, too. Not right away, not in the same reckless, passionate tumble I'd experienced with Elian. But in a mature and stable way—one that would last. It's what I thought I'd wanted, and for a long time, things were good. Not amazing, not butterflies-with-every-searing-hot-touch, but good.

Then, just as I was finally getting my footing again, it happened.

A mutual witch friend who'd moved down south had heard about a club in New Orleans. Saints and Sinners, it was called. An abandoned cathedral bought and resurrected a few months earlier by a silver-eyed fae with a crooked grin and a clever tongue.

A man who'd allegedly done the impossible:

Escaped the deadly realm of Midnight after years of exile.

His name was Elian.

"I wept to know he was alive," I said. "Wept to imagine what he must've endured in captivity. Wept to think he might soon return to the Bay, or call or write me, and what would I even say to him? I was in a different place in my life at that point. Stronger. Older. Content with my wolf shifter. But I still cared for Elian. I wanted him to know he'd always have a friend in me. One who wanted him to be safe and happy, no matter how badly things had gone between us. But Elian… He never reached out, and I was too scared to make the first move. I figured he had his reasons—reasons he didn't want to share, or couldn't share, and I tried to accept that. But I couldn't.

"My witch friend had visited the club a few times since then—told me about the wild parties, the fae women, Elian at the center of it all like some giant supernova. I wanted to be happy for him, but all I could think about was the fact that in all her visits, for all that he'd rolled out the red carpet for her, he'd never *once* asked about me. It was like I'd stopped existing for him the same way *he'd* stopped existing for everyone else years earlier."

I ran my thumb along the blade of my dagger, accidentally nicking myself. Blood welled on my skin, and I stared at the little red beads. They glinted like rubies in the sunlight.

I pressed my thumb to the blade again, just enough to make it sting.

"I started waking up every night at three-thirty-three again," I said. "Started having nightmares about him being trapped in Midnight. The questions I'd *sworn* I put to rest were back with a vengeance, scampering around my mind all day and night like rats. I'd do my best to keep it together at home, then lose it in the shower, hoping my boyfriend didn't hear me. I didn't have the courage to tell him about

Elian—about how often I still thought of him. Missed him. It was tearing me up inside—I could barely function anymore. Eventually, I got fired from my job. I blew up my relationship, pushed away most of my friends. I sank right back into my old, desperate patterns, and it was only the barest shred of pride that kept me from hitching a ride down to New Orleans and making a scene so explosive, it would put Elian's craziest parties to shame."

Another breeze cut through the humidity, carrying the scents of jasmine and the still waters of the pond. I shivered, despite the heat.

The worst night of my life was slowly clawing its way back to the surface, strangling me in its icy grip.

I hadn't thought about it in a long time—not even when I'd finally seen Elian last night—but suddenly, it was all around me again. The darkness. The cold.

"My friend called me one night," I said softly. "Said she was at the club, and Elian was heading down to meet her, and did I want to give him a message? Feeling brave, I told her to say hello for me, and to call or text later if he wanted to say hello back."

I shook my head and groaned, the old shame rising inside. "You never think you're gonna be that girl, Gargs. The one who holds her phone and literally stares at the screen for three hours, waiting on the ping that never comes. And it didn't, of course. It was never going to. So, as the sun started to rise on yet *another* day without a word from the man who still owned my heart, I decided I was finally done. Just done. I chucked my phone in the toilet, stripped out of my clothes, and turned on the bathwater."

A deep, shuddering breath rattled through my lungs. I'd never told this story to anyone. Not to my sisters, not to my coven mates, not even to my journals.

Now, I was telling it to a statue beneath the gentle sway of Spanish moss, feeling safe and calm in a way I hadn't since my high school years in Nona's kitchen, doing homework at the kitchen table while she baked her world-famous lasagna.

"The next thing I was consciously aware of," I said, "I was naked in a scalding hot bath with a bottle of pills in one hand and a kitchen knife in the other, trying to decide which would kill me faster. Pills were unreliable, I figured, so I went with the knife. A vertical slit from wrist to elbow, as deep as I could stand."

I shivered and traced the tip of my dagger along the scar, a pink and silver ridge about the length of my pinky. The skin was numb there. It didn't want to remember that night, either.

"There was a lot of blood," I said. "More than I was expecting. And seeing it, that bright red mess... Something snapped inside, like someone just yanked off the veil and shined a flashlight in my face. Maybe it was Nona, or my dead parents, or the sisters I hadn't even met yet. Maybe it was fate itself, reminding me I still had important shit to do. But in that moment, I heard a voice in my head, clear as a bell. *Stop hoping*, it said. *Just stop.* At first, I thought it was encouraging me to give up, but it wasn't. It was saving me."

My friend's reports of Elian's party life in New Orleans had reignited hope inside me, and every day that passed, I was *hoping* I'd see him again. *Hoping* he'd finally explain. *Hoping*, above all else, he'd finally fucking acknowledge that what we'd shared had meant something to him, even if we had to let it go.

All that hope? I was poisoning myself with it.

"So I stopped hoping," I continued, "and instead tried to think of one simple thing—one *real* thing—I could appreciate. First thing that popped into my head? Nona's lasagna. I'd just made a batch the night before, and suddenly, I *had* to survive, if only to taste one last bite. So I made myself a deal: Get out of the bathtub, stitch up the arm, and warm up the damn lasagna. If I still wanted to opt out after all that, I could get right back in the tub. But you know what, Gargs? Once I had that first hot, gooey bite, I wanted another one. So I made a new deal: Stay alive long enough to eat one whole piece. One piece became the rest of the pan, which got me through another week. Then I found something else to appreciate. On it went, a few hours or days at a time, all these little moments of appreciation and bargaining until I finally realized I didn't want to get back in that bathtub. I was ready to fight again."

It felt like a thousand years ago, that fight. I thought it would've ended by now, but it didn't.

I was *still* fighting. Every single day.

Seeing Elian last night, as beautiful and alive as I'd ever known him, still rocking that stupid smirk and those eyes that could melt my soul...

I could very easily let him break me again. Slip right back into the darkest hours of my life. Slice the vein. Slide under the water. Goodbye.

But I'd survived that darkness. And in the years that followed, I survived other darknesses as well—the brutalities of the hunters. The deaths of friends and loved ones. The war in Blackmoon Bay.

Now, I had to survive Midnight.

And survival, I was starting to realize, wasn't an endpoint you reached. It was a process you endured—an endless cycle of trying and sometimes failing, but ultimately getting up again to fight another day.

Maybe I'd never be completely free of those ghosts. Maybe looking into Elian's eyes or saying his name would always cut me open. Maybe I'd start waking up at the witching hour again, my heart bleeding, the pain so deep it would drive me to my knees.

Didn't mean it had to control me, though. Didn't mean I had to give up fighting.

The love I had for him, the love I lost, the darkness... All of it had shaped me into the woman and witch I was now—a witch who'd called upon the dark goddess and wielded that incredible magick to save her family. A witch who'd found the strength to face the man who'd nearly broken her, just so she could repay her debts and save them again.

So, pain? Darkness?

Yeah. Maybe surviving meant learning how to appreciate those things, too.

Sitting in the sun-dappled grass with the gargoyle, I carved a pentacle into the soft ground at the edge of the pond with my dagger, then wrapped my hand around my blade and jerked it hard, cutting a deep slice.

It wasn't mutilation, though. It was magick. A blood spell for strength and courage. A thank-you to myself for not giving up. For learning, day by day, to spin the pain of experience into the gold of wisdom.

I made a fist, squeezing the blood onto the pentacle.

I will not give up. I will not stop fighting. I will not drown.

It felt like a promise. A sacred oath between my heart, my soul, and fate itself.

The blood glowed bright, then sank into the ground with a quiet hiss.

The softest breeze carried away my silent vow.

And in its wake, a dozen black roses bloomed in the mud.

Saint was my boy and all, but damn. My boy was a fucking liar.

He'd told me about the witch last night—about this Midnight run we'd all signed up for, come hell or high water. But now that the woman was pouring her heart out —not to mention her blood—I realized he'd glossed over a few key details.

Like the one about how he'd jacked up her life. Broke her heart so bad she'd made a date with Death and damn near sealed the deal.

Fucking Saint.

I'd never learned why or how he'd ended up in Midnight. Same with Jax. Just wasn't the kinda group therapy bullshit you shared in a place that had you running for your life more often than kicking back with friends over a few beers. Out there, no one had a past. No one had a future. All you ever got was the moment. Sometimes, not even that.

But now? I wanted to know all of it. Every gritty detail.

What the hell was so bad about his old life that it'd driven him to bail on a woman like Haley? A woman who'd clearly loved his dumb ass?

Still loved him, if the heartache in her voice was a sign—and in all my centuries of taking accidental confessions just like this one? Yeah. It usually was.

I wasn't able to *feel* anything in my stone form—no human touch, no sense of my own body, no rain, not even the fly-by bird shit that hit me on the regular—but I could sure as hell see and hear everything, and my brain worked just fine too.

Saint had really done a number on her.

Babygirl was a fighter, though—had to give her credit. Pulling herself out of that dark hole? Showing up here asking for his help? That took a serious set of lady balls, and hers were made of steel.

Even with them crocodile tears slipping down her cheeks, she still looked like a warrior.

She reached out and fingered one of her roses.

"Fuck," she whispered, her mouth rounding into a soft little o. "What the fuck is *wrong* with me?"

Wasn't often I shared a smile these days, but hell. If I was in my human form, I definitely woulda had one for her.

I'd been alive for damn near a thousand years, and I'd seen enough crazy shit to make even the most depraved, twisted sonofabitch gouge out his own eyes.

But this?

This was something else.

She and the others might not realize it yet, but I saw the truth in them black roses. Behind Haley's bright green eyes, a spooky-ass little monster girl lurked in the shadows. She was a fighter, yeah. A survivor, just like she'd said.

But she was a hell of a lot more than that, and she was only just *beginning* to taste her full power.

"So listen, Gargs." She glanced up at me and smiled, warmer than the sun on my stone heart. "Didn't mean to get so heavy on you on our first date. But you'll keep my secrets, won't you? You're a vault. Yes, I realize I'm confiding in a statue, and yes, I realize I'm probably having a breakdown—one more secret for you to keep. Oh! Along with my horticultural disaster. Wow. Haley Barnes, everyone. The crazy just keeps on coming!"

She reached for a big ol' clump of Spanish moss that'd fallen in the grass and hastily covered up her roses.

Too bad. Beauty like that deserved to be seen.

Satisfied with the mossy camo, she sheathed her blade, strapped the holster back around her thigh, grabbed her coffee cup, and got to her feet.

Her dress was the color of apples. A quick breeze blew

it up around her waist, giving me a shot of white lace panties and the leather holster. Haley just giggled, though.

"Hey hey," she teased. "Confession *and* a show—lucky you!"

If I wasn't already stoned, the sight of her woulda made me *rock* fucking hard. How the fuck was I gonna keep my shit together around her after sunset, when I was back to being a man?

No wonder Saint was tripping over his own balls just to help her. Pretty sure Jax had fallen under her spell too, though he'd be the last to admit it. That demon always liked to play it cool.

So yeah, *this* adventure was off to a good start.

Smoothing out the dress, Haley beamed up at me and said, "Thanks again for climbing aboard my crazy train. I think it's safe to say we've reached our final destination— I'll try to keep the breakdowns to a minimum. Let's just hope Saint's house is stocked with as much booze as his club."

Then, she leaned in real close—close enough I could see the golden threads in her green eyes—and ran a hand along the edge of my wing.

Aw, hell.

If I could've spoken, I would've told her *I* was the one losing my damn mind.

Because right then? The touch of her hand? The magnetic pull of those eyes?

Everything just fucking changed in a blink.

Everything.

Fuck.

Fuck.

No. No fuckin' way. I had to have imagined that. Right?

Touch me again, babygirl. Just need to be sure...

The softest breeze ruffled her hair.

"Did you just...?" She cocked her head and narrowed her eyes. "I could've *sworn* I saw your wing twitch."

If that's true, shit just got a whole lot more complicated...

Haley shook her head and laughed. "I'm totally blaming the heat on that one. It's gotta be at least two hundred degrees out here, and your girl is *wilting*. How do any of you survive this place? Guess I dodged a bullet, huh? Okay, I need to get inside that house before I melt. Assuming I make it through the day without getting arrested for murdering a fae and a demon, I'll stop by and visit again later. Maybe find some hedge trimmers for those creepy roses."

She reached for me once more, this time placing her hand flat against my chest, her palm still wet with blood.

A bolt of electricity shot right through me, jolting my heart and sizzling across nerves I didn't even know existed.

She felt it too—I could see it in her face. Her eyes widened, and she sucked in a sharp breath.

Thing is... In my stone form? I shouldn't have been

able to feel it. Shouldn't have been able to hear the sudden jackhammering of my heartbeat.

It shouldn't have started beating at all. Not until the sun dropped and I shifted into one of my other forms.

But there was no denying it. Inside the stone shell, I was fucking alive.

She kept on staring at me with them wide eyes, her hand trembling against my chest, and I *knew*. Sure as I knew every chip in my stone gargoyle form, every notch and tear in my wings, every scar and line of ink tattooed on my human chest.

I hadn't experienced anything like it in nine centuries. Nine fucking centuries, and I'd damn near forgotten how it felt. Forgotten I was even capable of it. Forgotten it was a real thing and not just some story I'd picked up along the way and turned into a false memory.

But suddenly, at the press of her hand and the touch of her blood on my stone, there it was.

The bond.

If I could've roared right then, I would've.

Unlike Jax and Saint, I was born in Midnight. Bred in captivity to serve as a guardian to the original Midnight royals—the most honorable gig our kind could've hoped for in that hellhole.

Fucked up as it was, the place was home—only one I'd ever known.

Until two years ago when I was betrayed by my own

kind, and Saint smuggled me out to save my ass from being pulverized. Not even Jax knew the whole story, but we weren't about to leave him behind. Saint made the arrangements for all of us.

Blood before roses—the three of us were tight like that.

So last night, when my boy said he needed help with this mission? I was all in, no question. Ain't never turned my back on him, not once. On top of that, throw in a chance to go back and hunt down the motherfuckers that'd taken everything from me? Done and done.

But now? Shit just got real in a whole different kinda way.

The bond only meant one thing.

Haley was fated for me.

My charge.

My twin heart.

My mate.

No, I wasn't talking about love and marriage and all that happy horseshit. Fate had a fucked-up sense of humor, and it didn't always work out the way you thought it oughta. More often than not, a gargoyle and his fated mate *despised* each other.

Didn't make a damn bit of difference to the bond, though.

Whether she ended up hating me or loving me, whether she wanted to be my friend or something else entirely—good or bad—fate had just sent me a message.

I was chosen as her guardian. She was chosen as mine to protect.

Non-negotiable.

Starting right now.

"Haley!" Saint suddenly called out, heading across the lawn. He was carrying a few bags of restaurant food—I recognized the smell of Cajun Jeb's.

Haley gave me one more smile. Felt like a gift. Then she lowered her hand and turned to face him, taking that electric zing with her.

"Sorry to keep you," he said, charming as ever in a fitted suit the color of sand, white shirt open at the top. "I was out picking up lunch—took a little longer than I'd hoped."

"Totally on brand, Elian. But... bright side?" She plucked one of the bags from his arms and peeked inside. "This time, you only left me hanging for an hour instead of five years. And you brought food. Hallelujah praise the goddess, maybe you *can* be trained!"

On the inside, I was laughing my rock-hard ass off.

Good girl.

"Haley... What happened to your...?" He reached for her wounded hand, but stopped just short of touching her.

She flexed her fingers and shrugged. "Just a little blood spell. It'll heal up in a few minutes."

"But... on its own? How?"

"Blood magick. It's is a hell of a drug." She flashed

Saint a killer smile he didn't deserve, keeping her other hand—the one with that fat scar along her wrist—tucked under the food bag.

Something told me he hadn't seen it last night, either. Might not have been so smug if he had.

Saint glared at me now, a warning flashing in them nickel-plated eyes like I needed to know something, and fast.

What the fuck he was trying to warn *me* about, I had no idea. Didn't care, honestly.

Homeboy shoulda been warning himself. 'Cause here's what I *already* knew: He'd hurt her in the past. Bad.

And as soon as the sun set and I was back to being a hot-blooded man again?

Fuck Cajun Jeb's jambalaya. That fae-fucking sonofabitch was gonna taste my fist.

I followed Elian into the house, as grateful for the air conditioning as I was for the food.

Phew. New Orleans needed a level-ten boob sweat warning stamped right there on the welcome sign.

The interior was even more picture-perfect than the outside, completely remodeled but still retaining its original charm. Lush draperies hung over floor-to-ceiling windows, and crown molding wrapped around the tops of the high walls, everything done in an elegant palate of creams, sages, and black. Nothing was out of place—I'd be surprised if Saint had even spent much time here.

I took a moment to look around, bracing for the same gut-punch that'd socked me outside. It didn't come, though. My spell seemed to be working, keeping me grounded. Keeping me sane.

Just a beautiful old house, I reminded myself. *Just a means to an end.*

The kitchen was a massive affair of exposed brick walls, granite countertops, and stainless steel appliances, ending in an eating nook with French doors that led out to a sunny patio.

At the center of the nook, Jax was seated at the table reading the newspaper—like, a *paper* newspaper, not a tablet—which was about the quaintest thing I'd ever seen. He'd ditched last night's white button-down for a faded black Dead Weather T-shirt that clung to his muscled chest, his hair damp from a recent shower.

He looked and smelled good enough to lick—a situation that was *not* helping me recover from the heatstroke.

Maybe NOLA needed a warning sign for him, too.

"Hey there, sinner," I said with a smile. "Fancy meeting you here."

He glanced up from the newspaper and flashed a grin —there and gone again—and I practically swooned.

Pay no attention to the diamond-hard nipples your lush mouth has suddenly inspired...

"Angel," he said neutrally, returning his attention to the newspaper. "I trust you didn't have any problems checking out of the hotel?"

"Funny enough, someone had already paid my bill." I turned and glared at Elian, who was busy retrieving plates and silverware for our feast. "Any guesses who?"

"Don't read into it," he said. "The owner's a demon. He owed me a favor."

"Don't we all," Jax grumbled.

"What are you doing here, anyway?" I asked Jax. "Come to see me off?" I set the bag on the table and started pulling out the takeout containers. Southern, spicy goodness wafted up, making my stomach grumble. "I think I love you."

"After one night?" Jax ruffled his newspaper. "Didn't realize I made such an impression."

I rolled my eyes. "Yeah, I was talking to the jambalaya."

"She does that," Elian said. "Talks to her food."

Jax looked up at me and lifted his brows, like, *Are you going to let him get away with that shit?*

No, I was not.

"I think we need some ground rules here, Elian," I said. "Rule number one—don't do that."

"Don't do what?"

"Point out all my cute little quirks and foibles like you've got the inside scoop on all things Haley Barnes. It was a long time ago."

"But that's... that's a thing you still do," he protested. "You literally just did it."

I grabbed the biggest container and popped off the lid, then took a seat right next to the demon. "Do you mind if I make out with you a little, just to piss him off?"

Jax leaned over, his breath stirring my hair. "Just so I'm clear... Still talking to the jambalaya?"

"Obviously." Ignoring the shiver of pleasure that rolled across my shoulders at the demon's proximity, I snatched a spoon from Elian's hand and dug in, skipping the courtesy of dishing it into a bowl. Elian had made me wait in the hot sun for an hour without so much as a note taped to the door. Manners were no longer high on my list.

By the time I glanced up from my jambalaya snog-fest, the room had fallen silent, and both guys were watching me as if they'd never seen someone have an orgasmic culinary experience before.

"Want some?" I asked, though it came out more like "wan thub" on account of the red-hot deliciousness filling my mouth. I scooped up another spoonful and lifted it toward Jax, but the demon didn't bite. Just glared at me in that unnervingly hot way of his.

"Jax is *here*," Elian finally said, "because he's coming with us."

"As is Hudson," Jax said. "Our other... associate."

Coming with us? Other associate?

"I'm not following," I said to Elian. "Why would you drag more people into this?"

Elian and Jax exchanged a loaded glance. They seemed to be having an argument without words.

Apparently, Elian lost.

Through a tight jaw, he sighed and said, "I wasn't the

only one to escape Midnight, Haley. Jax and Hudson were with me. We survived the streets together, and when the time came to leave, we made it out together."

"So now you're going *back* together? I don't think so, Musketeers." I shoved the spoon into my mouth, but the spicy food wasn't enough to rival the hot guilt bubbling inside me. "Elian, I can't do this without you. We both know that. But I can't ask your friends to—"

"We're not friends," Jax said, at the same time Elian said, "It's already done."

I turned to Jax, my eyes misting. "Don't be crazy. You don't even know me. Why would you agree to this?"

"I have my reasons." He grabbed the spoon from my hand and dipped it into the container, then lifted it to my lips. With another smirk, he said, "Eat, angel. Or you'll be fighting Hudson for the scraps."

I did as he asked, my eyes locked on his mouth, my skin heating up in a way that had nothing to do with the spices *or* my guilt.

Elian grumbled under his breath, but that was another thing I wasn't about to let him get away with.

Keeping my gaze locked on Jax, I grinned and said, "Elian, that's a *great* idea—thanks for offering. I'd love something to drink. Lemonade? Preferably spiked? And something for the demon as well. I think he's a little... thirsty."

Jax laughed. "Oh, I think I'm keeping this one, Saint."

Good.

Because I was pretty sure I'd be keeping him, too.

11

After I'd demolished most of the food and sucked down just enough boozy lemonade to fortify all those emotional buttons Elian liked to push, we cleared the table and got to work.

For all his many, *many* flaws—and I do mean *many*—Elian was at least taking this seriously. In the time since I'd dropped the Midnight-or-bust bomb last night, he'd already sketched out a map for me, and now he spread it out on the table and gave me the grand tour.

It was a vast realm, rippling with jagged mountains and drowning in nearly bottomless lakes, some made of blood, others made of fire. Aside from a few small outposts established by the soldiers of the many ongoing wars, there was only one urban center—Amaranth City—built in the north along the shores of the Sea of Tranquility. The

Razorback Mountains protected its western border; a range called Dead Claw protected the east.

The remainder of the realm stretched out to the south, each section of the map more treacherous than the last—tar pits, ice cliffs, meadows filled with poisonous flowers and razor-sharp grass. At the southernmost edge was Boiling Glass Sands, a desert so hot the ancient sands had long ago turned to glass. Elian said the Midnight fae had relinquished the region to the dragon lords millennia ago, but no one knew for certain whether the fire-breathers still existed; anyone who got close to the glass simply... melted.

Three-thousand-degree heat would do that to a body.

Blackbone Forest lay about thirty miles south of the city. According to Elian, it was mostly just bare trees and scorched earth, very little flora or fauna, largely ignored by the many factions fighting for control and the many beasts that would otherwise devour our bones.

That's where we'd be portaling in. According to Elian, anything closer to Amaranth had a higher probability of being watched, or—considering how often war erupted there—was too much of an unknown quantity. We couldn't risk portaling into the middle of a battle.

As for the city itself? Amaranth was warded against portals.

"And all these rebel factions," I said. "They actually *want* these lands? Talk about shady real estate dealings."

"Wars have been waged over less," Jax said. "By monsters and men alike."

I studied the map intensely, trying to picture myself trekking across such an inhospitable place.

Guess I won't be needing any more cute dresses now...

"Your primary objective in Midnight," Elian said, "is to locate Keradoc, get close enough to work your magick, and steal his blood, all without him detecting our presence."

"Oh, is that all? Easy peasy." I dropped my head into my hands and groaned. Seeing the map just made the situation all the more real.

The Goddess had to be *nuts* to think I could pull this off. *I* had to be nuts.

Maybe that's what she'd been counting on.

Bring me your demented, your unstable, your overly-eager-to-prove-their-worth-after-suffering-years-of-crushingly-low-self-esteem...

Damn, I really wanted another drink. But I was pretty sure a hangover would be about as useless as the cute wardrobe for getting me through Midnight.

"Hey. I know it's overwhelming," Elian said, coming around to my side of the table. "Looking at it all at once, sure. It feels damn near impossible."

"Not just near, Elian. *Actual* impossible."

He crouched down beside me and put a hand on my knee. Not sexual, not dominating, just... encouraging.

The gesture made my eyes glaze with emotion. It was

like a glimpse of the Elian I used to know. A glimpse into the past.

"The best way to tackle something like this is by breaking it down into several smaller missions," he said. "The first mission? Packing up, which we'll do tonight when Hudson gets here with the supplies. The next mission is getting through the portal to Blackbone Forest. After that, we get a new mission. See how this works?"

"Lasagna," I whispered, the knots in my stomach loosening. It was just like I'd gotten through the dark days after the bathtub incident. First, warm up the lasagna. Then take one bite. Then a piece. Then the whole pan.

"Is that one of her things too?" Jax asked Elian. "Calling out random foods?"

"I'm... not sure. Maybe she's hungry again?"

"How is that possible? She ate all the jambalaya and most of the cornbread."

"Not to mention the dirty rice," Elian said.

I laughed as the two of them studied me like some kind of zoo exhibit. "I'm good. I promise. Let's get back to these near-but-not-quite-impossible missions, yes?"

Elian got to his feet again, pacing in front of the table as Jax and I returned our attention to the map.

"Other than the soldiers," Elian said, "the majority of the population lives here in Amaranth." He leaned over and circled it on the map. "You want to get to Keradoc? We'll need to get inside the city first."

"Isn't he out fighting battles and slaughtering innocent villagers?" I asked. "I mean, warlord, right? One job."

"There are no innocents in Midnight," Jax said.

"And Keradoc's not a soldier," Elian said. "He's a politician who *plays* at being a soldier, waging his wars from behind a desk safely locked away in a fortified tower. The only time his weapons see any action is when he's bored and orders his minions to bring him something to decapitate or set on fire."

"You're saying he's got a thing for vampires," I said, and Jax laughed. I was truly starting to like the guy.

Ignoring us both, Elian said, "We won't be able to figure out Keradoc's current location until we're in the city. There, even the walls have ears. So, our first order of business in Midnight is getting from the portal..." He made an X over Blackbone. "...to the city. The southeastern quadrant is the weakest point, so that's our objective." He made another X near the city, then circled it.

"Is there a checkpoint or something?" I asked. "Watchmen? Or do we just... show up?"

He drew a curved line with several Xs running along the bottom of the city, all the way from the Razorback Mountains to Dead Claw.

"Vanderham's Wall," he explained. "And the watchtowers. The wall itself," he said, drawing another curve just beneath the first, "is protected by a trench that spans thirty feet across, thirty feet deep."

"Beggar's Moat," Jax said. "Just about the *last* fucking place you want to be."

"A moat?" I asked. "Seriously? As in, alligators?"

Jax ran a finger across the moat. "Worse. Way worse."

"It'll take about two days to reach the wall," Elian said. "There are primarily two ways in." He drew a line from the center of the wall out across the moat. "The drawbridge, which is lowered from the gatehouse twice per night, allowing Keradoc's soldiers to come and go, along with any other assholes unlucky enough to be in his service. Mostly military and their outfits—medics, cooks, and the like. Suppliers and traders come and go as well, maybe a few hunters looking for their next trophy from Dead Claw, although most of those fools never make it back."

"So the rest of the people inside the city are prisoners?" I asked.

"Aside from Keradoc and the other pureblood Midnighters, *everyone* in the realm is a prisoner. The ones who make it through the wilds and into the city are more protected, but they're not free, Haley."

"So why does Keradoc let them stay?"

"Every emperor needs his peasants," he said. "The working class keeps the city running, which keeps the ruling class in power. The rich get fat and happy off the sweat of their labor, then toss them a few bones once in a while to lull them into complacency. If they start to grumble about inequality, the ruling class simply starts another war, finds them another scapegoat, makes them fear and loathe and turn on each other to divert their attention from the true injustices baked right into the system."

"On and on the machine grinds," Jax said. "Until it grinds us all to dust."

I blew out a breath. For all its reputation as a vile, terrifying kingdom of bloodthirsty exiles, Midnight didn't sound all that different from the rest of the world here at home.

"Anyway," Elian continued, "one of us alone could easily sneak in with one of the supply caravans. But with a group, our best bet is option two—going *over* the wall."

"Over it?" I asked.

"That's Hudson's area of expertise," he said. "We don't need to worry about the details right now."

I shot him a dubious look, wondering just what sort of "associate" this Hudson guy was. Did he build catapults? Was he a dragon? How the hell was he going to get us over that wall?

Leaving it for now, I said, "Once we're in, that's it? We figure out where Keradoc's secret warlord hidey-hole is and storm the castle? Make it home in time for Mardi Gras?"

"Not exactly." Elian capped the pen and tossed it on the table. "Once we're inside Amaranth City, we'll need to reassess the situation on the ground day by day. Tracking down Keradoc won't be easy—he's not one to leave the city's protective boundaries, but that doesn't mean he's easy to find. We're talking setting up tails, stakeouts, bribing everyone from house servants to guards."

"And let's not forget, *brother*," Jax said with a sneer. "Not everyone in Amaranth will be rolling out the red carpet for their three favorite fugitives."

Elian sighed. "No, they won't be."

"Why?" I asked. "What did you guys do?"

When he looked at me, all the confidence drained from his eyes, leaving only sadness and regret behind. In a soft, broken voice, he said simply, "We got out, Haley. And they didn't."

Again I wondered what his life had been like in Midnight. What he'd even done to get exiled in the first place. As I understood it, unless you were a pureblood, there were only two ways into Midnight—portal magick from a dark goddess or witch, or committing a crime against the high fae so vile, they had no choice but to banish you from all the decent places of the world.

Which of those two tickets had Elian punched? Or Jax, for that matter? What about Hudson?

I came to New Orleans begging Elian for help—partly because the Goddess ordered me to and partly because I didn't have any other options for getting into Midnight. Elian was my shot. My one shot.

But underneath all that logic, there was another part of

me that'd truly wanted to see him. That wanted to believe, however naïve and ridiculous, he'd still have my back.

Now, more than ever, I needed that to be true.

But I was also staring down the prospect of a long-term stay on planet hell—months, from the sound of it—facing more dangers than I could possibly imagine, and my only escorts were a man I hadn't yet laid eyes on, a battle-scarred, one-eyed demon who'd *clearly* seen some shit, and the vampire-fae who'd already betrayed me once.

What if they led me into a trap?

What if things got heavy and they turned on me to save their own asses?

What if Elian bailed on me again?

I sighed. Legit concerns, maybe. But ultimately, none of them mattered. I needed to get to Midnight, and I couldn't do it alone. That ship, however rickety, had sailed.

Absently, I rubbed my thumb along the scar on my wrist.

Come on. You've survived worse. You're surviving right now —present tense. Whatever it takes. You've got this. You've fucking got this...

"Hey." Jax got to his feet and glanced out the window. Headlights cut a path through the trees. I hadn't even realized it'd gotten so late. "Looks like Hudson's back."

I got to my feet too, nerves tingling down my spine.

This was it. The third guy. My final escort to Midnight.

And quite possibly to my doom.

12

A huge beast of a man pushed through the kitchen door, arms laden with bags from a local hunting and sporting goods store.

Presumably the promised supplies—I spotted a couple of tent boxes and some sleeping bags, along with some outdoor gear. I didn't see any ingredients for S'mores, though, which didn't bode well for our Blackbone camping excursion.

I tried not to show my disappointment.

Sacrifices, girl. We're all making them.

The guy dropped the bags unceremoniously on the floor, then stood up to his full height, casting a shadow that went on forever. His eyes met mine across the distance, and my stomach dropped into free-fall.

"Hudson," Jax said. "Haley. I believe you two have already met."

"Um." I scanned the guy from head to toe and back again, which took a long time because dude was *massive*. Six-and-a-half feet of solid muscle, white V-neck tee stretched across a torso that looked like it was sculpted from marble, every inch of visible skin on his arms and neck covered in tattoos. Sun-streaked, messy blond hair fell to his shoulders, setting off eyes the color of milk chocolate. He had a beard too, slightly darker than his hair and just this side of scruffy, practically *begging* for someone to run her fingers through it.

Not that I was volunteering.

Out loud.

Anyway...

"Pretty sure I'd remember if I'd met *you*," I said, heading over to shake his hand.

The moment our palms connected, an electric zap shot up my arm, straight to my heart.

I let out a gasp, and Hudson's lips twitched. Not quite a smile, but close.

There was something oddly familiar about him. About that little spark.

"Are you going to tell her," Jax said to Elian, "or should I? Preferably before he proposes?"

"Oh, for fuck's..." Elian sighed. "Haley, you spent the afternoon mooning over him in the garden. Hudson's the gargoyle. That's how we're getting over the wall—gargoyles fly."

"Like the one out by the pond?" I asked, still dazed by his hulking presence. "And the one at Saints and Sinners?"

"*Same* one," Elian said, gesturing at Hudson like he was Vanna freaking White showing the good people what they'd won. "Garden statue, cathedral ornament, man about town."

A hot rush raced up my entire body, toes to eyeballs. "Wow. So that whole time I was out there spilling my guts, you were just... And I... Right. This is *super* fucking awkward."

He squeezed my hand and winked, both gestures so quick and easy I almost missed them.

He still hadn't spoken a word, but somehow, I understood him.

Don't worry, he seemed to be telling me. *Your secrets are safe with me.*

I relaxed and finally released his hand, but that little spark lingered in my heart.

Jax grabbed a beer from the fridge and tossed it to Hudson, who caught it with one hand and popped the top in a move so smooth I felt like I was in a beer commercial.

Good with his hands, check and check...

"Are you from New Orleans originally?" I asked, and he shook his head.

"He's not much of a talker," Jax said, and I wondered if that applied in all situations or just social ones.

Like, did he talk in bed? In a dirty way? *Could* he? If I

strategically positioned myself beneath him without clothes on and asked nicely?

I wonder how that scruffy beard would feel between my thighs...

God, what was wrong with me? First, I was lusting after the demon. Now the gargoyle, too?

This was all Elian's fault. Why the hell did he have such hot friends?

I glared at him as if he might answer my unspoken question.

He glared right back, firm and commanding and *not* fucking around.

My thighs clenched.

Shit. How the hell did he still have that effect on me?

No matter. Elian was a high-speed, hot mess express, and even though I maybe, possibly, very probably still had feelings for him—stupid ones, obviously—that didn't mean I had to act on them. I had *zero* interest in climbing aboard that train-wreck-in-waiting.

Restraint. That was my word of the year.

For Elian, I mean.

Jax and Hudson? I'd have to figure out different words for them.

"Well," I said with a bright smile, "he's covered in tattoos and his very presence seems to be irritating the fuck out of Elian, so obviously Hudson's one of the good guys."

Hudson raised his beer and smiled. A tiny one, barely peeking out from behind the facial hair, but the sparkle in his eyes said it all.

I trusted him immediately.

"So you three were... friends?" I asked. "In Midnight?"

"*Were*," Jax said, at the same time Elian said, "more like brothers."

I glanced at Hudson, who nodded but still hadn't said a word. So far, he had my vote for the sanest guy of the bunch, but for all I knew, that would change the minute he opened his mouth.

I was starting to get the sense they *weren't* friends—not exactly. Especially Elian and Jax. But clearly, something still bonded them, even years after they'd escaped Midnight. There was a deep loyalty there, a ride-or-die current running just beneath all the sniping and heated tension.

That, at least, was comforting.

"Hey," Elian said softly, and I jumped. He was close now—so close his breath tickled my neck. I hadn't even heard him approach. "You know we're going to see this through, right?"

I turned to face him. Searched those silver eyes. Searched my own heart.

Once, Elian had been that guy. The one who could make a promise like that without hesitation. A promise that could carry me through anything.

But now?

I swallowed hard, my throat suddenly tight. "How do I know I can trust you?" I whispered. "All of you? I still don't even understand why Jax and Hudson agreed to this."

"Well, Jax is a demon," Elian said, "and demons don't like being in debt. He's essentially doing this for me. Ergo, if he fucks you, he fucks me, and then—"

"Not literally, of course," Jax added, coming to stand beside Elian.

"—*and then* he ends up back in my debt," Elian continued. "So, for the sake of self-preservation, Jax can absolutely be trusted. And Hudson? He's a gargoyle. You couldn't ask for a better guardian. Strong, loyal to a fault, mean as hell in a fight, and he's *always* got my back, which means now he's got yours, too."

The gargoyle crowded in next to Jax and put his giant hand on my shoulder, giving it a squeeze.

I still couldn't explain it, but something about him made me feel instantly safe. Protected, just like I'd felt in the garden.

Maybe it was all part of his gargoyle vibe. Before tonight, I'd never actually encountered one.

I put my hand on top of his. Squeezed him right back.

Sometimes you spent every day with a person for years, yet you really never knew them.

Other times you spent five minutes with someone and it was like you'd known them a lifetime.

That's how I felt about Hudson. Like I'd just been reunited with my oldest friend.

To Elian, I said, "I notice you didn't rattle off *your* qualifications for a position in our circle of trust."

This got a smile from both the demon and the gargoyle. Even Elian himself grinned, crooked and sexy as ever.

Damn it, thighs. Enough with the clenching. You're going to chafe.

"I'm an excellent map-maker," he said, counting off on his fingers. "I'm fast, have superior senses, and can carry a pack more than ten times my body weight." Then, his voice turning as serious as his eyes, "I won't let you down, Haley. Not this time."

I let out a long, slow exhale and looked over each of them in turn.

Hudson, the strong and silent gargoyle protector.

Jax, the demon fighter who called me angel and gave me the best kind of shivers.

Elian, the vampire-fae who'd once taken my heart and still hadn't returned all the pieces, suddenly back from the dead.

My escorts. My monsters.

Every one of them had a dark past. Every one of them had probably done things—terrible, horrifying things I couldn't even imagine. Things that ate them up inside, no matter how tough they played it on the outside.

We weren't so different, my monsters and I.

But right now, standing in that New Orleans kitchen as we prepared for the most dangerous mission of our lives, our pasts didn't matter. All that mattered was the promise Elian had just made me.

A promise I was making to them as well.

I looked into Elian's eyes once more and I smiled.

"Yes," I said. "We're going to see this through."

Jax nodded.

Hudson nodded.

Elian held my gaze for another beat, then he nodded too. "Excellent. We leave before first light."

I forced a laugh. "No rest for the wicked, huh?"

"No, sparrow." His silver eyes turned fierce. "No rest for *any* of us until we get you back here in one piece."

13

ELIAN

My sweet little sparrow hadn't earned her nickname touring the karaoke bars of Blackmoon Bay—as much as I would've *loved* to see that.

No, her singing was more of an involuntary reflex. A *post-orgasm* reflex that'd driven me fucking wild since the first time I'd discovered it, not long after she moved into my place in Blackmoon Bay.

Here in New Orleans, Haley had just wrapped up an hour-long shower in my guest bathroom—the last indoor plumbing she'd get to enjoy for months.

And now, the sparrow was singing again.

Fuck.

I knew a bad idea when one blindsided me—hell, I was the *king* of bad ideas—but this was a wreck I couldn't fucking divert.

My hand was already on the doorknob. Logic? Reason?

Those assholes were long gone. All I had left was the Devil's Dream dissolving on my tongue and the moron sitting on my shoulder, laughing his balls off.

It's your fucking house, he goaded. *Do whatever you want.*

I didn't bother knocking. Just turned that knob, pushed open the door, and waltzed right in.

"Shit, Elian!" she shrieked, clutching the towel she'd just finished securing around her body. Her hair hung in a dark wet curtain, dripping over her shoulders. "I'm half-naked in here! What is *wrong* with you?"

I cursed myself for my terrible timing. Thirty seconds earlier, and the view would've been a lot better.

"I heard you singing," I said.

"Was I singing a song called 'Elian, please barge in here uninvited and annoy me in that oh-so-special way only you can do?' No? Of *course* not, because I'm still working out the lyrics for that one and it's not ready for prime time. Now, if you don't mind..." She fisted the front of my shirt and tried to push me out, but I wasn't budging.

I grinned at her, and her eyes softened just a fraction.

I stepped closer. Gazed down into her heart-shaped face. "I know I'm not supposed to keep pointing out all your little Haley-isms, but—"

"But you think I'll find your refusal to honor my wishes endearing? Because—*bzzt!*—thank you for playing! Please try again."

"*But,*" I continued, stepping closer until I had her

backed up against the sink, no escape. "I remember *exactly* what it means when you sing in the shower, little sparrow. And I just had to know... What inspired tonight's musical selection?"

Her cheeks flamed, but she didn't look away. Didn't flinch. Didn't go for the dagger she'd left beside the sink. Just glared up at me with those fierce green eyes, water beading across her shoulders, a few drops rolling down the hollow above her collarbone.

It took everything in me not to lower my mouth to her throat and lick.

Suck.

Bite.

"If you remember what it means," she hissed, "then you should also remember your services *aren't* required. I've already taken care of things, thanks."

"A little self-love in the shower? Definitely not enough to satiate *your* appetite." I put my hands on the edge of the sink, caging her between my arms. Heat radiated from her freshly showered skin. She smelled, as always, like strawberries and cream. "I remember that too, sparrow."

"New rule—you do *not* get to call me that anymore. Furthermore, you can't just... Holy shit, Elian. What the hell happened to your face?" She reached up and grabbed my jaw, jerking my head to the side. "Looks like someone picked you up by your feet and used your head as a croquet mallet."

"It'll be back to normal soon enough," I said. Then, tossing out the words she'd thrown at me earlier, "Vampire healing. Hell of a drug."

"What are you healing *from*?"

"Hudson. He and I had a few... words."

Well, that wasn't entirely true. *I* had words. He had mean glares and a hard-as-rock fist, which gave me even *more* words as I connected the dots on his sudden flare-up of psychotic over-protectionism.

It was a little crazy, even for Hudson. Didn't take me too long to figure out what was going on.

He'd bonded with her.

Fucking gargoyle. Nine hundred years without a bonded mate, and fate decided to offer up Haley? *My* Haley?

My blood still boiled just to think of it.

"Elian," she demanded. "What the hell did you do to him?"

"*Me*?" I laughed. "Thanks for the sympathy. *I'm* the one with the nearly dislocated jaw."

"I'd bet my favorite stake you had it coming. Hudson's a total sweetheart—he wouldn't hit you for no reason."

"You've known him all of an hour."

"Oh? Is there an official amount of time for when you can say you've known someone? A few years, maybe? Or is it that you're supposed to live with them, fall in love, and plan a whole future together first? Because that plan didn't work out so hot for me, so I'm thinking maybe time and proximity aren't always factors in how well you know a man."

I closed my eyes. Bit back a curse. Gave her a little space.

"I deserved that," I said.

"Maybe, but..." She bit her lip and lowered her eyes. "I'm sorry. I can't keep blowing up at you about the past. You're helping me now, and that's enough."

I moved in again. Tucked my finger under her chin until she met my gaze once more. "There's a lot you're not saying. Don't think I'm blind to it."

She nodded. "But I told myself I wouldn't ask you."

"Ask what?"

The breath left her lungs in a rush, stirring the steamy air between us. "What you did to get exiled to Midnight. You... you must've had your reasons for leaving that night, but... Anyway, it doesn't matter now. No going back."

Yeah, I had my reasons. At the time, I thought they were good ones. Honorable, even.

If I could go back and change things...

No.

As fucked up as it sounded—as much as the woman's very presence was tearing me up inside—I still couldn't say I'd do things differently with a second chance. Going to Midnight... It was something I had to do back then, just like I had to do it now.

Hurting Haley, though... That was the one thing I *would* undo.

"Haley, you have to know I—"

She held up her hand, cutting me off. "I told you, I'm not interested in rehashing the past. I don't need to know how you got to Midnight. But there is something I *do* need to know. Something we didn't cover earlier."

"Anything," I breathed.

"How the hell did you guys get *out*?"

"Midnight's... Well, it's not much different from any other place. A few bribes here, an exchange there, an agreement or two..."

"I guess everyone has a price," she said.

"Absolutely. The question is... Are you willing to pay it? Can you bear that cost for the rest of your life?"

She held my gaze for a long time, searching my face as if the answers she swore she didn't want were written there.

If she noticed my blown pupils, she didn't mention it.

Instead, she said sadly, "What did it cost you?"

"More than you can imagine."

Tears tracked down her cheeks, and I reached for her, cupping her face and swiping them away with my thumbs. She didn't pull back.

"I never stopped thinking about you, little sparrow." I held her face in my hands and drew closer, whispering against her lips. "Not once."

It was a confession I never would've bared if I'd been off the Black, but the inhibitions were down and the words were out and—like everything else in my fucked-up existence—I couldn't take them back.

"Elian..." She lowered her eyes again.

"Tell me you didn't think about me too," I said softly. "Tell me you banished me from your mind the night I walked out on you. Tell me you weren't thinking of me in the shower tonight, and I swear to you, Haley, I'll walk out of here right fucking now and never bring it up again."

She shook her head, a broken laugh escaping. "I can't."

Damn it. I was playing with *serious* fire, but having her this close again, her tears on my skin, her breath in the air, I couldn't let her go.

Just another minute, I promised myself. *Two tops.*

I wasn't so stoned I couldn't tell the difference between reality and my own twisted bullshit. I still knew I wasn't allowed to kiss her, to touch her any more intimately than I already had, but the Dream gave me just enough of a push to keep me walking along that razor-sharp edge.

Ask her, the moron on my shoulder said. *You know you want to.*

"Do you remember the first time I caught you singing in the shower?" I whispered.

She nodded, the blush rising in her cheeks. "I wanted you. Needed you, actually, but you were fast asleep and I didn't want to wake you."

"But you woke me, anyway. The sweetest, most off-key melody I'd ever heard stirred me from my dreams. I headed into the bathroom and found you leaning back against the tiles in the shower, your hand between your legs, your skin flushed. Even through the steam on the glass, I knew you'd just made yourself come."

"I was thinking of you. The way you kissed me. All the things you..." She swallowed hard, the blood racing through her veins, calling out to me just as her songs still did. "...the things you did to me earlier that night."

"You opened your eyes and caught me grinning at you," I whispered, afraid anything louder would shatter the moment. "I was so hard for you, I thought I might explode." My own words painted the fantasy, mixing with the Dream in my system to bring it to life as if it were unfolding right here, right before my eyes. I was hard for her again, my balls aching. "You weren't shy about it, though. You smiled right back at me, you wicked girl. And when I stepped into the shower, you *begged* me to touch you."

A teasing smile touched her lips, her eyes glassy, as if she was tripping right along with me. "You refused."

"I wanted you to make yourself come again. I wanted to watch. And you know something, sparrow?" I leaned in close, lowering my mouth to just a hair's breadth from hers. "You *wanted* me to watch, didn't you? Wanted to tease me and drive me wild."

Her breath caught. She nodded, unable to deny it.

"Do you know how many times I've played that movie in my mind?" I asked, tracing a fingertip along her jaw, following the path of another rivulet of water down her throat. "How many nights I've stood in the shower, still hard for you, remembering the sight of your fingers sliding over your wet skin? The taste of your kiss on my lips? Your breathy moans as you brought yourself right back to the edge?"

"Elian, I... I..." She closed her eyes and shook her head. Muttered a curse.

When she glanced up at me again, the haze had cleared, her eyes flashing with anger.

"Stop," she commanded. She leaned back against the sink, her hands instinctively going to her dagger, as if the damn thing were a security blanket. "Just stop."

I raised my hands and stepped back, shrugging as if it didn't matter to me one way or the other. As if it didn't feel like she'd just punched a hole through my chest and yanked out my heart.

"I'm not one of your clients, asshole," she snapped. "So stop incepting me with your hypnotic fae illusions and creepy vampire... *whatever* it is you're doing."

I didn't have the heart to tell her the only power I was using was words. The story of our shared memories unearthed from the deep and brought back into the light.

What Haley and I had shared? It didn't need a

vampire's influence or a fae's trickery. It was powerful and magickal in its own right. And even though I'd fucking destroyed it, it still tethered us. Across the years. Across the realms. I could still feel her under my skin. In my soul.

Yeah, I was an asshole to barge in on her tonight. An asshole to push things as far as I had.

But I couldn't leave it like this.

If she knew what this was doing to me right now...

No. Vulnerability was the surest way to get yourself killed.

I plastered my smile back in place, as cocky as she'd ever known it.

"Too bad you feel that way," I said. "Might be your last chance to, ah... *sing* for me before we ship off to hell."

"Pretty sure I'm already there."

"If that's true, then why is your blood racing?" I held my palm in front of her chest, close enough to feel the heat of her skin, but not touching. "I can hear it, little sparrow. Zipping through your veins like it's trying to escape."

"Hmm. Are you sure it's *my* blood you're hearing?" Haley laughed. Then, with a cocky grin of her own, she slammed her hand against my chest.

Blood leaked from a fresh gash on her palm, soaking into my shirt.

The magick hit me at once, a hot flush that burst from my chest and skittered across my skin like fire. Stars blinked before my eyes, and the edges of the room darkened. The ground spun out from beneath my feet.

I caught myself on the edge of the sink just before I fell.

"It worked!" She clapped her hands and bounced on her toes, so fucking cute I couldn't even be pissed at her for whatever mojo she'd just unleashed.

"What... did you do?" I panted, still dizzy. Weak. Not a good look for a vampire-fae, I'll tell you that much.

"Oh, is there something you *don't* remember about me? That I'm a blood witch, maybe?" She laughed, the sound of it echoing off the tile walls.

"But this is..." I clutched my chest, the breath slowly returning to my lungs. "This is different."

"Yeah, that particular spell is a *new* Haley Barnes trick." She waggled her fingers in front of my eyes, showing off a silver ring with a polished dark-red stone. "Bought it from a blood priestess last night in Tremé. She said the bloodstone was spelled to enhance my natural gifts and allow me to temporarily manipulate blood flow in an assailant. Don't you just *love* when a product works as advertised?"

I nodded, still trying to blink the stars from my eyes, though at that point I couldn't be sure they were from the magick and not from the whirlwind of Haley Barnes.

"But now that you've had the pleasure of nearly losing consciousness at my command," she added, her smile bright, "you can add it to the list of things to remember about me. Write it down. That way, the next time you barge into my shower uninvited, you'll know what to expect."

With that, she pressed her hand to my chest again and shoved me and my still-raging hard-on right out of the bathroom.

"Save your fucking fantasies for someone who wants them," she snapped, "because I sure as hell don't."

The door slammed in my face.

My breathing returned to normal.

I leaned my forehead against the wood and sighed.

Fuck.

Haley didn't want my fantasies? Yeah, they weren't for her. They were never for her.

They were for me.

Because like I'd told her, the price I'd paid to leave Midnight was higher than she could've imagined. And now, a fantasy was the closest I could ever come to making my little sparrow sing for me again.

14

KERADOC

ieutenant General Oona of Midnight stood before me at the council of war, her sky-blue hair pulled tight, her face grim. "We've lost Hanging Lake, sir. The Road of Silence has been overrun."

The other generals and commanders seated around my table grumbled, but I kept my face impassive.

Named for the mutilated corpses the raven gryphons hung from the surrounding trees, Hanging Lake was actually a swamp, a fetid pit of despair that stretched on for miles along the southwestern borders of Midnight. The swamp's value was purely strategic; it surrounded both sides of the Road of Silence that led into Razorback range, keeping all but the most intrepid travelers and traders from wandering too close to Amaranth City.

Most could neither outrun nor outwit the vicious raven

gryphons, and the slaughtered remains of those who'd tried had long served as a deterrent to any upstarts.

So how the hell had we lost control?

"Darkwinter?" I asked, though I already knew the answer. The Darkwinter fae were the toughest of the rebel factions—the only faction we truly needed to fear, assuming the others didn't unite under a common banner. They'd been steadily gaining ground for months, portaling in all across the realm, each new platoon stronger and more fearsome than its predecessor.

"Yes, sir." Oona held my gaze, her spine straight as an arrow. "Reports from the northern front have also confirmed additional Darkwinter vessels moving in across the Sea of Tranquility."

So the enemy fae had found dark witches powerful enough to portal in not just their men, but their ships as well?

Again, I fought to hide my displeasure.

Despite its moniker, the northernmost sea was anything but tranquil. Roaring as high as a mile above sea level, its waves were notoriously savage, pulverizing most ships within seconds. What the water could not destroy, the sub-zero air temperatures and brutal hurricane-force winds usually did, not to mention the array of fiendish sea creatures circling the depths, always in search of a feast.

Long before Amaranth City was built, the Sea of Tranquility protected Midnight's northern border from invaders, fae and demonic alike. It was so untraversable, our own people had never even built warships. We scarcely knew the true depths of that perpetually storm-tossed sea or the terrifying creatures that inhabited its watery kingdom.

"How are they even navigating it?" one of the commanders asked.

"Our troops claim their ships are unassailable," Oona said. "They cut through the waves like hot knives through butter, allegedly impervious to both the cold and the threats of Tranquility's native monsters."

"We *must* mount an attack," he replied.

I shook my head. "Our gargoyle squadrons simply aren't capable of an aerial assault in the extreme cold."

"Unchallenged, they will surely reach this city," he said. "This castle."

"Yes, and we must defend both at all costs." I turned my attention back to Oona. "I want more men moved to the outposts along the shoreline. Find out what they need in terms of additional weaponry, and see to it they get it. Assume a prolonged siege."

"And if the arriving Darkwinter troops are as fortified as their ships?" another general asked.

"We will face them nevertheless."

"The Fog of a Thousand Knives, sir," Oona said. "The shoreline outposts are closed until it lifts—two to three more weeks, at least."

A chill crept into the room.

The Fog of a Thousand Knives descended upon the shoreline twice annually, lasting anywhere from four to six weeks. No one knew what caused it exactly, or how long it'd been haunting the north. No one who'd been caught in the mist had ever survived to tell the tale; anyone trapped in its white claws was immediately liquified. By the time the Fog receded, the beach would be stained with the blood of its victims.

My composure finally unraveled. "Do any of my commanding officers have a damned bit of *good* news to report? Have we managed to reclaim any territory from Darkwinter? Made any new gains in the east?"

Silence.

All eyes were downcast, save for Oona's.

There was a reason she was my most trusted advisor— one that had nothing to do with blood ties.

"See to it our additional troops are prepared to move north as soon as the Fog allows," I commanded. "In the meantime, send reserves to the Road of Silence. I want a full assessment of the situation, as well as ongoing reports on Darkwinter's movements. Every time one of those bastards so much as shits in the Haunted Wood, I want to know about it."

"Yes sir," came the chorus of replies.

"We'll reconvene in three nights' time," I said. "Dismissed."

As one, the council rose from the table and saluted, fists pressed together over their hearts.

I gestured for Oona to remain.

"What of our prisoner?" I asked when we were finally alone. Other than two very handsomely paid dungeon guards, Oona was the only one I trusted with knowledge of his existence.

But even she didn't know his true identity.

"Weaker by the night, sir."

I nodded, twisting the ring on my finger. Through the magick that bound me to him, I could feel his body failing, his soul aching for release. But if that happened before my armies reclaimed full control of the realm...

No. I wouldn't even allow for the possibility. Mine was a plan *years* in the making. Executing it had required exceptional vision, strategy, precision, and commitment.

I'd come too far to surrender now.

"See to it that his health is stabilized," I said. "Ask the guards to relocate him if you must."

"Relocate him?"

"The dampness and mold are likely impacting his lungs. Move him to the second level and increase his food and water rations as well. I want him alive and healthy, but not strong. Not clear-headed. Understand?"

"Yes, sir."

"What news of the Hollow?" I asked. "Have the peasants decided to revolt yet?" At this, I allowed a small smile, which Oona returned.

"Not yet, sir, though we're seeing increased signs. Dwindling access to food and water is causing unrest. Petty squabbles are turning more violent. Drugs and weapons seizures are on the rise from sources we've not sanctioned for the trade." She sighed. "If I may speak plainly, sir?"

"Please."

"It's been three years since the last Feast of Midnight. Perhaps it's time to host another? Give the people something to celebrate?"

I closed my eyes and sighed.

The Feast of Midnight.

In days of old, the ruler of Midnight began the tradition, hosting what would then become an annual gathering. For reasons that had always evaded me, he invited the filthy rabble of Amaranth City off the streets and into his home for a night-long celebration of food and sex and wine, offerings for our continued victories over the forces —natural and otherwise—constantly seeking to destroy us. The ruler, along with wealthy guests who'd paid for the privilege, would attend a more exclusive version of the event on the upper levels of the castle.

Feast of the Beast, as it was colloquially known, though I was never certain whether the beast referred to the host, the copious amounts of exotic meat he served, or the base impulses of the masses.

I'd always found it barbaric, but the people loved it. The ruler's feigned generosity gave them hope, and the briefest taste of luxury easily put them back into the barely conscious slumber from which the ruling class so readily profited.

The idea turned my very blood to ice, especially since it was now *my* home that would be opened to every street rat and urchin in Amaranth City, *my* feigned generosity put on full display.

But Oona's thinking was sound. The people needed something to celebrate. Something to pacify them.

"Very well," I said. "We shall give them their meat and ale. Let them cling to their ridiculous traditions."

"A wise choice, sir," Oona said. "I'll appoint advisors to see to the arrangements and keep you apprised of the plans."

"Thank you." I rose from the table and gazed out the tower window.

Situated in the center of the city on a rise that offered a three-hundred-sixty-degree view, the Castle of Midnight had been in the family for millennia, an architectural marvel as well as a fortress. In the long dark of Midnight's many wars, the Castle had never fallen.

Now, gazing south across Amaranth City and beyond Vanderham's Wall, I wondered how long that would remain true.

As if in response to an unasked question, red lightning

flickered on the southern horizon, sending an unexpected jolt of fear skittering along my spine. It settled in the pit of my stomach with a dull fizz, like sparkling wine gone suddenly flat.

"Sir?" Oona asked. "Are you unwell?"

I stared out at the dark sky. Nothing moved but the clouds scudding over the two visible moons. No more lightning. Not even a flicker of starlight. The third moon wouldn't rise for hours.

"Father?" she pressed, finally dropping the pretense of military rank as she placed a hand on my arm.

The touch drew my attention, and I glanced into her eyes, violet like her father's.

In that moment, she was no longer a lieutenant general. Just a concerned daughter. Daughter of the monster who ruled this land with fists and swords and manipulation, no atoning for the blood he'd spilled along the way.

The concern in her voice softened my hard heart, but I wouldn't allow her to glimpse it. Oona wasn't accustomed to gentleness. She'd grown up the target of threats and abuse that had only grown worse with time, with the pressure of our many endless wars.

Showing vulnerability now would only confuse things. For both of us.

"Your concern is misplaced," I said firmly.

"But I thought—"

"See to our prisoner, Oona. And let the cooks know I'll be taking dinner alone in my chambers tonight."

"Shall I join you there? We could review the maps, maybe look at alternate routes around—"

"What part of *alone* was unclear to you?"

She didn't flinch. She was too good a soldier for that.

But I'd seen the flicker of sadness in her eyes, and it cut me in a way I preferred not to dwell upon.

"Of course," she said. "Goodnight, Father. Sir." She bowed her head, then stood up straight and saluted.

"Dismissed," I replied, and then she was gone.

Guilt simmered, but Oona was strong, just as her mother had been.

I glanced out across the wall once more and sighed.

I only hoped her strength would be enough to save her.

There's beauty in darkness. Remember that when we get where we're going.

—H

I stared at the note, scrawled hastily on the back of a receipt for wool hiking socks and MREs, tucked under a vase of fresh flowers that someone had left in the guest room while I'd showered.

Not just any flowers, either.

Black roses. *My* black roses.

I couldn't help the smile that spread on my face or the warmth that followed.

The biggest, baddest guy of the bunch, and when it came down to it, Hudson was just a big ol' squishy teddy bear in the body of a stone giant.

Maybe I should've been mortified to discover I'd bared

my soul to *him* in the garden and not an inanimate statue, but I wasn't. That covert wink had said it all. He really was a vault—safe and secure. Reliable. Strong.

Besides, I'd taken him on a deep dive into my ocean of crazy, and even after he'd shifted into a man with functioning legs, he hadn't gone running for the hills.

He was a rock.

And honestly? Between the old flames Elian was stoking back to life and the new ones Jax was igniting, a rock was just what I needed.

Not that Hudson didn't have the power to stoke flames.

Just that not everything with every hot guy had to be about sex.

Even though I hadn't really... ahem... *sung* for anyone other than myself in a long time. And I was a thirsty bitch who would've loved to share my vocal gifts with a partner. Hell, at that point, I was ready to put on a full-blown concert, complete with T-shirt cannons and pyrotechnics and a Madonna-style cone bra, if that's what it took.

Alas...

Duty called.

I folded up the note and tucked it inside the pack I found on the bed. There were some clothes laid out as well —cargo pants, sports bra, a fitted moisture-wicking shirt, hiking boots, all in my size. They'd thought of everything.

I dressed quickly, finishing up just as someone knocked on the door.

"Come on in," I said, knowing it wouldn't be Elian. He wouldn't have bothered with the knock.

It was Jax, the scent of campfire and lemon trailing in with him as he stepped inside and closed the door.

"Looks good on you," he said. "Not that you can trust the opinion of a one-eyed demon, but..."

"Thanks," I said with a smile. "I'm used to a different sort of look."

"Short dresses?"

"Sometimes, yes. My other favorite is leather and metal. All depends on whether I'm hunting down blood-suckers—"

"Or trying to drive your ex crazy?"

I laughed. "Yeah, well. Pretty sure my crazy-driving days are over. I'm Rocky Mountain Barbie now."

"Pretty sure you've still got some crazy in you." Jax's smile faded. "You about ready?"

"Does it matter if I'm not?" I sat down on the bed, fingering the strap of my new pack. "Wait—let me rephrase: no, hell no, not even close."

"Haley..." Jax ran a hand through his black hair and sighed, then came to sit beside me. "What Saint said about trusting us... Look, I won't pretend to know what the two of you went through before he showed up in Midnight, and I sure as hell don't know what's waiting for us when we get back. But he was right about one thing. We *will* have your back."

"I know. I'll have yours, too."

"Is that so?" he teased.

"Of course! What the hell kind of a witch do you take me for?"

"No idea, but something tells me you're kind of a badass."

I propped a hand on my hip and glared. "*Kind* of?"

"Okay, okay. Full-on badass." Jax smiled, then grabbed my hand, shocking the hell out of me.

His touch was strong and reassuring, and in the wake of its warmth, I rested my head on his shoulder and closed my eyes.

"You think I'm crazy, don't you?" I whispered.

Jax's breath stirred my hair. "I think... I think you're doing what you believe is best to save the people you love."

"Nice save, demon." I laughed. "Who knew hellspawn could be so diplomatic? Maybe you should consider running for office."

Jax wasn't laughing, though. He pulled back and gazed into my eyes, a sadness rising in his that made my heart squeeze up. "Saving the people you love is never crazy, Haley. Just be sure you don't lose yourself in the process."

I nodded and promised I wouldn't, but could I even keep a promise like that?

How could I make sure I didn't lose myself when I'd never even found myself in the first place?

"Take a few more minutes and do what you need to

do," Jax said, giving my hand one last squeeze before letting go. "But we need to get going. We don't know how long the portal transition will take, and if we don't get enough of a jump on sunrise, we'll have to wait until Hudson can shift back again tomorrow night."

"How does all that work, exactly?" I asked. "With his shifting?"

"Daylight always turns him into stone. Any other time, he can shift at will among three forms—human, stone, or his winged warrior form, which is sort of crossed between the two, but more massive and with wings."

"Stone by daylight. Okay, I need to set a watch or something—that seems like an important thing to keep track of."

"Won't be an issue in Midnight. The sun doesn't rise there—just three moons."

"Seriously? I was hoping that was just hyperbole."

"Nothing you've heard about that place is hyperbole." He put his hand on my shoulder, his gaze stern. "Remember that, angel. Because the minute you forget, it'll get us all killed."

Loaded up with our gear, the four of us stood on the damp earth on the far edge of the pond, gazing into the thicket of live oaks in the shadows just beyond.

"Will it hurt?" I asked, one hand clutching the portal spell, the other nestled tightly in Hudson's grip.

"No," Elian said. "Just hold on to us, and don't let go. As long as you focus on keeping the portal open, and the three of us keep visualizing Blackbone Forest, the magick should guide us straight there."

"From your lips to the Goddess' ears." I took a deep breath, inhaling the fragrant scent of night-blooming jasmine, realizing it could very well be the last time I ever smelled it.

I closed my eyes and whispered a prayer for my sisters, sending them all my love.

Then, with nothing left to say, I opened my eyes, tossed the vial to the ground, and stomped on it.

The portal shimmered to life before us, swirling with reds and golds and black, just like it had inside the glass. Hudson's grip tightened, nearly crushing my fingers. Jax moved closer, lacing his fingers through my other hand. Elian hooked his fingers through the back of my waistband.

And together, my monsters and I stepped into the light of the portal.

Into the darkness of another realm.

And into a volley of flaming arrows sailing right toward us.

16

"Down! Now!" Elian shoved me hard from behind, and we all dropped to the ground as the arrows whizzed overhead, leaving trails of smoke behind them. All around us, fires burned unchecked.

Ash and fire choked the air, making my eyes water. Through the haze about fifty feet out, I counted a dozen soldiers moving through the bare trees, their arrows knocked for another volley, bows aimed toward the sky.

"Fae. They're not after us," Elian said, and we all looked up at once. Two dark, winged figures cut through the glow of a blood-red sky, letting loose an earsplitting cry that sent shivers down my spine.

"Raven gryphons." Jax cursed as the beasts flew closer. "What the fuck are they doing this far east?"

"Hold!" came the command from the fae troops. "Hold! On my mark!"

I watched in a state of shock and wonder as two monstrous black birds the size of large SUVs swooped down to the treetops. They had the heads and wings of ravens, the limbs and tails of lions, and talons that looked like they could tear through concrete.

"Fire!" shouted the commander.

The troops unleashed another volley, their arrows whistling. The gryphons soared higher, avoiding a direct hit.

"Holy shit, they're fast," Elian said.

They screeched into the night, circling once before swooping back down, heading right for the fae.

The commander shouted again. "Fire at will! Fire at will!"

This time, some of the arrows actually hit the wings, but they had little effect on the huge gryphons, the fires fizzling out almost immediately. The winged beasts crashed through the dead trees and snatched up three fae, rending them apart in a shower of blood and gore that sent the others scampering off toward us.

"Get up!" Jax hissed, helping Elian to his feet. "We need to move before we're spotted by the gryphons *or* the fae."

Before I could say another word, Hudson hauled me up by my pack and set me back on my feet, his hand clamping around mine again.

Heads ducked, the four of us took off in the opposite direction of the advancing line. I chanced a quick glance behind us; the gryphons were busy turning the soldiers into their own personal buffet.

All around us, the bare, pitch-black trees of Blackbone Forest rose like skeleton fingers reaching up toward the stars. The sky glowed orange-red with the fire that raged behind us, chewing through the underbrush with a sound like a runaway train.

I choked back a cough, forcing my lungs to keep breathing despite the acrid air. My heart pounded, ears ringing with the roar of the fire and that awful screeching, all of it now mixing with the terrified cries of fae soldiers as the gryphons continued their relentless attacks.

It felt like we'd been running for hours when Jax finally stopped us at the top of a rise, bending over to catch his breath. Hands on his knees, he glanced up at me and said, "You okay?"

"Midnight makes one hell of a first impression," I said, finally letting loose that cough. The air was marginally cleaner up here, but the sky still held that ethereal orange glow. In the distance, I could just make out the silhouettes of the two gryphons, their forms growing smaller and smaller until they finally vanished.

I was pretty sure none of the fae had survived.

"The Midnight welcoming committee could use some new blood," I said. "Because that *completely* sucked. Didn't you say this forest would be deserted?"

"It should've been," Elian said.

Certain we were alone, we took a moment to check over our packs and each other for any signs of loss—gear, blood, or otherwise. All signs indicated we'd survived the literal trial-by-fire. After a quick water break, we started moving again, heading deeper into Blackbone.

Jax stayed by my side, with Hudson taking point and Elian bringing up the rear. We walked in silence for a few minutes, our gear clinking, boots hitting the scorched earth with soft thuds.

Then Elian said, "You were right about the gryphons, Jax. They shouldn't be roaming this far east. Their domain is the Hanging Lake."

Jax nodded, turning to glance at Elian over his shoulder. "Things have changed since we left."

"War will do that to a place," Elian said. "I wonder what other surprises we'll find. I don't—"

"Guys!" I gasped as a new shadow moved over us. "We've got company!"

A third gryphon glided overhead, passing us before it circled back for another look.

Fuck. My gut told me we had mere seconds before he spotted us.

Jax grabbed my arm, but I shook free and dropped into a crouch, unsheathing my dagger and drawing a pentagram in the dirt. A quick slice of my palm and a tight fist, and my blood spilled onto the symbol.

The gryphon let out his war cry and dove, and I called out my spell.

> *Beast of darkness, beast of night*
> *My blood is your weakness, my blood is our*
> > *light*

I slammed my palm against the dirt. The pentagram glowed as bright as the fae arrows, then exploded in a flash of red light, rising like a wall before us just seconds before the gryphon crashed through the trees.

The beast hit the wall head-on. Magick sizzled across his feathers, lighting him up as if he'd been electrocuted, unleashing a cry of pure agony.

I jumped to my feet. "Move! It won't hold him for long!"

We darted down the other side of the rise and into a new section of Blackbone. The bare trees offered no cover, and minutes later, the gryphon was back in the air and hot on our trail, the smell of scorched feathers so strong it made me gag.

Even at a run, I saw his dark shadow slithering along the ground. Felt the air current shift above me as he dove.

My heart jumped into my throat.

"Haley!" Elian shouted from somewhere behind me. "Get down!"

I dropped and covered my head, and in a blur of

vampire speed and grace, Elian catapulted over me, his sword held high.

The gryphon cried out, a great flapping of wings sending a hot current rushing over me.

Blood rained down, splattering my hair, my pack.

I didn't even have time to process what'd happened before Hudson barreled into me, tucking me against his chest and rolling us away mere seconds before the muti-lated gryphon dropped from the sky, plowing into the ground where I'd just been crouching.

Still caged in Hudson's arms, I thrashed frantically, scanning the scene.

"Elian!" I called out. "Elian!"

"Here," came the reply. "All hail the victorious gryphon-slayer."

He emerged over the top of the dead beast like a cham-pion dragon-slayer of old, pack dangling off one shoulder, his sword at his side. Blood ran down his face and covered his clothes. He looked like a demon straight out of hell.

But the vampire-fae merely tossed his pack to the ground and laughed, white teeth flashing in the dim. "You should see your face right now, sparrow. Priceless."

"For fuck's sake, Saint," Jax said, staring at the gryphon and its killer in disbelief. "How the hell...?"

Hudson finally released me, and I jumped to my feet, charging right for the cocky fae.

"Seriously?" I glared at him, hands on my hips. "I totally weakened him for you."

"Yes, and that was quite an impressive bit of hocus-pocus, witch."

"I know, right?" I flipped the bloody hair over my shoulder and preened, more relieved to see that stupid fae than I cared to admit.

Elian kicked at the creature beneath his feet. "You know, these assholes wouldn't be half bad if I could figure out how to compel them. Maybe strap on a saddle."

"Hard pass," I said. "But you go right ahead. In the meantime, I need to change this bloody shirt before I puke. Any idea where the ladies' room is?"

Elian laughed, but before he could shoot out his next retort, his face paled, his eyes going wide.

A dark shadow swept over him.

I sucked in a breath and blinked, and just like that, another gryphon swooped in. Before he could even raise his sword, the beast plucked Elian from the dead gryphon like an owl plucking a mouse from the field.

His sword fell to the ground.

And the gryphon soared into the smoke-filled sky.

17

HALEY

G o!" Jax shouted at Hudson. "I've got Haley. Go help Elian!"

Hudson met my gaze for an instant, my eyes wide with fear, his own pained, then took off at a sprint, his human form already beginning to morph. His muscles stretched and elongated, bones shifting, his body gaining in height and mass as the warrior form took shape. Hands and feet became talons not unlike those of the gryphons, and as his clothing fell away, his skin turned a deep slate gray. By the time the massive leathery wings burst from between his shoulder blades, Hudson was already airborne.

I watched him soar higher and higher, following the path of the gryphon until both of them vanished into the darkness. I spun around in circles, head tipped, searching in all directions for any more assailants.

"I think we're in the clear," Jax finally said. "They don't usually hunt in packs. That they were here at all is a fucking mystery."

"But Elian's... That thing took him and..." I swayed on my feet, images of the dismembered fae soldiers flooding my mind.

Jax caught me and held me upright, his mouth close to my ear. "Pull it together," he whispered. "Elian's stronger than he looks, and Hudson's already on his way. We've fought these things before—they just took us off guard tonight. It won't happen again."

"But—

"They'll be back before you know it. Trust me—we know how to survive Midnight. That's why you came to Elian for help, right? So stop freaking out before you lose your shit and make a mistake that gets us killed."

I nodded, blowing out a shaky breath.

Jax was right. They were practically locals. *I* was the newbie here. And this was only day one. Hour one. *Disaster* one of what was probably many more to come.

If I lost it now, the mission would be over before it'd ever really begun.

Digging another water bottle from my pack, I did my best to rinse the gryphon's blood from my hair, then swapped my shirt for a clean one.

"Hungry?" Jax asked, searching through his pack. "I'm

guessing that blood spell took some of the wind out of your sails."

I nodded, offering a grateful smile. "If I ever say no to food, *that's* when you need to start worrying."

"Fresh out of jambalaya, but I've got an oat-and-honey granola bar and some beef jerky, if you're interested."

That got an even bigger smile. "Throw in a Fallen Angel, and you've got yourself a deal, demon."

"Don't tempt me."

"Is that even possible?" I teased, happy for the distraction it provided. Without it, I'd start thinking about Elian and Hudson and that freakshow fucking bird. "Aren't demons supposed to be the tempters in this operation?"

"Free advice?" Jax tossed me the food, then readjusted his eye patch, his mouth pulling into a surly scowl. "Don't *ever* give a demon reason to tempt you."

I tried not to shiver at the dark warning in his voice.

I gobbled up the jerky, then the granola bar. Feeling a little more grounded, I left Jax to brood alone and headed over to check out the gryphon carcass. The thing was even more terrifying up close. The beak alone was as long as I was tall, lined with two rows of black, razor-sharp teeth.

A fresh wave of fear barreled into me, and I turned back toward the demon. "Why aren't they back yet? What's taking so—"

"Um, Haley? Less talking and more..." He grabbed my shoulders, then stepped us a few feet to the left.

A heartbeat later, another dead gryphon crashed to the ground with a thud.

Two figures emerged from the trees behind it.

Hudson was back in his human form, naked and glistening with sweat, his powerful muscles rippling beneath his skin, and yes, friends and neighbors, the answer to the question on *everyone's* minds...

Those tattoos really *did* go all the way down.

He caught me staring. Winked.

Cheeks flaming, I managed to drag my gaze away from him long enough to check on Elian, who was still wearing that same smug, victorious grin he'd had after taking out the other gryphon.

"Two for two," he said breathlessly, stumbling toward us. "If anyone's keeping score."

"You're okay," I breathed. I scanned him from head to toe, not entirely sure I could trust my eyes. "I thought you were a goner, you dick."

"All good, sparrow. Just... just a little..." He blinked, then fell forward, collapsing into my arms.

"Jax! What's wrong with him?"

"Fuck. He needs to feed," Jax said. "Come on, let's get him on the ground."

As Hudson dressed and checked our perimeter, Jax helped me get Elian situated against a tree. We cleaned the blood from his face, then fished out a couple of blood bags from the stash, helping him feed. But even after downing two in a row, he still looked pale and listless.

"It's not going to be enough," Jax said. "I was afraid of that."

"We've got plenty more."

Jax shook his head. "He burned through too much energy fighting the gryphons. They've got their own sort of dark magick, and it takes a bite out of you just as sure as those claws and teeth. Cold blood isn't going to cut it. He needs to feed from the source."

"Source?" Alarm spiked in my chest. "Are there even any humans in Midnight?"

"In the city, yes."

"Jax. That's a two-day hike. He'll never make it."

"You got a plan B? I'm all ears."

"No, but..." I bit my lip, not sure if this was a good idea or a fucking disaster-in-the-making, but at that point, I was pretty sure things couldn't get much worse. I pushed up my sleeve and made a fist, bringing my veins to the surface. "How about a plan B-positive?"

Jax glared at me, his blue eye boring right through me. "*No.*"

"Why the hell not?"

"Once he starts, he might not be able to stop. If he takes too much, you'll—"

"He won't. You'll keep a close watch. If it looks like he's about to O.D. on the good shit, just cut him off."

"Have you ever tried to cut off a starving bloodsucker mid-feed?"

"Have you ever tried to tell a Scorpio-sun, Aries-moon blood witch that she can't do something?"

Silence.

I glanced at Elian. His eyes were closed, his head lolling to the side. I tucked one of his silver braids behind his ear, my hand trembling for more reasons than I wanted to think about.

In a quiet voice, I said, "I told you before we left New Orleans, Jax. I've got your backs, same as you've got mine. So either help me or stand aside, because I'm not letting him die here tonight."

Jax sighed, but finally agreed. Kneeling beside us, he gave me a quick nod, then gripped Elian's shoulder. "Careful, Saint."

I took a deep breath. Pressed my wrist to Elian's cold lips.

He tried to swat me away, to turn his head, but he was too weak to fight me.

"Bite me, bloodsucker," I said, cupping his chin to hold him steady. "Or you're going to give me some weird complex about how my blood is undesirable and I'll end up in therapy and I don't have health insurance so I'll have to—"

Fangs pierced my skin, a sharp pain shooting up my

arm. But before I could even cry out, the pain receded, chased by a pleasure so intense, I almost came.

"*Damn*," I whispered, and Elian's gaze locked on mine, new life flooding into his eyes, their silvery depths swirling with desire as he licked and sucked.

Tasted.

Devoured.

Left me weak and panting and—

"Slow down, Saint," Jax said, but Elian ignored him, sucking harder, his eyes fierce and fiery, my skin burning under the instant press of his mouth.

"That's enough."

I was vaguely aware of the demon's command, but I didn't dare pull away. Didn't dare deny Elian the blood he needed. Didn't dare deny myself the exquisite pleasure of—

"I said that's *enough*."

I hadn't even felt Jax reach for it, but before I knew it, he had my stake out of its thigh holster, the pointy end pressed to Elian's throat.

Elian shot him a vicious glare, but—with a final swirl of his tongue against my skin—he released me.

Blood shone on his mouth, his lips pulling into that crooked grin I loved as much as resented.

"Haley, you good?" Jax asked, sliding my stake back into place.

Blinking, I tore my gaze away from Elian's ruby-red

mouth and glanced down at my wrist. The wound throbbed, every beat of my heart sending a matching pulse of desire through my core.

But unlike the asshole vamps who'd bitten me at Saints and Sinners, Elian had infused the bite with his healing magick. The bright red punctures immediately began to close, leaving nothing behind but a smear of blood and a deep, endless ache between my thighs.

"I'm fine," I told Jax. Then, forcing a bright smile, I looked at Elian once more and said, "And you? All better, gryphon-slayer?"

He held my gaze for a long moment, flickers of desire still flashing in his eyes. He reached for my hand, gave it a quick squeeze. "Rest assured, sparrow," he whispered. "Your blood is *highly* desirable—no therapy needed."

We packed up in silence, hiking another couple of miles through Blackbone before deciding to stop for the night.

Well, for whatever constituted "the night" in a place with three moons and no sun.

The guys insisted on setting up camp, so while they hammered tent stakes into the ground with mallets and generally played out their macho outdoorsman fantasies, I found a quiet spot nearby and took a seat.

Other than the occasional smack of a mallet or the

snapping of branches for firewood, the forest was oddly silent. We'd moved far past the main area of the fires; all that remained was the vague scent of woodsmoke. It reminded me of Jax.

All around me, the finger-bone trees reached out, black and barren, strangely beautiful. There were no crickets or night birds, no rustling of leaves, no skittering of nocturnal creatures.

Yet the place held its own beauty. When I placed my palms against the dirt, I felt the hum of its magick running just beneath the surface, wild and untamed. Dark. Enchanting.

I took a deep breath and tried to figure out that strange, foreign feeling settling over me.

Peace.

Despite the beating we'd taken on arrival, something about Midnight had called to my soul in a way not even Blackmoon Bay ever had. Now, in these quiet moments, I could almost hear my soul whispering right back.

This is where I'm supposed to be...

But that was impossible. Crazy. Midnight was the worst place that'd ever existed.

Wasn't it?

"Good news and bad news," a smooth voice said from behind, and I turned to see Jax approaching, a mug of something hot in his outstretched hands. "Good news, we got the fire going, and I thought maybe you could use a—"

"Yes." I didn't even care what it was—I was so happy for a mug of hot liquid, it could've been straight out of Elian's blood bags and I would've dogged it. I took a sip, pleased to learn it was actually mint tea. "Tea is excellent news. So what's the bad?"

He crouched down beside me and frowned. "We lost two of the tents in the chaos, so there's only one left."

I laughed. "Bad news for you guys. That tent's *all* mine."

"But—"

"Hey, you're the one who was all, 'trust me—we know how to survive Midnight.' Since you're so intimately familiar with the place, you should have no problem sleeping out in the elements."

"You're not willing to share? Not even with one of us?"

"Yes. Hudson."

Jax laughed. "He doesn't sleep. He'll be keeping watch."

"Then he'll be watching me sleep in the luxury of my own private tent." I beamed at him and took another sip of tea. "This brew is excellent, by the way. Did you make it yourself?"

Jax shook his head, but there was no malice in his eye. "I thought it might help you sleep. In your own private tent. While the rest of us freeze our assess off outside. Why the fuck did I ever agree to help Saint with this shit?"

"Aww, you'd better stop saying such sweet things, sinner. Otherwise, I'll start getting the wrong idea."

"And what idea might *that* be?" he grumbled.

"That you *like* me."

He held my gaze for a beat. Two.

"Finish your tea," he said with a smirk, "and get your ass in that tent before Elian beats you to it and I have to stake his ass for being rude."

"Yes, sir." I took another sip, then turned to him and said, "Thanks, Jax."

He let out a huff. "For being so damn sweet?"

"Among other things."

And I meant it, too.

Especially an hour later, when I was safely tucked inside my tent and zipped up in my sleeping bag, far from prying eyes and superior vampire senses.

Because for the first time in five years, when I quietly slid my fingers between my thighs, the name I whispered into the darkness wasn't the name of the accursed silver-eyed fae, but a grumpy, blue-eyed demon whose smoldering gaze made me feel like I had a delicious new secret, all for me.

18

I had every intention of sneaking out of camp without making a fucking nuisance of myself.

But as soon as I passed Haley's tent, the soft, off-key melody of a badly butchered Led Zeppelin song floated to my ears, and I fucking tripped over my own stupid feet.

"Fuck," I muttered, barely catching myself before I face-planted into the still-smoldering fire pit.

Gods be damned, Haley Barnes. Forget the dangers of Midnight. You and your insatiable appetites are going to kill me before any of them get another shot.

The tent unzipped with a whoosh.

And there she was, blinking up at me with a wide, dreamy gaze, her cheeks stained with some new blush.

I knew *exactly* how that color had gotten there, too.

"Fuck," I muttered again, because when it came to Haley, there just weren't enough of them to cover it.

"Elian?" Her voice was soft and low in the quiet dark. "I thought you guys crashed already. What are you doing?"

Resisting the urge to climb into the tent, tear off your clothes with my teeth, and fuck you with my mouth until you're singing loud enough to wake the dead of Midnight...

"Just wondering if you're taking requests, little sparrow." I smirked and tapped my lips. "Radiohead, perhaps?"

Her sweet blush darkened, making my cock twitch. The taste of her intoxicating blood still lingered in my mouth—reason number one why I had to get the hell out of Blackbone Forest—and soon.

"Oh my God!" she whisper-shouted. "Were you *spying* on me?"

"There's a rumor Thom Yorke is fae—that's how he's able to hit those otherworldly notes."

"Elian!" She huffed out an exasperated breath, but she couldn't hide the smile curving her lips.

I tried not to gloat. The naughty little witch *liked* that I'd caught her.

The more things change, the more they stay the same...

Her green eyes flashed with mischief, then narrowed, finally noticing my pack. "Going somewhere?"

"Amaranth City."

"Alone? Now? In the middle of the... well, whatever the hell time it is?"

"I can move faster on my own."

"But... Why? We'd planned on a two-day hike. We haven't even talked about our next mission yet."

"Jax was right—the cold blood bags aren't cutting it. It's not just the gryphon attack—it's this place. It's more draining than I remembered." I hauled my pack higher on my shoulder and glanced around. The trees were still and silent. Fucking eerie, this place. I was pretty sure I'd never get used to it. "The longer I go without access to a live blood source, the more danger I'm putting everyone in."

"Right. I'll be sure to expedite your Martyr of the Year nomination." She rolled her eyes and pushed up her sleeve, revealing her creamy skin and the blue veins pulsing beneath. "You need a top-off? I'm good to go —promise."

My mouth watered at the sight of it, at the soft pulse throbbing in her veins. It echoed in my eardrums, damn near hypnotizing me.

Bite her, the asshole on my shoulder said. *She's offering the vein—fucking take what's yours...*

I closed my eyes. Bit back a curse.

I wanted nothing more than to drop to my knees and do just that. Fucking take it. Feed on her in all the ways I still fantasized about. Ways that would leave us *both* breathless and ruined.

But that was a sure path to disaster.

"Thanks," I said, meeting her eyes once more. "But it won't be enough. We can't risk it, Haley. I need to go."

Or I'm going to drain you dry...

Yeah, the scent of her blood was pushing me to an edge I did *not* want to cross, and I needed another food source. But it wasn't the only reason I had to get away.

Being this close to her again after so many years... It was screwing with my head. The way she looked at me was just...

Fuck.

Long before I'd ended up in Midnight the first time around, I'd spent decades surviving through lies and trickery. Then I met her and my world turned inside out. She'd seen me right from the start—right through all the masks, the bullshit.

After, when I got out of here and landed in New Orleans, I'd promised myself I'd make it real easy. No close ties. No intimate relationships. I'd built our Empire on fake smiles and the promise of escape, and people loved me for it. Fae, vampires, demons, witches—they all wanted in on the party. All wanted to be friends with the Saint of New Orleans, the fae who could take away their pain and absolve them of their sins.

It was all bullshit, nothing real, but it was easy. I knew what they wanted. They knew what they were getting. Add in a few smiles and comp VIP tickets, and I'd never want for company.

But people like Haley Barnes would always need more than I could give now. Not because they demanded it, but because they fucking deserved it, and to offer them anything less was un-fucking-acceptable.

Now, when she looked at me with those big green eyes, I tried to imagine what she saw.

And I fucking *despised* it.

So yeah, maybe that made me a coward. But I couldn't afford to be distracted—not out in the open like this, where my complete inability to get my shit together and function like a real man would put everyone at risk.

Especially her.

I crouched down in front of her. Pulled the sleeve back down over her wrist. Took her hand, just for a minute. "I'll see you in the Hollow in two days. By then, I'll have everything set up for us. We'll be safer in the city—all of us."

She pulled her hand away, tucking it deeper inside her sleeve. "What's the Hollow?"

"Our old... neighborhood, for lack of a better word. We've got someone on the inside—she knows we're coming. She's just waiting for me to make contact."

I heard the skip in her heartbeat at the word "she," but she didn't ask for details.

"Okay," she finally said, though her eyes had lost some of their sparkle. "And Hudson and Jax—"

"They know I'm leaving. They'll get you there safely." I got to my feet, readjusted the pack.

Haley stood up, too. "Will you do me one favor, if possible?"

As long as you don't ask me to kiss you...

"Anything, sparrow."

"The blood source... Will you ask first?"

"Ask *what*?"

She glared at me like I was the realm's biggest idiot. Which, admittedly... Yeah. I was definitely in the running.

"Permission," she said. "Consent is sexy, Elian."

"I'm a vampire now. Pretty sure 'sexy consent' doesn't apply to feeding."

"Yes it fucking does, and I'm asking you—against all odds—to at least *try* not to be a murderous asshole, if at all possible."

"And if it isn't possible? If I can't find the *one* human in all of Amaranth City who might be happy to offer up the vein? Would you rather I starve?"

"Of course not. If push comes to shove... Fine. Bite whoever you need to bite. But *only* if it's a break-glass-now kind of emergency."

I laughed. "Good to see you're still adhering to that rock-solid moral compass, Haley. Downright inspiring. In fact, maybe I'll write a song about it. And speaking of songs..." I nodded at her tent. "Don't let me keep you. Seemed like you were having a pretty good night, all things considered."

She glared at me a minute, then narrowed her eyes and said, "You sure you know what you're doing, *Saint*?"

Considering I'm about to walk away from you again? No, not in the slightest.

"Guess we'll find out, won't we?" I winked at her.

She pressed her lips together and sighed, clearly holding back.

"Haley, listen to me. I know I haven't always... I didn't..." I struggled to find the damn words. Words I actually meant, even if they weren't all the ones she deserved. "You said you needed my help getting you into and out of the most dangerous realm in the known universe, and you've got it. So everything else you feel about me, everything I did in the past, everything you *think* you know... I need you to put all that shit aside. Right now, the past no longer exists. Blackmoon Bay, New Orleans, the lives we had before—dead. There's only this shithole and the things we all need to do to get through it, and one of those things is you trusting me." I gripped the straps of my pack with both hands, because if I didn't, I'd grab her instead. "The guys will take care of you. Stick with one of them at all times. You hear me?"

She let out another sigh, but eventually nodded. "Yeah, I hear you."

"Good. Okay. Right. So, anyway... Yeah. I'll... I'll see you soon."

No response.

I turned on my heel. Heard the change in her heartbeat —the telltale spike.

"Elian, wait."

I blew out a breath. Turned around, even though I was terrified of what I might find in her eyes next. Terrified she might give me a reason to stay.

But Haley merely smiled at me. A small one, but real. Real enough, it almost had me tripping over my damn feet again.

"Be safe out there," she said. Then, with a new twinkle in her eye, "And for the record? Thom Yorke is *definitely* fae."

The three of us left camp a couple of hours after Elian when we figured out none of us could sleep, anyway.

The hike kicked off slow and groggy, but things started looking up when we found a freshwater lake. We took turns washing up, doing our best to ignore a group of imps on the shore taking turns flaying one another's skin off and feeding it to some creature they'd trapped.

Fucking Midnight. Sometimes, it was even worse than hell.

Considering Haley had never set foot in this fucked-up nightmare world, though, she was holding up pretty well. *Better* than well; after the bath, she perked right up, her cheeks pink, her eyes bright as we continued on through the endless night.

About a mile beyond the lake, Hudson took off to scout

ahead. Haley and I climbed another rise, and a small meadow opened up on the other side, silvery-blue in the moonlight, streaked with black vines and tiny white flowers—a plant I'd recognize anywhere.

"Corpsevine," I said, gazing out across the expanse. A small wooded area edged the back side. "Fuck."

"What's wrong?"

"Corpsevine is the raw material used to make Devil's Dream—a potent hallucinogen. Most of the fields are already marked off. This one looks untouched—it probably hasn't been noticed or cataloged. Which means—"

"As soon as people find it, they're going to be fighting over it."

"Exactly."

"What's the deal with the drug? Do people smoke the flowers or something?"

"No, they're dried and processed into pill form. It's sold in Amaranth City and... Well, New Orleans, primarily."

She blinked up at me, the pieces clicking into place behind her eyes. "So, *that's* why Saints and Sinners is so popular."

"One of the reasons, yes." I turned away from her, looking out again across the vine-laced meadow. "We're smugglers, Haley. We've got people here in Midnight handling production and portaling, and we sell it back in our realm. Everyone gets a cut."

"Is that how you three met? Dealing in Amaranth City?"

There was no judgment in her tone, just an earnest curiosity, which I appreciated. Last thing I wanted to do was justify our survival methods to a tourist who hadn't even seen the *real* shitshow of Midnight yet.

"It's... kind of a long story."

"Look around you, sinner. All we've got is time."

I let out a long breath. She was right, and something told me if I didn't spill it, she'd pester me for the rest of the hike.

"Those of us exiled to Midnight are the worst of the worst," I began. "Most of us are portaled into the realm far away from the city, dropped into battles more often than not. Military duty isn't exactly a volunteer thing here."

She shivered next to me, and I resisted the urge to pull her close.

"Anyway," I continued, "if you make it as far as Amaranth City, you stand a better chance at surviving. But surviving behind the wall requires a different set of skills."

"Skills you obviously have," she said. "Okay. So you, Hudson, and Elian made it to Amaranth after your arrival."

"Well, Hudson... He was born here. And don't ask me any more than that—it's not my story to tell, and I don't even know most of the details. But yes, Saint and I made it to the city. Different timelines—I'd been here a while by the time he showed up—but eventually, our paths crossed. Not long after that, we met Hudson. We all hit it off. Didn't take us too long to put our heads together and figure out we had some... complementary talents."

She flashed a wicked grin, her eyes sparkling with new mischief. "Oh, I *bet.*"

The look in her eyes sent a shock of heat straight to my cock.

Bad idea, asshole. Bad, bad idea...

Dismissing the sudden onslaught of images featuring Haley on her knees and me telling her to suck harder, I said, "Saint was a smuggler and a con who could just about charm a corpse out of the ground. And Hudson—"

"Let me guess. Muscle?"

"Exactly. Also a good scout. Flying is dangerous in Midnight—you risk being shot down by a solider's flaming arrows or attacked by a raven gryphon—but gargoyles are fast, strong, and extremely agile flyers. That worked out in our favor, especially when we had to meet up with people we didn't know very well."

"Okay, so Elian was the mouth, surprising no one. Hudson was the eyes and the muscle. That makes you..." She glanced up at me and narrowed her eyes, assessing. "The brains?"

"I have certain... abilities," I hedged. "Manipulation techniques that allow me to read things about people—things they don't always want to broadcast."

"Such as...?"

Don't even ask, angel.

Glaring at her, I ignored the question and started down the rise, leading us to the edge of the field.

"Okay," she said, seemingly content to move on. "You guys hooked up behind the wall and decided to parlay your talents into a drug-smuggling operation?"

"No, we didn't start out dealing in Dream—that came later. At first, it was just... well, whatever people needed. Saint had a way of finding things for people, or finding other people who could get the first people what they needed. Through that, he developed a reputation as the guy who could get anyone anything—weapons, booze, sex, spells, poisons and hexes, information—and he built this whole network of associates who came to trust and rely on him."

"When does the mystical fae crack come into play?"

"Drugs were already rampant in the city, same as anywhere else—people want their medicine. Something to take away the pain, you know?"

She nodded.

"But Saint... He was always one step ahead of the game. By the time some new designer drug hit the streets, he was already looking for the next big thing. Eventually, we found it. One of the trading caravans came through Amaranth selling corpsevine flower as a cure-all. Total bullshit, but we started experimenting with it. And we figured out if you dried the flowers under the full triple moon—it only happens once every two months or so—you could activate the hallucinogenic properties with dark fae magick. From there, you could process it into pills."

"Wow. Not only do you sell it, but you *invented* the crack? It's like I'm standing in the presence of drug-dealer royalty."

"I wouldn't go that far. But yes, we discovered it."

"Devil's Dream," she said. "Interesting name."

"D2, Black, Dark Delight. There are a lot of names for it, but the end result is the same: it takes you right out of your mind and into another place entirely. Swallow enough, and eventually, you'll no longer be able to tell fantasy from reality."

With a soft sigh, she dropped her pack and crouched down for a closer look. "This is the stuff you guys import back home?"

"No. This is the raw material—completely inert." I crouched down next to her and plucked a flower from the vine, then handed it over. "We can't do anything with it on the earthly realm. It has to be processed here first—the moonlight and the fae magick are what make it possible."

"Why do they call it corpsevine?"

"It grows mostly on old battlefields where many dead have fallen. Their blood and bones nourish the soil. It's said the potency of Devil's Dream lies in its connection to death—that it brings you as close to the other side as you can get without actually stepping over."

"And people put this into their bodies? Willingly?"

I nodded. "The euphoria is like nothing you've ever felt, Haley."

She looked at me, her brow furrowed, but there was still no judgment there. "You've done it?"

"At this point, you'd be hard-pressed to find anyone in Midnight who hasn't."

"And Elian?" She turned back to the field and ran her hands just above the flowers, not quite touching them. "It explains a lot. I've seen him popping pills. Seen the fog in his eyes."

I didn't respond. His was another sad story that wasn't mine to tell.

"It's not dangerous to touch this stuff, right?" she asked. "The flowers won't fuck me up or anything? Because hey, no judgments, but the only hallucinations I'm into are the ones induced by early onset food coma after I go all in on a plate of nachos."

I couldn't help but laugh, grateful for a break in the heaviness. "You're fine, angel. The plants themselves are harmless."

"In that case." With another of her sexy-as-sin mischievous grins, she got to her feet and bolted out into the middle of the field.

I stood up and watched her, that bright smile beaming at me across the expanse.

Holy fuck, she was beautiful. Crazy, just as I'd suspected. But she was definitely getting under my skin, and I wasn't sure I could keep her at arm's length much longer.

Wasn't sure I even *wanted* to keep her at arm's length, which was... problematic, to say the least.

"Get your demon ass out here, sinner. You're missing the best part." She got down and stretched out on her back, arms and legs splayed like a child making a snow angel.

Unable to resist, I dropped my pack and trotted out there.

The first moon shone down on her, catching the highlights in her dark hair, casting her in an otherworldly glow, and for a second I swore she looked like she was born here.

"Less staring," she said, "more getting down here with me. You've *got* to see this view."

Rolling my eyes, I dropped down into a crouch beside her and looked up.

She grabbed my arm, tugged me until I fell on my back.

I opened my mouth, all set to give her some smart-ass comment about tricking me into getting horizontal for her, but the view stole the words right out of my mouth.

Gazing up at the sky, I lost all sense of time and place.

Way out here, far from the torchlights of Amaranth City, even farther from New Orleans, the red-and-gold stars of Midnight were infinite.

It was better than Devil's Dream. Better than any drink I could whip up at Saints and Sinners. It was fucking majestic.

"Kind of amazing, isn't it?" she said softly. "Before we left New Orleans, Hudson told me—well, *wrote* me—there's beauty in darkness. This is exactly what he meant, Jax."

I barely had the words to respond. "I... I've never... seen it. Not like this."

"Really? How long did you live here?"

I let out a deep sigh. "Eighteen years, four months, and six days before Saint pulled me out."

A soft gasp slipped out from between her lips, but she didn't say anything. After a beat, I felt the soft touch of her hand against mine as she linked our pinky fingers.

Something jabbed me then, right in the heart.

We stayed like that, side-by-side on our backs on the field of the dead, and I'd never felt so alive. My body burned with the need to do something, to touch her, but...

Fucking Saint.

I closed my eyes. Forced those ridiculous notions right out of my head.

But then, out of nowhere, Haley said, "Jax? I kind of want to kiss you."

20

JAX

*A*nother unplanned, uninvited smile stretched across my lips. I turned on my hip to face her, shocked to find she was already facing me, her eyes glittering, her body surrounded by the ethereal white flowers.

"You're not talking to the jambalaya again, are you?" I teased.

"Not this time. And granola bars and MREs don't inspire the same level of affection."

"I see," I said, hoping like hell she couldn't hear my heart slamming against my ribs. "Is this a what-happens-in-Midnight-stays-in-Midnight thing?"

"It could be."

Sure, it *could* be. Just a little fun, right? No harm, no foul. A lot of women believed they could have that with me.

On some level, I got it. The scars, the mystery of the

missing eye, the whole bad-boy-who-goes-good-for-you fantasy. And if Saint was any indication, I fit the profile; Haley had a thing for walking disasters.

But while I'd promised him I'd take care of her—and something about the woman brought out my protective instincts like nothing else ever had—that didn't change who I was at the core.

A demon. A killer. A monster.

Being in this place only served to remind me of that.

I didn't know what Haley saw when she looked at me the way she was looking at me now, but it wasn't the truth.

"As tempting as your offer sounds..." I shook my head and flipped onto my back, swallowing my disappointment. "You don't want me to kiss you, angel. Trust me on that."

"I didn't say anything about *you* kissing *me*. I said *I* wanted to kiss *you*."

"*You* want your doom."

"Maybe I do," she whispered, shifting closer and sweeping her fingers through my hair.

Her touch was electric, and it made me shiver.

Fuck.

I was already fucking hard.

"Jax," she whispered, her soft breath tickling my cheek, just below the eye patch.

And that was it.

I rolled on top of her, propping myself up to keep from crushing her completely. Her body was warm and soft in a hundred different ways—a hundred ways I hadn't felt in so long, I barely remembered how good it could be.

What are you doing to me, angel?

"What's *this* new game?" she teased, wriggling beneath me. "You've got me at a disadvantage here, but I think I'm okay with it."

"No more games," I said. Then, staring at her lush mouth, I whispered, "Tell me what you *really* want from me, angel. You sure it's just the kiss of doom?"

"You think you can give me what I want, demon?" she teased, her nipples hardening beneath me.

"Oh, I *know* I can give it to you. But be warned—you might not like it once you've got it."

She slid her hands behind my neck. Then, in a hot whisper against my mouth, "Why don't you let *me* be the judge of that?"

Fuck me. I'm done.

My resistance shattered, along with my instinct to protect her from my demon side, and any remaining shreds of loyalty I had for Saint.

I crashed into her lush mouth, stealing the offered kiss before she could change her mind.

The taste of her... It shot through me like a spark, igniting a fire inside that threatened to consume us both.

But after just a few seconds of pure bliss, she was already pushing against my chest, struggling to break free.

I pulled back. Tried to hide my frustration.

"Giving up already, angel?" I teased, though I knew *right* where this was heading. I'd known it from the moment she'd said she wanted it.

One taste, and she'd be running for her life, just like everyone else.

"Oh my God," she gasped, her eyes wide. "You're... you're a *fear* demon."

"Finally figured that out, did you?"

She touched her fingertips to her mouth, a shiver racking her body. "It's... so cold... I feel like... like I'm drowning and... Jax?" Panic filled her eyes. "What's happening to me?"

"That's the fear," I said. "The closer I get to someone, the greater the effect. Intimate contact? Sorry, angel. You just got the highest dose possible, outside of me intentionally forcing it on you."

"Were you... were you born like this or...?"

"Breathe, Haley. You need to breathe. You're freaking out on me here."

"Move." She shoved against my chest. "Move!"

I rolled off, and she got to her feet. Took off running without another word, crashing through the field and into the wooded area just beyond.

A wicked grin slashed across my mouth, matching the wicked fire in my balls.

Sorry, angel. You've just signed your death warrant.

About a mile out from Amaranth City, atop the towering White Cliffs of Oshen, I looked out across a largely unobstructed view of the moat crossing and gatehouse at Vanderham's Wall.

Flat on my belly, I crawled to the edge of the cliff and peered through my binoculars, trying to suss out the situation.

Clusterfuck.

The drawbridge was down, but the crossing was jammed up by a caravan that trailed back about a quarter-mile. By the light of their magick torches, I counted about a dozen shepherd wagons pulled by twice as many Mares of Night—massive, horselike beasts that looked more demonic than equine, with all-white hair and bright red eyes that glowed in the dim. Midnighters had figured out how to tame them with iron and magick centuries ago, but the wild ones were so feral they made the raven gryphons look like winged kittens.

All of them were waiting for entry into Amaranth City.

Had to be a trading party. I had no idea where they'd come from, but it was a miracle so many had survived the trek without a military escort.

It was the first bit of good news I'd gotten since I left Haley back at camp. Traders—even ones strong enough to cross the realm—weren't warriors. They were merchants.

In other words, con artists—my favorite fucking kind of asshole.

Con artists always thought they had the upper hand, which made them easy to kill; they were always so busy trying to separate you from your wallet, it rarely occurred to them you were planning to separate their heads from their bodies.

I tucked away the binoculars and made my way down the steep rise, doing my best to conserve my dwindling energy. The mile-wide swath of land that stretched from the bottom of the cliffs to the edge of Beggar's Moat was bleak and barren, nothing but obsidian sand and the bones of those deemed too fetid for even *these* cursed grounds to swallow.

There were no shadows cast but those from the wagons. No places to hide.

I'd have to rely on my vampire speed and, if someone spotted me before I wanted them to, my influence.

I checked my pack. I'd sucked down all my extra blood bags hours earlier, but I couldn't afford to screw up now. I needed one last burst of energy and speed—along with a little trickery—to get to the caravan.

At the bottom of the cliffs, I dropped the pack and dug out a change of clothing—an Amaranth guard uniform I'd stolen before we'd left last time. I had no idea if they were still using the same ones, but the travelers might not notice, anyway. Just had to look close enough to the part, turn on the charm, and hope they weren't as clever as they believed.

After I walked as far as I dared across the black sands, I blurred to the very last wagon, pressing myself against the back and taking a minute to catch my breath. Pinpricks of light danced before my eyes. I needed to fucking eat, and soon.

The entire caravan fucking stank. Rotten food, dead animals, personal waste, road reek. Somewhere near the rear was likely a cart carrying the few of their dead they'd managed to recover from whatever shit had befallen them on the trek, but that was always a wasted effort. Soon as they got to the bridge, the guards would force them to dump the corpses into the moat.

Amaranth City had enough of its *own* dead to contend with, *fuckyouverymuch*.

I wondered how many travelers from their original party were left. Seemed kind of quiet—just the soft nickers of the mares and a few grumblings from the people who'd left their mounts and ducked inside the wagons to wait out the traffic jam.

From what I could pick up, it sounded like Keradoc had ordered extra patrols, though no one seemed to know why. I heard snatches of everything from "Darkwinter fae enemies" to "arrival of a weapon that would turn the tides of the war" to "Keradoc's balls were hanging a little too far the left tonight, so he decided to take it out on his city watch and give them all extra work to do."

Whatever the reason, it sounded like I'd be here for a while.

Most of the wagons were fitted with three doors—one in the back and two smaller doors on the sides to allow for shift changes on and off the mares without having to stop. It was also fun to flip off the guy behind you and piss out the back, but that wasn't what I'd come to do tonight.

Certain no one had seen me, I stashed my pack under the wagon, then slipped in through the back door.

Two men—a human who looked about as old as the grains of sand outside the door and a fae whose face had recently been chewed on by something bigger than him—glanced up from a card game in progress, immediately reaching for the daggers on their hips.

"You're no guard of Amaranth," the fae said, taking in my red-and-black uniform. "They wear blue."

"Good to know," I said. "Would you mind standing up?"

He got to his feet and unsheathed the dagger. "What the fuck do you—"

I grabbed his head and snapped his neck, then turned the quivering old human into a juice box—not about to look *that* gift horse in the mouth.

The blood rejuvenated me at once, bringing with it a flash of guilt I quickly dismissed.

Wasn't exactly consensual, but... I was pretty sure it would meet Haley's qualifications for a break-the-glass emergency.

Working quickly, I stripped the fae and swapped my uniform for his traveling clothes—not much more than a pair of dusty cargo pants and a dark gray hooded cloak. I stashed the bodies in one of the hollow storage benches that lined the walls, just in case someone decided to poke their head in the door looking for these two.

I found a rucksack too, and when I left the wagon I'd forever think of as my dining car, I retrieved my pack and shoved it inside.

I looked like one of them now. Smelled like them, too. Made my eyes burn.

I hoped like hell the place Gem found for us had running water.

Keeping my head low, I walked up the line, passing the corpse cart and another wagon that seemed to be filled with medical supplies, for all the good it did them. A few travelers were hanging out outside, trying to get a peek at whatever was holding up the line ahead. I grunted my greetings and kept on moving, not bothering to offer condolences for the bastard whose clothes I'd stolen.

By the time they all made it over the bridge and realized they'd left the last wagon in the dust, they'd be tucked away in one of Amaranth's many taverns, and some terror or another—one much bigger than a vampire-fae—would have already destroyed the wagon and claimed the two corpses inside it as a meal.

I kept walking, searching for my jackpot—a.k.a. the booze cart.

Every caravan had one—traders, hunters, and military alike.

A traveling bar and distillery was a source of comfort on a long journey. A place to gather after a long night's ride. A sanctuary to drink to the fallen they'd lost along the way.

More importantly? It was a fucking bomb on wheels.

I found it about four wagons from the bridge entrance and slipped unseen underneath it. Waited. Each time another wagon moved onto the bridge and the line crept along, I crept right along with it.

And then, it was finally time. We were at the bridge, about to start the crossing, no chance for another traveler to pop in for a drink.

Just before the wheels started turning again, I slipped out from under the wagon and let myself in through the side door.

The occupant, a low-level crossroads demon, was busy rearranging liquor bottles, his back to me.

"Sorry, friend," he said, not even turning around. Apparently, my foul stench marked me as one of their own, no visual confirmation needed. "We ain't open. You'll have to wait till we get across the—"

I punched a hole through his back and tore out his spine just as his horseman whistled to the mares. The wagon bumped onto the drawbridge, its wheels somehow managing to find every crack and divot in the old wood.

I waited until we reached the center of the bridge, then opened the side door and pitched his remains into the moat.

The guards never cared about shit like that, and most of the other travelers were too worried about their own business to notice. People were always falling off the wagon, so to speak, or getting thrown off, or—for those looking for the *worst* way to go—jumping.

It was an unexpected treat for the ghouls that dwelled there. I didn't have to watch to know what was happening; the second the demon hit bottom, they converged, rending skin and muscle from bone, consuming it until there wasn't so much as a drop of fucking blood left.

Then they dropped to their knees and wept, a sound so

haunting it always made me want to retch, cry, and punch something at the same fucking time.

They looked like rotting skeletons, the ghouls, draped in nothing more than a vaguely transparent layer of tattered skin suggesting the person they once were.

Such was the fate of the soldiers of Midnight. *Keradoc's* soldiers. Outside the city walls, all who died in battle were left to rot. What the beasts of Midnight didn't pick clean eventually decomposed in the fields. After that, the poor bastards would rise again in Beggar's Moat, cursed to forever guard the city that'd turned its back on them.

Demon attendant properly disposed of, I pulled out the liquor bottles and dumped them, dousing the interior of the wagon, no surface left dry.

Minutes later, we reached the end of the bridge and pulled to a stop at the gatehouse for the inspection, which was little more than a payoff.

One I wouldn't be making tonight.

The guard didn't knock. Just opened the side door and stepped in, probably already salivating for the cash—and the liquor—he'd been counting on.

What do you know—the uniforms really are blue now.

He caught my eye. Nodded, real friendly, like they always were when it came time to get their palms greased.

"Nice night for a barbecue," I said. Then I flicked my Zippo to life, tossed it at the guard's feet, and slipped out the other side in a vampire blur so fast, even the most reliable witness would've had trouble convincing a jury he'd seen anything other than a smudge in the night.

I was a safe distance away when the fucking thing exploded, undoubtedly sending the rest of the guards into a tizzy, no time to pay heed to any possible rumors of a stowaway.

Hey, I liked covering all the bases.

Pulling my hood up, I tucked in with the rest of the rabble in the street, my stink unnoticeable in the river of filth and shit that was Amaranth City.

One last glance over my shoulder, and I smiled.

I'd fucking made it.

That old guilt soup started boiling in my gut again, but this time, I didn't ignore it. I welcomed it.

Used to be shit like this was easy. Pleasurable, even. But those days had died the night I left Midnight, vowing never to return.

Now that I had?

I didn't want it to be easy anymore. Killing someone—human, fae, demon, guard, innocent, guilty as sin—it *shouldn't* be easy. Ever.

But one thought of the witch with the off-key songs and the power to make me dizzy with a murmured spell and her little magick ring, and I knew I'd keep right on killing—anyone, anywhere, anytime I deemed it necessary to keep her safe—no matter how much it ate me up inside.

Making sure I hadn't been followed, I cut down a familiar alley, slipping into the shadows once again.

But something moved behind me.

And before I could turn around, the short sword was at my throat, a stake pressed between my shoulder blades.

$\mathcal{Y}$ou've got some nerve showing up here, bloodsucker," a female voice hissed, low and gravelly.

Demon, maybe?

I wasn't sure. Too many other smells and sounds in this putrid asshole of a city to get a good read.

"You know how to use that sword, assassin? Or is this some kind of fucked-up gang initiation that's only going to get you killed?"

"Bit of both, perhaps?" My assailant laughed and lowered her weapons, then stepped in front of me and pushed back her hood. Chin-length purple hair curled around a smile as bright as the blaze I'd left behind. "By the moons and stars, it's good to see you again, Saint."

I wrapped her up in my arms, crushing her against my

chest. "For fuck's sake, Gem. I was about to *waste* your beautiful ass. I thought you were a demon."

"And I thought you'd at least give an old friend the courtesy of showering before manhandling her, but you know what they say—nothing in Midnight is ever what it should be."

"You'd think I'd remember that by now." I released her, stepping back to take a good look. Other than Jax and Hudson, Gem had been one of the only people I'd ever trusted in Midnight. Hell, one of the few I'd ever trusted *anywhere*. "How the hell did you find me so quickly?"

"Really?" With a laugh, she glanced over her shoulder, where a fiery orange light glowed in the distance, flickering against the roughly hewn black stone buildings that surrounded it. "Where there's smoke—and an explosion, and murder, and a lot of baffled city watchmen bumbling around with their dicks in their hands—there's fire. And in this case, by fire, I mean you."

"What can I say? I love to make an entrance."

"Speaking of entrances, where are the rest of my boys? Don't tell me they sent your scrappy ass back here alone."

"They're still a day behind. Had to leave them to make the trek with Haley," I said, my heart kicking me in the ribs at the reminder. I knew they'd take care of her, but damn. Leaving her behind—again? I *really* needed to stop making that a thing. "I need blood, Gem. Human. Live."

"Don't worry, bloodsucker," she said with a grin. "You know I've got you covered."

Haley's words echoed.

Again.

Consent is sexy, Elian...

I sighed. Fucking woman was going to get me killed.

"Hate to ask," I said, "but... Willing?"

Gem lifted a brow. "Don't tell me you've gone soft on me, Saint."

"Never. Just... trying to mitigate rumors about a vicious new vampire on the scene. People start nosing around, asking too many questions... That could be bad news for us. I'm trying to keep a low profile this time."

She glanced back at the inferno still raging near the gatehouse. "Low profile, sure. Looks good on you, Saint. Really." With another laugh, she looped her arm through mine and sighed dramatically. "Oh, all right, I'll free the guy I've got tied up in the apartment and find someone a little more... agreeable. If you insist."

"I knew I could count on you, Gem. Always."

"Saint, I..." She hesitated, something darkening her eyes, but before I could ask her where her mind had wandered off to, she was back with a conspiratorial grin. "Tell me about this mission of yours. I want all the details."

"That, I'm afraid, will cost you." I put my arm around her. "A few drinks, perhaps?"

"You mentioned something about a witch in your message. That's Haley, I presume?"

"Yes," I said. "She's a blood witch. She has business in the city."

"She must be the reason you're not tearing off my clothes. Not that I'm jealous or anything. Just need to make sure I'm not losing my sparkle."

I laughed. For all our years of flirting, Gem and I never actually hooked up.

"Pretty sure you could never lose your sparkle," I said.

"Good answer. Now come on—I've got you all set up. A place not far from your old digs. You ready to be back?"

Back. In Amaranth City.

In the place where at least a third of the population wanted me dead, another third would definitely sell me out to the first group if the price was right, and the last third would be more than happy to stand on the sidelines with some beer and popcorn to watch the slaughter.

I took a deep breath and nodded.

"Ready as ever, Gem. Lead the way."

23

HALEY

It was no conscious decision on my part—I simply ran. Ran like my life depended on it, my heart close to bursting, my lips still icy from the demon's kiss.

The moment we'd come together, I felt it, like a fist punching right through my chest and yanking all my worst fears to the surface. They'd flashed before my eyes—losing my sisters. Getting trapped in Midnight. Watching Elian die. Flashbacks to the prison compound the hunters had trapped me in. Shit from my childhood—from before I was adopted—I wanted to leave in a fucking graveyard.

The more distance I put between us, the better I felt. When the chill finally subsided, I stopped to catch my breath in the woods, hands on my knees, eyes shut tight. I hadn't gone far—I could still see glimpses of the silvery-white field through the trees.

No Jax, though. Maybe he'd decided to give me some space.

I wasn't sure exactly how it worked—how much of it Jax could control—but kissing him seemed to unleash it all. Logically, I wasn't scared of *him*—not really. I'd simply reacted to the images of my own fears shoved in my face. But in that moment, it'd all felt so real.

I opened my eyes and stood up. My hands were still trembling.

Fucking demon.

A twig snapped, and I glanced up to see Jax slowly approaching, our packs slung over his shoulder. His face was unreadable.

"I tried to warn you," he said, stepping closer.

I crossed my arms over my chest and took a step back, still fighting off a shiver. "You could've been a little more specific."

"Would you have even believed me? Would it have stopped you?"

Heat pooled between my thighs—another reaction. Purely instinctual. Purely... *fuck.*

Horror-movie slideshow notwithstanding, that kiss had been...

I blew out a breath, forcing away the memories of his hot mouth. The smoky taste. The fire that had raged inside me when he'd finally given in and...

No.

I couldn't go back there. Not in my mind. Not in my reality.

Didn't matter how sexy he was or how damn fine he'd tasted. Kissing demons in the dark was far too fucking dangerous.

"I didn't need to see that stuff," I said. "I can't... I can't be worrying about all my old demons, no pun intended, when I'm trying to focus on this crazy-ass mission in the most crazy-ass place in the universe. This isn't about me, Jax. I've got sisters. Three of them. I didn't even know they existed until recently, and if I don't see this through—if I don't get this dude's blood and get back to the Temple of the Dark Moon—Melantha will kill them."

He dropped the packs and closed the space between us, reaching out to cup my face. Sympathy flashed in his eye, but it quickly turned to something else—something wicked and predatory.

"I know," he said darkly.

"You know?"

"I'm a fear demon, Haley. Everything you saw just now? I saw it too. I can sense your fears. All of them—fears about the future, fears you experienced last year, right down to the fear of drowning you've had since you were a child."

I pulled away from his touch and shook my head.

"Your whole life," he said, "you've been afraid of your birth mother. She murdered your father—her own husband. She tried to drown you. She tried to steal your magick—your legacy."

Ouch. Right to the fucking bone, that one. It felt as if he'd shoved a knife into my gut.

"Stop," I whispered.

Still, he kept coming. Another step, too fucking close. Another reminder. Another twist of the knife.

"You suffer from an almost debilitating fear of abandonment," he continued, "firstly from your mother, but also because your adoptive parents and grandmother died, leaving you behind. Saint bailing on your relationship only further served to—"

"I said *stop!*" I unsheathed my dagger. "Get out of my fucking head!"

"Haley, I'm telling you," he warned. "If you don't deal with this shit, you're—"

"Fuck off and deal with *this*." I sliced my palm and slammed it into his chest, the spell already on my lips. He stumbled backward, then fell on his ass, and I pounced.

Straddling him, I gazed down into his face, his eye wide, his breath short and ragged.

"You feel that, Jax? The lightheadedness? The muscle weakness? Your heart's beginning to slow. If I don't call off the spell, you'll pass out. Maybe even die. Scared yet? You fucking should be. Fear demons aren't the only ones who can unleash terrors."

"Haley," he whispered, reaching for my face with a shaky hand.

But he wasn't scared—I could see it in his eye. Just sad and a little pale.

And, as much as it pained me to admit...

Hard.

For me.

Fucking asshole.

I could've pushed it further. Could've rerouted the blood to leave his dick as limp as an overcooked lasagna noodle.

But now, with that rock-hard bulge pressing urgently against my core, all I wanted to do was...

No.

Jax was a fear demon. If merely kissing him for ten seconds had sent me fleeing for my life, what would a dose of that red-hot demon dick do to me?

I was in so far over my head, I might as well be drowning all over again, just like my birthmother had intended.

I sighed. My spell was already fading. It wasn't intended for long-term use, anyway—just a quickie to help you escape a jam, like if you were about to get jumped or groped.

But the thing about escaping was you had to actually, you know, *go*. Away. You couldn't just sit on top of your would-be assailant, subtly grinding against him, dreaming about that sweet, sweet Demon D.

After a beat, Jax sucked in a breath, the color finally returning to his cheeks.

I slammed the dagger back into its sheath.

Before I could move to let him up, Jax wrapped his hand around the back of my neck and pulled me down close, a new spark alighting in his eye. "You shouldn't have done that."

Another shiver snaked down my spine, but it wasn't his touch that was cold. He was as warm as any other man. But his touch? It brought out the cold from deep inside me— and that's where the *real* terror lived.

Where his power lived.

Jax squeezed my neck. Arched his hips, ever so slightly, making me feel it. Feel him.

Time stopped. The world stopped. Right now, there was nothing outside the trees that mattered.

"Jax," I whispered, but it was too late.

He flipped us so he was on top, his weight pressing me into the soft ground, hands clamped down over my wrists, his body warm and solid and delicious and...

Oh, hell, I was fucked.

"What... what are you doing?"

"You were right, angel. I couldn't give you what you wanted. So now I'll have to give you what you need."

He claimed me in another kiss—bruising, fucking

incredible. The fear rose again, but this time it had no face. No images. Only a feeling of ice-cold dread and dagger-sharp edges slicing right through me, a contrast to his hot mouth and fiery touch.

Resisting the urge to run again, I slid my hands up inside the back of his T-shirt, clawing at his shoulders as he continued to own me with his mouth.

He finally broke our kiss. "Think you can hurt me again, angel?" he growled in my ear. "Do your worst."

"I hope you feel this all fucking night." I raked my nails hard down his back.

He hissed in my ear, then licked his way down to my neck, biting me so hard he drew blood. I cried out, but the pain quickly turned to pleasure as the warm trickle slid over my skin.

Like a man unhinged, he grunted and tore open my shirt, kissing and biting his way down my chest, my stomach, his mouth searing every inch of exposed skin. When he got to my pants and underwear, he didn't even bother taking them all the way off. Just yanked them down to my knees, then buried his sexy demon face right between my thighs.

I moaned and fisted his hair, which only encouraged him to go harder, tongue lapping my clit as he shoved two fingers inside me and fucked me fast and furious.

I gasped and writhed, his mouth and fingers driving

me closer and closer to the edge, harder, faster, so intense I couldn't even catch my breath before...

"Right there. I'm... yes! Jax!"

A starburst of blinding, white-hot ecstasy exploded inside me, waves of pleasure rolling through my body as the demon sucked my clit and curled his fingers, hitting the perfect spot, making good on his promise to give me *exactly* what I needed.

"Jax," I whispered again, the night sky tilting sideways, and he got to his knees and glared at me, his mouth glistening with the evidence of what he'd done.

I hadn't even finished shuddering through the last aftershock when he flipped me onto my stomach, grabbed my hips, and hauled my ass up in the air.

He was behind me now, one hand on my backside, the other unzipping his pants.

His cock teased against my still-dripping pussy.

"Okay?" he growled.

One question.

One answer.

"Fuck yes," I breathed, and he slammed into me from behind, letting loose a deep, possessive growl that made me weak.

He fucked me hard and deep, fingers digging into my hips as he claimed me, owned me, marked me.

I arched my back and he fisted my hair, pulling it hard and forcing me up onto my knees as he continued to rock against my ass. I reached behind with both hands and clawed at his sides, and he returned the attack with a bite on my shoulder, then pushed me back onto my hands and knees, taking his fill any way he wanted it.

We were animals in the dirt, scratching and biting, fighting, fucking, and I'd never felt anything so raw. So primal. So perfect.

The heat was rising inside me again, building, winding me tight as he sped up his thrusts. He slammed into me one last time, growling as he shuddered against me, coming in a hot torrent that sent me right into another spiral. I choked out his name, and he pulled out and brought his bare hand down on my ass with a crack that echoed through the trees, and I came so hard I had tears in my eyes.

ou're singing," Jax said as we continued walking north through the woods.

"Humming, technically. Is that a problem?" I laughed. "After all the noise we made earlier, I didn't think a little music would suddenly give away our position."

"It's not a problem. It's... cute."

Heat crept into my cheeks, and I knew I should've left it at that.

But I just couldn't help myself.

"It's... a thing I do," I confessed. "After."

"After...? You mean... oh. Oh! Well, *damn*." He arched an eyebrow, mischief flashing in his eye. "Is that why Saint calls you—"

"Yes. Can we move on?"

He stopped and grabbed my hand, pulling me close.

With a hot kiss behind my ear, he whispered, "No. I want to make you sing again."

"Too late," I teased. "You ruined the mood with all the talking."

"Let me make it up to you." He kissed his way down my neck, reaching for the zipper on the shirt I'd changed into after he'd ruined the last one. I was just about to give in, just about to let him drag me to the ground for another go, when a rustling in the trees ahead stopped us cold.

"Jax?" I whispered. "Did you—"

He clamped a hand hard over my mouth and dragged me to the ground, but not for anything fun.

"Stay here," he whispered, hot and low in my ear. "Don't make a sound. I'll be right back."

I nodded, watching with my heart in my throat as he took off in the direction of the sound. Seconds later, a young fae soldier emerged onto the path about twenty feet in front of me, stopping to scan the area.

Shit.

I slid the dagger from my holster. I had maybe five seconds before she spotted me.

A noise behind her caught her attention, but it was too late.

Jax was already on her. He grabbed her head, and I held my breath for the telltale pop of a snapped neck.

It never came.

The fae's arms went limp at her sides, and she dropped

soundlessly to her knees, Jax crouching down behind her, still holding her head.

Even from this distance, I could tell she was beautiful. Ethereal.

Staying low, I crept a little closer.

What the fuck is he doing?

Suddenly, all the color drained from her face, her eyes wide with fear. I'd never seen anyone look so flat-out terrified. I wanted to run to her. To shove that demon away and save the poor creature from whatever torment he was undoubtedly inflicting.

But movement in the trees a dozen feet behind them caught my eye.

Another soldier. Female, just like the first.

She lifted her bow. Knocked an arrow. Aimed it right at Jax's head.

I didn't think. Just whipped my dagger at her, straight and true. It zinged through the air, blade over handle, and hit the mark—the soft hollow just above her collarbone.

She let out a strangled gasp, then dropped to her knees.

Jax turned around just in time to see her faceplant.

Without a second thought, he pulled a dagger from his boot and sliced his fae's throat.

"Jax!" I bolted up from the ground and ran to him, but pulled up short when I saw the fiery rage burning in his eye.

"I told you to stay *put*," he growled. "What the *fuck* were you thinking?"

Excuse me?

I folded my arms across my chest and took a step backward, glaring right back at him. "I'm sorry. Was that demon-speak for 'thanks for saving my ass?' Because yeah, you're welcome."

"Fuck, Haley. You killed her. You fucking killed her."

"Um…" I gestured at the dead fae at his feet. "Hello?"

"I didn't want to kill them. Leaving a trail of bodies—Midnight soldiers—is a sure way to get tracked."

"Then what the hell were you doing to her? Before you sliced and diced her, the poor thing looked like she was about thirty seconds from dying of fright."

He sighed. Glared. Waited for me to catch up, which…

Holy. Fuck.

"You fear-mojo'd her."

"My intention, had you let me take care of things, was to scare her so badly she'd take off, forgetting she'd ever seen us."

"And her little friend back there? Did you think she'd just wait in line for her turn?"

Jax said nothing.

"You didn't even know she was there, did you?" I asked.

Silence.

"Okay, so why did you end up killing her after all that?" I asked. "Why not let her go?"

"Because the trauma of seeing her partner assassinated might've been enough to shock her out of the fear-haze and alert the rest of her squad to our presence."

I walked around the dead fae slowly, still trying to process what I'd seen.

She really *had* looked like she was about to die of fright.

"What did you show her?" I whispered, almost afraid of the answer. "What was her worst fear? How does it even work? When we were together, I didn't... I didn't feel anything *close* to that. I mean... She was *terrified*, Jax."

He gripped my jaw and leaned in close, his grin turning cruel. "You just got front-row seats to the kind of terror a direct hit from a fear demon can unleash, and that's not even the worst I've got. Still think you can outrun your demons, angel? Or are you ready to wise up and stay the fuck away from me?"

"Fuck off." I jerked away from his touch and stalked off to go retrieve my dagger.

He grabbed my arm, hauling me back. "Leave it."

"But it's—"

"I said leave it. We need to move. Now." He held my gaze for another beat, shaking his head as if he couldn't have been more disgusted. "Before you do something *else* to give away our position."

HUDSON

Stone City wasn't a city, but that's what they called it—a mountainous region dotted with caves named for the wild gargoyles who called it home. It was all part of the Dead Claw range that stretched far to the north.

It was also where my people lived. Where I'd been born.

While Jax and Haley'd had their little... *ahem*... private moment in the woods, I'd headed east for a quick flyover of the homeland. Quick, because anything out in the open like that could get you noticed *real* quick. But still, I needed to see it.

Between our current route and Stone City, I spotted a few skirmishes on the ground. I recognized the Dark-winter insignia on some of the uniforms—looked like they were making a push toward Dead Claw, probably hoping to find a way into Amaranth through the mountains, but they'd have to face the gargoyles, too. Wouldn't be an easy victory.

Keradoc's soldiers were holding them off for now, but from what I could tell, the ground was soaked with just as much Midnighter blood as Darkwinter.

Whole thing was fucked.

Once I reached Stone City, wasn't long before I started getting that feeling like I was being watched and had to double back. But I got a glimpse, which was a start. The place was still there, still just as overcrowded as I remembered. Lots of old memories, but no obvious signs of the fuckers that'd sold me out two years ago.

Not a problem. I'd track them down soon enough.

Once Haley got what she needed from Keradoc and we put her on the express train back the fuck to New Orleans? Yeah, I had some personal business to take care of here. An old score to settle. I suspected it was the same for Saint and Jax, but like I said, Midnight wasn't a group-therapy kind of place. Whatever those guys were up to, they were keeping it to themselves for now, same as me.

It would all come out eventually, though. Always did. And the longer we stayed in this place, the more we were gonna need each other again, just like old times—*that* was a fact.

But right now, the main thing that bound us was Haley.

Her mission had become ours. Keeping her safe and helping her see it through was our only priority.

I'd just gotten back when I spotted her and Jax tumbling out of the woods, looking like they'd done a hell of a lot more than roll around half-naked in the dirt.

First came the demon, storming away from her like she'd just dipped his balls in kerosene and was packing a flamethrower.

Haley stalked out next—no flamethrower, but man, did she look pissed.

Still in my warrior form, I glided down and landed in front of her. Gave her a good once-over, just to make sure she wasn't bleeding or broken.

Then I just stared at her, waiting for her to spill it.

"I'm fine," she insisted, even though she wasn't.

I could wait her out, though. One thing I'd learned about Haley in our short time together? Babygirl couldn't keep it locked up for too long. Not with me. Not when something was eating her up inside.

"Okay, so I'm assuming you saw all that?" she finally said.

I shrugged and rocked my hand in a so-so gesture.

"Just... don't tell Elian, okay? I mean, not that you're... talking. But... you know. Don't leave him any notes or give him any winks or gestures."

I cocked an eyebrow. Tried not to smirk.

"It's none of his business what I do, where I do it, or

who I do it with. Plus, he's just gonna go psycho on Jax, and for no reason, because there's *nothing* going on between us. And even if there *was*, why should Elian care? He's the one who ended things with me. No, I take that back. He didn't end things. He just walked away, leaving *me* to tie up all the loose ends and I... You know what, Hudson? I love talking to you, but I think it's a little early in our relationship for the post-woods, walk-of-shame, justifying-my-bad-life-choices convo."

She tried like hell to hold on to that anger, but we both knew it wasn't meant for me, and eventually, she gave up. Just lowered her eyes and shook her head, her cheeks blushing.

"Sorry, Gargs. I know you're just trying to look out for me."

I reached out. Tugged a few sticks from her hair and smoothed it out so she didn't look like such a hot, freshly fucked mess—as much as I appreciated the look.

It was a small thing, that touch. Barely anything, really. But damn, my fingers were on fire.

Frustration simmered in my blood. Just this once, I wanted the damn bond to be more. To actually mean what all the fairytales said. Mates, in every sense of the word. True partners. Lovers. Friends. The whole kit-n-caboodle, right down to the cheesy framed photos and matching monogrammed bath towels.

No idea if regular couples did that kinda shit, but if so, I was fucking in.

She pursed her lips. Shot me a look that I wanted to memorize for the rest of my immortal life, that perfect mix of sass and sweetness.

"You okay?" she asked. "You look a little... pensive. More than usual, I mean."

I forced a smile. Nodded. Turned away from her before I did something even more stupid—more dangerous—than touching her damn hair.

"Hey, will you do me a favor?" she asked. When I turned back to face her, she held out her hand and said, "Will you stay on the ground with me? Just for a little while?"

I probably shoulda left her, right then. Gestured to the sky, my duty, and taken off, keeping an eye on the path ahead, staying far above it all.

But one look into those green eyes, and my stone heart was as good as melted goo.

I took her hand, so tiny in mine, doing my best to ignore the fire shooting up my veins as we walked on in peaceful silence. Every few minutes, a light breeze would blow her hair, and the silky strands would tickle my arm, and Jax got so far ahead of us I lost sight of him completely.

We caught up with him not long after in a clearing at the base of a sheer rock face, a freshwater stream cutting through the middle. It was a good place to stop, so we set up camp and made a fire. Haley wasn't hungry for dinner —just wanted to crash.

I waited until she was tucked safely into her tent. Waited until Jax gave me the look—the *what the hell did I do?* look.

Then, with no more warning than a low growl, I slammed the fucker against the rock, hand around his neck, his feet dangling a good foot off the ground.

"Ease off," he said, more annoyed than frightened. "This shit between me and Haley has nothing to do with you."

I lifted my eyebrows. Pounded a fist into my chest, then into his, indicating our tattoos. The oath.

"You think I'd let a woman—a witch—come before my oath?" he shot back. "Saint may be a rotten fuck, Hudson, but I will *always* honor my oath. You should fucking know that by now."

I *did* know that, and his loyalty to our bond wasn't what I'd meant at all, the dumb fuck.

I pointed at the tent, then back to my chest, then his.

Haley was one of us—that's what I'd meant. She didn't need no tattoo or blood oath to prove it. It just *was*.

Eventually, the asshole got my meaning. I saw it rise in his eye like the moon, and I let him drop, shooting him one last warning glare, just to drive the point home.

"I won't hurt her," he said, his voice soft with a hint of regret. "Not again. You have my word."

I nodded, which was about all I could give him just then.

"Are you taking first watch?" he asked, rubbing his neck. He was lucky I hadn't broken it.

I shook my head and pointed at him.

Tonight, I was putting *him* on perimeter watch.

Me? I'd be keeping watch over that tent and the witch inside it, making damn sure she didn't end up with any more hurt in her eyes than the sonofabitch had already put there.

26

HALEY

fter a night with little sleep followed by hours of hiking in uncomfortable silence, Jax and I finally made it to the top of the White Cliffs of Oshen.

Hudson landed behind us moments later, and together, we peered out across the black expanse that led to the City of Amaranth and its imposing wall.

"Wow," I said, the sight nearly stealing my breath. "Looks like *someone's* architect has Mordor on his inspiration board."

Jax let out the faintest laugh. I smiled in response, but didn't show it to him. He'd been a total jackass to me, so no, he wasn't getting any of my personal sunshine tonight.

Or any of my screaming orgasms either...

Ignoring the pulse of heat between my thighs, I turned to ask Hudson about the plan for getting over the wall.

But before I even opened my mouth, the rain started.

And it... burned?

"Um, guys? Is this normal?" I held out my hand, catching a few glowing drops. They sizzled into my palm like sparks.

"Shit! Starshowers!" Jax grabbed me and pulled me close just as Hudson stretched his massive wings over us, shielding us from the rain.

"Are they really falling stars?" I asked as the red-and-gold sparks hissed into the grass around us.

"Just a name," he said. A few of the sparks were starting to catch, igniting a series of little fires in front of us. "We can't stay here. We need to move."

"But what about the plan? How are we—"

"No time for a plan, Haley. Let's go."

"But—"

"Hudson has to take us over the wall. It's the only way. *That's* the plan, okay? So do me a favor and just... Just hold still and don't freak out."

The showers picked up in intensity, and a gust of wind sent a spray of sparks flying into my chest, a hundred points of heat biting into my skin. I patted myself down, tamping out the embers.

It was raining fire. It was fucking raining fire.

Flames surged up from the grass behind us, and without another second to waste, Hudson lifted me and Jax off the ground, tucked us in close, and took off at a run, leaping from the cliff and soaring out into the falling-star night.

I couldn't scream. Couldn't even catch my breath. All I could do was cling to Hudson's massive arm and do my best to ignore the vertigo, the bite of the starshowers nipping at my legs, and—if I was being totally honest—the thrill charging through my bloodstream at the sheer fucking wonder of it all.

Midnight was deadly and dark and terrifying, sure.

But it was also fucking amazing.

We swooped down across the abyss, skimming along the black sands before taking a sharp turn upward at Beggar's Moat, where I caught a brief glimpse of the creatures dwelling in its shadowy trench, lit up by the starshowers.

Skeletons. Shambling, shivering skeletons.

I bit back a gasp. Definitely worse than alligators.

We zoomed up Vanderham's Wall, sparks pinging off Hudson's leathery wings as he cut through the air. When we reached the top, two guards spotted us, shouting and pointing but making no move to leave the relative safety of their tower—especially not for a lone gargoyle and a couple of carry-on bags with no visible weapons.

We sailed up and over, then dropped down to street level on the other side, Hudson landing with a graceful thump.

Thankfully, the starshowers fizzled out fast. People

who'd clearly just run for cover spilled out onto the streets again, dousing small fires with buckets of water that seemed to be kept on hand for just that purpose.

Jax led us through a maze of alleys to a no-name pub in the Hollow neighborhood—the rally point, he'd said. Elian would supposedly find us there.

While he went inside to check things out, Hudson and I ducked under a tin overhang, and I took a minute to catch my breath and take in my surroundings.

The city was black and craggy, as if the surrounding mountains had started crumbling and the inhabitants decided to carve out homes rather than clear away the rocks. Newer buildings had been erected too, and now the city was a mix of crumbling rock-hewn structures, sleek black skyscrapers, and a mass of single-story shacks with tin roofs, all of it thrown together with no rhyme or reason. From our spot beneath the overhang, I could just make out the rise in the city center, the castle looming at the very top.

And the people. So many people. Every supernatural race, every age, every social status—whatever that even meant in a place like Midnight.

I couldn't stop staring.

The air smelled like roasted nuts and raw meat and garbage and fire and so many different things I could scarcely separate them all. There were no cars in the streets, no modern transportation, but I spotted a few wagons drawn by demonic-looking horses, along with some rickety old bicycles and a few rickshaws for rent. It seemed that most of the city's residents got by on foot.

Everywhere I looked, magick and firelight flickered in the windows, bright eyes in a face of shadow and rock. The same light burned in the streetlamps that lined the alleys.

My own magick surged, tingling along my arms and legs, making my heart race.

Amaranth City was filthy and cramped and louder than a concert, but it was easily the most breathtaking place I'd ever seen.

And when a familiar face finally stepped out from the pub and into the flickering torchlight of the streetlamp above me, Amaranth City started to feel, inexplicably, like home.

"Elian," I breathed, my knees nearly buckling with relief.

"Glad you finally made it, sparrow. Welcome to the Hollow."

His eyes were glassy, his smile too wide.

My heart sank.

I glanced over at Jax, who'd just exited the pub behind Elian. His jaw was tight. He gave me a quick shake of his head.

Fucking Devil's Dream.

I had no idea whether Elian had brought a stash with

him or scored one the minute he got to Amaranth City, but obviously, he'd found a way to get his fix.

Was this why he'd left camp? Not for blood, but for pills?

I blew out a deep sigh, trying not to let my disappointment—or my worry—fester.

I *hated* Elian for what he'd done to me all those years ago.

But more than that, I hated him for what he'd done to himself. For what he'd done—was *still* doing—to the man I once loved.

"So, what happens now?" I asked, if only to take my mind off everything else.

Elian flashed his cocky, crooked smirk. *That*, at least, hadn't changed. "Now, little sparrow, we go home."

The third-floor apartment was located inside a modern, plain black building about a block from the pub. It was a no-frills kind of place, but it was a lot more spacious than I'd expected. It looked like dozens of other apartments I'd seen in Blackmoon Bay, with plain wood flooring and white walls, minimal decor, and appliances just a little smaller than average. The entrance was off the kitchen, which opened into a common area with two fold-out couches and a small bathroom off to the side. Down a hallway at the back of the apartment, I spotted a large bedroom with its own private bathroom.

"What she lacks in elegance she makes up for in hot water, indoor plumbing, and electricity," Elian said, showing me around. "Gem managed to scrounge up some shampoo and conditioner for you—luxury items in these parts."

"Hot water?" I gasped. "*Conditioner*?" All my exhaustion drained away in an instant at the prospect of a real shower.

Jax let out a low whistle. "You must know people in high places, Saint."

"Once a deal-maker, always a deal-maker." Elian held Jax's gaze for a beat, a million unsaid words passing between them.

I had no idea how he'd managed to score such a place either, but right then, I didn't care.

"Work it out, boys." I claimed the bedroom as mine, dropped my pack on the bed, and headed right for that hot shower.

As much as I wanted to luxuriate in all my sudsy glory for the next three to five days, I also knew we had work to do. I wrapped it up quickly, then changed into a fresh set of clothes from my pack.

By the time I got back to the common area, Jax and Elian were already heading out the door.

"Where are you going?" I asked, twisting my wet hair into a bun.

"Back to the pub to meet up with Gem," Elian said. "She might have some intel on Keradoc."

"Great! I'm coming with you."

"No, you're not."

"You got me into Midnight, Elian. And Jax and Hudson got me to Amaranth City. But if I'm going to pull off a blood heist, I'll need as much information about Keradoc as I can get. Every little piece of gossip or news could end up being important later, and the more ears we have to the ground, the better our chances of picking up on something useful. So, yes. I *am* coming with you. And you're going to shut up and take it like a man, or I'm going to tell your friends about the *adorable* nickname we had for your—"

"Wow, would you look at the time?" He huffed out a nervous laugh and offered me his arm. "We'd better get going if we want to find a good table!"

I smirked at him and squeezed his arm, more than happy to gloat.

Haley Barnes, you've still got the touch.

27

ELIAN

As an immortal fae, I'd lived a lot of fucking lives. A childhood I barely remembered in the royal fae court of Autumnshire, back before we lost my brother Evander. Our family's banishment to the material realm. The darkness that eventually landed me in Blackmoon Bay, where I finally met Haley, my light. The all-too-brief years we'd shared that were still—of all the lives I'd lived before and since—my fucking favorite.

After the Bay came my first tour of Midnight.

Then New Orleans, Saints and Sinners, the empire that Jax, Hudson, and I built.

And now, I was back in Midnight once more, all of my lives converging and colliding like someone had tossed them into a blender and hit puree.

Felt like they'd tossed me right in there, too.

We sat huddled around a sticky table inside the dark,

dank pub, the whole place reeking of bodies and spilled ale. It was a long way from the cool refinement of Saints and Sinners, but something about the nameless pub in the Hollow would always feel like home.

Still, I couldn't risk being recognized. Right now, Gem was the only resident of Midnight I trusted, and until I could determine otherwise, I'd be operating under the assumption that everyone else was an enemy out for blood.

I sank a little in my chair. Drew my hood low, throwing my face into shadow.

"It's so nice to finally meet you, Haley Barnes," Gem said, beaming at her. "Saint's told me almost nothing about you, a fact which speaks even louder than words."

Haley laughed, but I didn't get the joke.

"Save it, Gem," I warned. "I'm not paying you for your comedy."

"Well, you should be. I'm pretty hilarious." She laughed again and tipped back her ale, but I knew the woman. Part of it was an act—blending in, playing the easy-going party girl. Her eyes were sharp though, darting around every dark corner, cataloging every new patron that walked in and every old one that stumbled out.

Gem was one of the Midnight elite, a pureblood fae witch who could travel freely between this realm and our home realm. She could also travel freely between Keradoc's ruling class and the class of miscreants and reprobates that made up the majority of this city, which came in handy for picking up intel from both camps.

In the time I'd known her, she'd gained a reputation as a tough and loyal friend who looked out for the real people of Amaranth and did what she could to keep Keradoc's nose out of our fucking asses, which was the only reason Jax, Hudson, and I were able to get our empire off the ground and keep it running in NOLA.

She took her cut, of course, just like everyone else, but that was fair. She earned it.

And now she'd be earning a little more.

Since I'd left Midnight, she'd stepped in to fill the void, serving as the woman who could get anyone anything, anytime—for the right price.

The most valuable of her offerings?

Secrets.

"What's the word, Gem?" I asked. "I'm hearing whispers that Keradoc's losing his touch. Can't keep his territories."

She glanced around the pub, then nodded, leaning in close. "Darkwinter's got him *real* twitchy these days."

"Darkwinter?" Haley's eyes widened, her neck turning blotchy.

"Are you familiar with the bloodline?" Gem asked her.

Adrenaline spiked in Haley's blood, mingling with a hint of fear. I could smell them both, souring her.

What the hell's got her so worked up about Darkwinter?

"Somewhat familiar," she replied cautiously. "My allies and I recently fought some of them in Blackmoon Bay. They'd been working with human hunters to hybridize supernaturals and create large-scale magickal weapons."

"Fuck, Haley." My gut clenched, guilt surging anew, reminding me just how much of Haley's life I'd missed.

Did this fight have anything to do with her debt to Melantha? With the reason she was here now?

"It's all good." Haley shrugged, forcing a smile. "We nailed the bastards and shut down the entire operation, but... Yeah. Darkwinter left a bad taste."

"Well, we've got ourselves an infestation here," Gem continued. "They've been spilling over our borders like bog roaches, mowing down Keradoc's troops faster than he can keep up. I just heard they took the Hanging Lake and the Road of Silence."

"Seriously?" Jax asked. "How'd they manage that?"

"No idea. They're allegedly moving in from the sea, too. Got some kind of crazy powerful ships."

"You think they're poised to take over?" I asked. "Turn this place into a Darkwinter satellite realm?"

"If I were Keradoc?" She nodded and lifted her glass. "That's what'd be keeping *me* up at night."

We shot the shit a little longer about the perils of Darkwinter, the festering lands of Midnight that were quickly falling under their control.

But Haley had gone completely silent after her

comment about the fight in the Bay, her heart still fluttering like a trapped bird.

I leaned in close. "You okay? You don't look so hot."

"What?" She turned to me and plastered on a smile. "No. I mean, yes, I'm fine. I'm just... You know, I think I'll head back to the apartment. I should probably... practice some of my spells." She rose from her chair and nodded at Gem. "Nice to meet you, Gem. Thanks again for finding us the apartment."

"Anytime, hon. You need help getting back?"

"I'll take her," Jax said.

I didn't want to make a big deal about her leaving, but what the hell? After the fight she'd put up about coming with us, now she was ready to call it a night?

Something was definitely going on with her, and I was pretty sure it had to do with Darkwinter and the shit she'd gone through back in the Bay.

Shit I should've been able to help her with, but couldn't, because I'd fucking bailed on her to come to this hellhole and...

I blew out a breath. "I need another drink. You good?"

"I could use one too," Gem said. "But let me get it. You stay here, Mr. Low Profile."

By the time she fought her way through the crowd at the bar, Jax had returned.

We settled back into the Darkwinter convo again, but

then out of nowhere, she said, "So, Jax. You gonna look up Oona while you're here?"

My heart almost seized in my fucking chest.

"Gem," I hissed. "Oona... She died."

Last thing we fucking needed was Jax tripping down memory lane. I needed him focused on Haley, not on the past.

Gem's face paled. "Died? But—"

"I saw it happen," I said. "Killed by her own father's guards. Fucking sick."

I felt Jax's eye burning right through me.

Fuck.

"I... I'm so sorry," Gem said, sounding genuinely astonished. "I had no idea."

"You know, I've been meaning to ask you about that night again, Saint," Jax said cooly. "Now that we're back at the scene of the crime, so to speak."

He flashed a grin that cut right to the bone.

Before he could spit out his question, I clamped a hand over his shoulder and said, "We've been over this, Jax. Oona's dead. Keradoc ordered the hit. How many more times do you need to hear it?"

"As many as it takes until I'm convinced you're not lying to me."

"Trust me, brother. You do *not* want to go chasing after ghosts. Not in this city."

"Maybe I fucking do." Jax pushed back his chair and got to his feet. "Good to see you again, Gem."

"Fuck you going?" I asked him.

He didn't answer. Just glared at me with the all-seeing eye, then took off.

"There's something you're not telling him about Oona," Gem said once he was gone. "Spill it."

With a grin, I picked up my mug and dumped some ale onto the floor, knowing damn well that's not what she'd meant by "spill it."

"For Oona of Midnight," I said anyway. "May she rest in peace."

Gem scoffed at me, but when it was clear I had nothing more to say on the matter, she let it go.

"All right, Saint. I've held out long enough. Time for you to tell me what you're *really* doing in Midnight, and why the hell you're asking me so many questions about Keradoc."

I finished my drink. Set down the mug. Looked hard into her eyes. "We need to get close to him, Gem. Tell me how to fucking do it."

A slow smile stretched across her face, lighting her up like the moons in the pitch-black sky. "Oh, I've got just the thing for you, Saint. And I've been waiting for a chance to see you and the boys in tuxes for a *long* time."

28

After a shower, I headed into the common area wearing nothing but sweatpants, thinking I'd have the place to myself for a bit.

But Haley was sitting on the floor, surrounded by potted plants and a few vials of blood and a bunch of them sharp knives she loved so much. The space was filled with candles, and a pentacle glowed on the bare wooden planks in front of her.

"Practicing," she explained when she caught me watching her. "Sorry if it's a little... extra. Then again, it's not like I ever claimed to be anything else, so... Working as designed?" She shrugged and wrinkled her nose, and I grinned, real big this time. She brought it outta me like no one else could.

"So, bare chest and gray sweatpants, huh?" She took in

the sight of me, her eyes roving down to my bare feet and back up again. "*Now* who's casting dark magick?"

Anyone casting spells around here, babygirl, it's you.

Ignoring her sinful little smirk, I grabbed two beers from the fridge, handed one to her, then took my favorite spot on the couch.

"You want some company up there?" she asked, already getting to her feet.

I shot her a look, like, *Do you really need to ask?* Then patted the spot next to me.

She curled up beside me, tucking her legs up, but I grabbed her feet and pulled her legs across my lap. I liked having her close. Liked being able to keep in contact—made me feel better about all the things outside these walls trying to hurt her, like maybe I could actually keep her safe from some of them.

"I was out with those guys earlier," she said, sipping her beer. "Trying to get some intel on Keradoc from Elian's... friend. Gem?"

I nodded. Gem and I went way back, even before Saint was in the picture. I knew they'd gotten close during his time here, so if Saint thought we could trust her on this mission? Then I backed him. After all, she'd helped us get out of this place when my ass was on the line. I'd always be grateful for that.

"She seems smart," Haley said. "Really knows her way around the streets, you know? I respect that."

She gazed down into her beer bottle. Ran her thumb up and down the neck.

I tugged on a lock of her hair. Smirked at her when she finally looked up.

"*What?* I'm not jealous. I'm just... cautious. New people... It's hard to trust, you know? Especially with something so important to me."

Yeah, I couldn't argue with her there. Trusting the wrong people had nearly cost me my life.

We sat in silence for a while, listening to the sounds of the city outside—fighting, mostly. Glass shattering. Thunder in the distance, though it was muted compared to the rest.

When I looked over at her again, I found her staring at the tattoos on my chest, mesmerized.

I curled my arm and flexed, and the sweetest blush crept into her cheeks.

"Sorry," she said. "I'm just... You're covered. And they're fucking incredible." She reached for my shoulder, fingers hovering just over the tattoo that took up most of my upper arm—two daggers crossing beneath an eye. "May I? I've always been fascinated by tattoos. Well, that and scars. I kind of see them as two sides of the same coin. Scars are the stories of the things that happened *to* us, things that were chosen *for* us. But tattoos are the stories we choose for ourselves. Both can be beautiful. A record of our lived experiences, you know?"

I leaned into her, and she brushed her fingers over my skin, making me shiver.

Her touch was... fucking indescribable.

The gray sweatpants suddenly seemed like a real bad choice.

But Haley wasn't paying attention to the situation in my lap. She was tracing the lines of my tattoos—my stories. The daggers and the eye. The raven gryphon feather. The triple crescent moons. The fleur-de-lis I'd gotten when we'd first ended up in New Orleans. The weeping skull with its mouth full of roses.

Blood before roses, it said beneath.

"I've only got a couple of tattoos," she said, and held out her wrist.

I ran my thumb along the writing tattooed there, bisecting the long, vertical scar. I'd noticed it that first day in Saint's garden, but hadn't been close enough to read it until now.

"This too shall pass," she said, soft and slow, like maybe she needed to hear it again.

Haley sighed.

I swiped a thumb across her cheek, erasing the tear that'd slipped out.

"I got it after... the bathtub incident," she said softly. "I wanted the reminder that pain like that doesn't last forever. But over time, I started taking it as a reminder that peace and joy don't last forever, either. Maybe that sounds morbid, but I find it comforting. It makes me appreciate everything a whole hell of a lot more than I used to because I know nothing is guaranteed. Not love, not health, not money, not friendship. But that doesn't make those things any less valuable, you know? In some ways, it feels even *more* valuable because it's fleeting, and…" She rolled her eyes and grinned. "Okay, I'm doing it again. Babbling your ears off."

I smiled at her and shook my head, letting her know I didn't mind. Matter fact, I could've listened to her babbling my ears off for another few centuries at least. Maybe even longer.

"Hudson, can I ask you something?"

I set my beer on the end table. Tucked a lock of hair behind her ear.

"How is it that we're in the most dangerous place in the universe," she said, "yet I've never felt so safe anywhere than I do right here? With you?"

I flexed my biceps for her again, and she laughed.

But just as quickly as the laugh had sprung up, it died, and a whole mess of tears spilled from her eyes.

I drew her close, wrapped her up in a hug.

A tremor rolled through her body, and I tightened my hold, wishing I could take away her pain. That I could go back in time, hunt down all them motherfuckers who'd ever put a crack or dent in her heart, and tear the flesh right off their bones.

But I knew Saint would be on that list.

And hell, maybe she'd be on his list too.

Sometimes things just got to a point with people where blame no longer served a purpose. Everyone was suffering the same damn misery.

Haley blew out a shaky sigh and pulled back, smiling at me once again. "Not only do I feel completely safe with you, but you're also the guy who gets me to reveal my deepest secrets and ball my eyes out, all without saying a word. Oprah could learn a thing or two from you, Gargs."

She tried another smile, but once again, it dropped right off her face.

This time when the tears started, she blinked them away, refusing to let another one fall.

She musta seen the worry on my face.

"I'm okay," she insisted, trying for another smile. "It's all good."

I touched her wrist tattoo again, and she nodded.

"Exactly. It'll pass, right? Always does. No point in falling apart over it."

I shook my head and frowned.

"Okay, it's... not all good? It's terrible and awful and we should probably just throw ourselves into Beggar's Moat and save fate the trouble?"

I shot her a stern glare and pressed my finger to her lips, and she nodded and quieted down, like she knew I needed a minute to gather my thoughts.

Just then, I felt like I needed an hour. A lifetime, and I still wouldn't have known how to do this.

I cupped her face, my big hands nearly swallowing her up. My heart thudded in my chest, blood rushing to my ears, the whole room going a little fuzzy.

Back in New Orleans, Haley had come to me—trusted me with her secrets—before she'd even known I was a real man. But that day in Saint's garden out back, something told me she sensed I was listening anyway.

Now, I knew she was listening to *me*.

Most people, when they encountered someone who didn't talk much... Well, most of them just started ignoring you after a while. Like, if you couldn't entertain them with your jokes and stories, if you couldn't ask them questions about their oh-so-fascinating lives, if you couldn't brag about how much money you had in the bank or what kind of car you drove, you weren't worth their time.

Haley was different, though. She listened to me in different ways—in all the subtle ways most people didn't bother with—like maintaining eye contact and noticing body language and being okay to just hang out in the silence together.

She always seemed to know what I needed.

Just like I always seemed to know what she needed.

She was mine to protect. If she needed *anything*—a hug, a loan, a kidney, a place to hide a fucking body—I was all over it.

Right then, with her still half-trembling in my arms, I knew the thing she needed most was for someone to tell her everything was gonna be okay, and mean it. To remind her that she didn't have to face the harsh world alone.

And suddenly, after more years than I could remember, I no longer wanted to just write it down on the back of a receipt. I wanted to taste the fucking words in my mouth. And I wanted to give those words to her—in my own voice.

I swallowed hard. Pressed one of her hands to my heart, still holding her face.

Another tear slipped down her cheek.

I took a deep breath.

And I opened my mouth.

"It's okay, babygirl," I said. "I got you."

The words rumbled through my chest, deep and gravelly, the sound of my old voice a shock to my ears. If I didn't know any better, I would've sworn there was another man in the room.

But it was just me and Haley, all alone in the candlelight, her eyes going so wide I saw the flames dancing in them.

This time when she smiled, it stuck.

"Hudson," she whispered, "thank you."

And I knew it wasn't just for the message, but for the words. For sharing them with her like some precious gift.

I kissed her forehead and pulled her back into my arms, and she snuggled in close like the whole fucking world could go to shit and it wouldn't matter, not a damn bit, so long as I kept my promise.

"I got you," I said again, only a whisper this time, because like she'd said—sometimes a fleeting thing was all the sweeter. "So fall apart if you need to, 'cause I *swear* I ain't letting you go."

I woke up in my bed a few hours later, half-smothered by a sleeping, tattooed giant in gray sweatpants.

It took a few minutes to extricate myself. My big teddy bear looked so sweet and peaceful, snoring lightly and taking up most of my bed, I didn't want to wake him. Something told me it was the first time he'd slept in a long time.

I closed the door softly, then crept into the kitchen, unable to help the smile that spread on my face.

Until I found Elian standing at the counter, arms crossed over his chest, glowering at me like he'd just discovered I'd eaten his leftovers and had been waiting hours to ambush me.

"Sleep well?" he practically grumbled. His jaw ticked, and his pupils were large and glassy.

Technically, there was no morning in Midnight, but it still felt too early for a little wake-'n-bake with the Devil.

I blew out a breath. I no longer had a say in Elian's choices—if I ever really did.

He kept on glaring at me, though, which was getting annoying.

Forcing myself not to roll my eyes, I said, "If you're not careful, Elian, you'll infect this whole city with your joyful attitude, and the next thing you know, they'll be painting rainbows and unicorns on the wall and breaking out in musical numbers in the streets. Is Jax back yet?"

"Why?" he snapped. "Worried he'll find out who you spent the night with, *angel*?"

"Okay, first of all? Don't call me that. Secondly, it's none of your business who I spent the night with. The only thing I want to hear out of your mouth next is confirmation that Gem stocked this place with coffee, or I can't make any more guarantees about your personal safety."

Elian turned his back on me to mess with something on the counter. When he faced me again, he held out a steaming mug of black coffee that called to my very soul. I hadn't even noticed the coffeepot behind him.

I took the mug with a nod of thanks and a genuine smile. Elian almost smiled back.

After a few sips, I leaned back against the counter next to him and said, "After we left you guys last night, Jax told me he was going up to the city center to dig up some more dirt on Keradoc. I figured he'd be back by now."

"Haven't seen him," he said. He shifted to stand right in front of me—all the better to glare down at me with those judgy silver eyes. "Haley? Honestly. What are you doing with Hudson?"

I took a few gulps of fortifying coffee, then grinned. "Oh, that's easy! If you head on over to Wikipedia and look up the entry for... What was it called again?" I tapped my lips. "Oh, right! Even More Shit That's None of Elian's Fucking Business. Can you spell all that, or should I write it down for you? I don't want you to miss out—it's a good entry. It'll save you from wasting your breath asking me shit like this."

He stepped close to me, crowding me against the countertop, his bergamot-and-rain scent making my heart rate kick up even more than the fresh jolt of caffeine.

Another second of *that* stupidly sexy nonsense and I couldn't even hold his gaze anymore—just dropped mine into my mug, grateful I had something else to focus on.

"It's the worst of the worst who end up in Midnight," Elian said, his voice low.

"Jax told me Hudson was born here."

"Doesn't mean he isn't just as bad as the rest of us. Or worse."

I laughed. "Oh, yes. Hudson's a real monster, all right."

"Haley—"

"As hard as it is to believe, some guys really *are* genuinely kind and sweet."

"And some are just good at putting on a show."

I patted his chest. "And thanks to all of *yours*, I've developed a keen bullshit detector. So, as much as I appreciate your opinion about my bedroom companions—which is not at all—I don't need a babysitter."

"I'm just telling you to be careful. I know you guys are getting close, and that's fine. Just don't piss him off. He's not—"

"If he's so big and bad, why is he even here?" I finally glanced up at him again. "I thought you trusted him. You said he'd always have my back."

"Yeah, within the parameters of this mission—protecting you and getting you in and out of Midnight. How was I supposed to know you two would get cozy?"

"You're being ridiculous."

"Really? Do you ever wonder why a thousand-something-year-old gargoyle looks like he could be the frontman of a motorcycle club?"

"His lifestyle choices have nothing to do with—"

"It's not a lifestyle choice, Haley. It's basic mythology. When a human dies by a gargoyle's hands—either by outright murder or by the neglect of his duty—the gargoyle incorporates part of that human's soul into his own, kind of like an atonement. He carries it with him for the rest of his eternal life. Hudson's whole big, burly teddy bear thing you love so much? That's not entirely *his*."

"You're saying he's just... acting out some other guy's life? A guy he *killed*?"

"No, he's not acting. His thoughts are his own, his values, the man he is at his core. But certain aspects of his personality, the way he looks and dresses, the way his words form into thoughts, the way he'd talk if he could... It's hard to explain, but a lot of what you're seeing and reacting to is essentially a piece of someone else."

"A piece of... someone he killed?"

"Not *someone*. *All* the ones. Including some you haven't seen yet. And *that's* what worries me, Haley. The ones you haven't seen. Because some of those aspects are downright—"

"Again. You're being ridiculous."

"I'm just telling you your sweet little cuddle-buddy isn't all he's cracked up to be, and all I ask is that you be a little smarter about that."

I shook my head. Nothing Elian had said would change the way I felt about Hudson. If this soul-incorporating thing was part of gargoyle mythology, then it was all just part of what made Hudson who he was—a friend I'd come to care about. One I trusted with my life.

One who was probably as tired of Elian's bullshit as I was.

"What are you doing?" I asked.

"Trying to protect you from—"

"No. You're not acting like a concerned friend. You're acting like a jealous ex. All this stuff about Hudson? You know damn well he'd never hurt me, no matter what kind of soul-mashup he's got inside. You're just pissed because you think I slept with him."

He huffed. "Didn't you?"

"Literally, yes. As in, I curled up against his chest, with all my clothes on, and fell asleep. And it was the best night's rest I've had since we got here, so please prepare yourself, because it might just happen again, and I wouldn't want you to get all hyper-protective and vamp out on me over—"

"For fuck's sake." He finally broke away from me, giving me some much-needed air, but it was only so he could reach into his pocket for another little black pill.

It was the first I'd seen one up close, tiny and unassuming, and I watched with fascination as he pressed it to his tongue, magick swirling briefly in his mouth before he snapped it shut and swallowed.

When he looked at me again, the tension had left his jaw, his eyes turning even darker and more glazed than before.

He was killing himself. Fucking killing himself, one little pill at a time.

Anger flared inside, but I tamped it down.

In so many ways, I understood him. That urge. That

sliding scale between desperately wanting to live, desperately wanting to die, and the dead center of not really caring one way or the other.

When I'd met Elian, we were both closer to the center. But now, it felt like he was sliding toward that black edge where he might just decide—one night when no one was watching—to hurry things along.

Elian didn't know just how close he'd driven me to that very same, very dark edge—and he didn't need to.

But I wasn't about to let him fall over it now.

"Do you want to die?" I asked.

He offered a lazy, crooked grin. "Do you want me to die?"

"Why do you do it?"

"All part of the fantasy, sparrow. You should try it— might help take the edge off if you escaped your reality once in a while. Might make you a little less uptight."

"You think I don't know how to escape reality?" A bitter laugh hissed through my lips. "It's ironic that you ended up in the fantasy-dealing business, Elian. That people actually *pay* you for this shit. Me? I never needed a pill or fae illusions or the thrall of a vampire. I spent so much time making up fantasies about *you*, half the time I couldn't even remember what was real."

"Yeah?" Guilt flickered in his eyes. His smile faded. He stepped closer. "What kind of fantasies?"

"All different kinds. Sometimes the one where I woke

up and found you in bed, just like always, and realized my life without you was only a bad dream. Other times it was the fantasy where you came home to me, telling me you'd finally remembered our life together after being in a coma for five years. There was the one where I'd be in a restaurant with some other guy, and you'd walk through the door and see me there, and you'd fall to your knees and beg me to forgive you and take you back." Emotion rose in my chest as all those old, useless dreams came rushing back. "Then there was the most painful one. The one I distracted myself with for hours on end, forgetting to eat, to shower, to sleep."

Elian swallowed hard. Reached up and tucked a lock of hair behind my ear, his glassy-eyed gaze turning soft. Sad. "Which fantasy was that, sparrow?"

"The one where you'd never even left me at all."

A tear slid down my cheek, and Elian followed it with his fingertip, lingering on the corner of my mouth.

"Three-thirty-three in the morning," I whispered. "It's the loneliest time in the world, Elian. When the rest of the city is asleep and you're wandering your own house like a fucking ghost. Do you have any idea how many three-thirty-threes I suffered through? Staring out the window onto the dark streets of Blackmoon Bay, trying to walk backward through time in search of the *one* thing I could've done differently, the *one* thing I could've said to make you stay?"

He cupped my face with both hands, his breath warm on my lips, sickly sweet from the drugs.

"I'm sorry," he whispered. "I never meant... I'm so sorry."

"Those were my fantasies," I said. "They gave me hope. And let me tell you something. Hope? It's a drug worse than your Devil's Dream. A drug that causes delusions so powerful, you re-route your whole life around them until all you have left are the bullshit stories you tell yourself just to get through another day." I closed my eyes and leaned into his touch, stealing a little of its warmth. "Those fantasies were killing me. So, I came up with a new one."

"Tell me," he whispered.

I opened my eyes. The guilt etched into his face was nearly overpowering.

I didn't want to carry it for him. Not a single ounce.

"The one where you *died*," I said. "Every other fantasy got locked in a box, because they were too painful to deal with. And now I'm standing here watching you pop your little pills and you're looking at me like that and we both know *damn* well I'm still in love with you—I always will be. But all I can think is... All I can think is that I wish it were true. I wish you really *had* died. Because grieving for a corpse is a hell of a lot easier than grieving for a man who's standing right in front of you, disappearing a little more each night." More tears fell, and I swiped at them hard. "So that's all I've got left for you, Elian. All the blood. All the broken pieces. The fucking mess. Take a good look, because this is the *last* time I'm shedding a tear for you."

He stared at me in silence, but didn't take too long to recover. He moved in close once again, pushing me against the counter, sucking all the air out of the room.

"You wished me dead, sparrow?" he breathed, looming over me. "Well guess what? I *was* dead. I died the night I walked out on you." He fisted my hair, his hips pinning me in place, the heat of his body radiating through his clothes and straight into my skin. "You want me on my knees? You want me to bleed for you? Fine. Here it is. I was a dead man. A fucking ghost. Then out of nowhere, you walked into my bar with your vampire stakes and your green eyes and that hot little lace dress, and for the first time in five fucking years, my heart started beating again. Damn near thought I was having a heart attack. You tell me you still love me? Fuck, Haley. I'd give *you* the last fucking breath from my lungs if it came down to it. But I can't. No matter how badly I want to, I just can't. So you go on pretending I'm dead if it helps you get through the night, but don't for a *second* think you're the only one staring out that window at three-thirty-three, wondering what the fuck you could've done to change things."

He didn't let me go. Didn't back up. Just kept standing there with his hands in my hair and his body so close I could feel his heart banging against his chest, could see my own reflection in the depths of those bottomless black pupils.

His gaze swept down to my lips, and he lowered his mouth to mine, the barest brush of a kiss...

A noise on the stairwell, and a second later, the kitchen door swung open.

Jax.

Elian closed his eyes. Slipped away from me.

And I went right on back to wishing he was already dead.

The tension in the kitchen was as thick as the Fog of a Thousand Knives, and one look at Haley and Saint told me it was probably just as deadly, too.

They broke apart immediately, but neither one of them said a word. Just kept stealing glances at each other when they thought the other wasn't watching.

Something churned in my gut like battery acid, but I wasn't about to name it. Not now.

"Everything okay?" Haley asked, putting on a bright smile. I would've loved to bask in it, but it wasn't her real smile. Didn't even light up her eyes, which I could see now were rimmed in red.

Fucking Saint.

What the hell had he done to her this time?

I glared at him, but one look into those eyes told me he

was so far into the Black, he probably couldn't even hold a conversation.

Ignoring him, I headed to the small kitchen table and set down my bag, retrieving the box from inside and handing it to Haley.

This time, I got a glimpse of the real smile, which made some of that battery acid evaporate.

"What's this?" she asked.

"This," I said, "is demon-speak for thanks for saving my ass. Something I should've said a while ago. But don't get your hopes up, angel. It's not an engagement ring."

She cracked up. "Glad you clarified that. For a minute there, I saw a box the size of a swordfish and got excited. For a ring, I mean. Not actual swordfish. Which, come to think of it, I haven't had in—"

"Haley?"

"Yeah?"

"Open the box."

She let out a little squeal, then popped the lid.

As soon as she saw the dagger inside, she gasped, removing it and wrapping her hand around the bone handle, turning it to inspect the blade. "This is gorgeous, Jax. *Way* better than a ring."

I laughed. "Yeah, well. I know it sucked when we had to leave yours behind. Soon as I saw this one, I wanted you to have it."

"It's perfect. Look at the detailing on the blade! And the weight... It's like it was made for me."

"There's a sheath in the bag, too. Should fit on your current holster, but if not, we can get you something else."

"Thank you. I love it!"

My chest puffed up. Couldn't be helped. "Yeah?"

"Seriously? Best present ever. Hands down."

Her eyes were all sparkly again, her cheeks pink, all evidence of the earlier tears gone.

The fact that I'd even noticed as much? Probably a warning sign, but I didn't care.

Haley was right that first night at camp. I *did* like her.

I watched her now, the smile curving her lips, the light in her eyes, and a feeling of rightness settled over me.

I'd come back to Midnight not just because Saint had dragged me into another of his epic fucking messes, but because I thought it would give me a chance to finally find some fucking answers. Answers about the night Oona died— about Saint's version of events that'd never quite added up.

But all night, as I'd walked the alleys of the city that'd claimed the woman I'd once loved, all I could think about was the woman I'd left at the apartment back in the Hollows.

My angel of darkness.

Oona's death had damn near destroyed me, and after years of chasing the ghosts of all those unanswered questions, after years of nurturing a festering rage at the unjustness of it all, Haley Barnes had taken me completely off guard.

She'd snuck up on me. Her laugh, her fire, the taste of her kiss, the feel of her fevered touches in the corpsevine field, the sound of her moans as I'd made her come for me...

I didn't know what the fuck it all meant, if anything. But right then, staring at her in our kitchen in the Hollow, I knew I wanted more.

More than just a mission.

More than just a roll in the corpsevine.

More than I'd ever admit to anyone—even her.

Especially her.

"Thank you so much, Jax," she said now, stretching up on her toes and kissing my cheek.

I sighed and ran my hand down her back, my thumb grazing the soft skin that peeked out beneath the hem of her T-shirt.

Saint, who'd gone so still and silent I'd forgotten he was even in the room, groaned. "While you were out on your little shopping spree, Jax, *I* actually managed to find some useful intelligence."

Still holding Haley in my arms, I glared at him, shocked he could even use the word 'intelligence' in a sentence, given how stoned he was.

"So, if you don't *mind*," he continued, rolling his eyes,

"I'm much more interested in discussing Keradoc than watching you fondle my ex."

"So don't watch," Haley said, flashing me a devious little grin that had my cock twitching.

Damn it. All I wanted to do was drag her ass into that bedroom and make up for the two days we'd wasted avoiding each other.

But if Saint had found good intel on Keradoc, we needed to hear it.

"Out with it," I said.

"The Feast of Midnight," he said with a flourish. "Also known as the Feast of the Beast. Also known as our best shot at getting up close and personal with the warlord we so know and love."

"Also known as a thing that hasn't happened in years," I said. "They don't do the feasts anymore."

"Ah, but they do!" Saint beamed. "Resurrected from the dead for one night only, and it's happening in less than two weeks."

"What's the Feast of Midnight?" Haley asked.

"Some bullshit party the ruler of Midnight throws to convince the people he gives a shit about them," I said. "It's the only time his castle is open to the public."

"Concurrently," Saint added, "he hosts a soiree for the upper-crust. Very exclusive, invite-only, lots of ass-kissing and deal-making. Those rich bastards are the only ones who'll get anywhere near Keradoc. They don't even host the parties on the same floors."

"So, what are you thinking?" I asked, my interest definitely piqued. "Can we bypass security? Have Hudson get us in from the top, maybe?"

"Not a chance. The place will be crawling with soldiers. The main floor is one thing—they'll be admitting every criminal and murderer from the Hollow to the Sea. But the exclusive party? Fourth-floor ballroom. And *no* one's getting up there without an invite."

I nodded, seeing right where this was headed. "You've already talked to Gem about this."

"She's already working on my list."

"What's on the list?" Haley asked.

"Two tuxes, three forged tickets to the soiree of the century, weapons to be strategically placed ahead of time by the most disloyal castle staff money can buy, a formal gown with easy access to said weapons and the ability to conceal a contraption that can extract someone's blood without that person's awareness. Oh, and the contraption itself—we obviously need that. Let's see... Floor plans for the castle, a list of additional guards and servants open to bribes, no less than three escape routes... Yeah, I think that about covers it. Oh! I forgot to ask her about shoes." He pulled a notebook out of his back pocket and scribbled it down, along with a few other notes.

"Pretty sure you're missing a tux and a ticket," Haley said.

"Hudson doesn't need one. He'll keep watch from the roof. If hell breaks loose, he'll swoop in and… well, break it looser. And whisk us out of there in a flash of those glorious wings and talons." Saint spread his hands like a magician revealing his final trick.

"You make it sound so easy," Haley said.

"The logistics are always easy. It's the execution that fucks people." He flashed the crooked grin that'd closed more deals and sealed more fates than there were stars in the Midnight sky, then returned his attention to his notebook, frantically scribbling once again. "Fortunately for us, I'm an *expert* at not getting fucked."

Haley and I exchanged a glance, both biting back a laugh.

Then, leaving Saint to his maniacal plotting, Haley grabbed her new dagger, and we snuck off to the bedroom to execute a few plans of our own.

No sooner had Jax peeled me out of my T-shirt and closed his hot mouth around my nipple did my bedroom door crack open, ushering in a sliver of light and a vampire-fae who seemed determined to piss me off.

We'd been sniping at each other for a week straight, ever since we'd started planning for the Feast of Midnight heist. First, it was an argument about the best way to infiltrate the party and get close to Keradoc, and wasn't there a way I could just steal his blood without actually touching him? From a safe distance across the room, perhaps? Then Elian decided I wasn't spending enough time practicing my blood spells. The asshole had even picked a fight about whether the gown Gem had procured for me would draw too much attention and blow our cover.

Yes, friends and colleagues, a little side-boob-and-shoulder combo is all it takes to raise the alarms of Midnight. I sure hope the embroidered potato sack I ordered as backup will arrive in time!

Idiot.

So forgive me, Father, for feeling less than hospitable while my jerky ex-boyfriend crashed my private party with my demon lover, but...

What the fuck did he want to fight about now?

"Haley, look," Elian said, his voice low and serious. "We need to talk. There's something you need to know."

Jax and I froze in the bed. Apparently, Elian hadn't noticed I was otherwise occupied, which shouldn't have surprised me. Elian was a selfish prick who rarely noticed anything unless it had to do with him, and those pills had put a serious damper on his vampire senses.

"A little busy right now," I finally said.

"Busy? But you're... oh. *Fuck*," he muttered, finally figuring it out. "I should've known."

"You should've *knocked*," I said. "What do you want?"

"I told you, I need to talk to you."

"*Busy*," I said again. I rolled onto my hip to face him. Jax drew closer from behind, lips hot on my bare shoulder, hand sliding invitingly around my hip and down between my thighs, teasing me through my panties. Only a thin sheet covered us—all that kept our intruder from getting a full show.

"You expect me to wait?" Elian asked, annoyance darkening his tone.

"She's worth it," Jax said, taunting him. "But you'll have to take a number—assuming she'll have you at all."

Elian let out a hollow laugh. "Didn't peg you as the share-and-share-alike type, brother."

Jax's fingers tightened possessively on my hip, but he shrugged and said, "Her bed, her rules."

"I need to talk to Haley."

"She's a little busy at the moment. Maybe try back in an hour?"

"I'll wait."

"You sure about that?" Jax kissed the back of my neck, his fingers skating lower, just behind the top edge of the lace.

I tried not to shiver.

Elian folded his arms across his chest and leaned back against the door. That asshole fae wasn't going anywhere. Not until he got his way, which I wasn't about to give him.

So, dropping all pretense of modesty, I slid out of Jax's hold, hopped out of bed, and waltzed right over to him.

Staring him down in nothing but my black lace G-banger, I folded my arms under my bare breasts and said, "What was it you needed to talk to me about, Elian? The weather? Tomorrow's breakfast options? My shoe selection for the party? Or are you here to warn me about my poor choices in men?"

Elian swallowed hard, his gaze locked on mine, cold and impassive. There was no hiding the hitch in his breath, though. The flare of his nostrils as he took in the scent of my bare skin.

There was no hiding the resulting throb of desire between my thighs, either, but like I said—we were well past the pretense of modesty.

"I told you I'd *wait*," he ground out. "So go ahead and get back to... whatever it is you're doing."

"Whatever it is I'm doing? Really? Is it unclear what I'm doing? Did you need a diagram or something?"

A buck-naked Jax joined me by the door, stepping up behind me and placing his hands on my hips, his hard cock nudging me. Kissing the sensitive spot behind my ear, he said softly, "A live demo could also be arranged."

I glared at Elian, my heart pounding as his rain-and-bergamot scent collided with Jax's smoke-and-lemons. I felt like I was caught between a storm and a fire. I didn't know which would kill me first.

Elian glared right back at me, his eyes flashing in the darkness, pupils nearly blown from the Dream, his breath quickening. A low growl rumbled in his chest, the warning of an apex predator.

He wasn't going to back down.

I closed my eyes. Tried to calm the frantic beat of my heart. Tried to talk myself into kicking Elian out, bolting the door, and climbing right back into bed with Jax as if we'd never been interrupted in the first place.

But deep down, where all my darkest truths lived, another secret rose to the surface:

I didn't *want* Elian to back down. I wanted him to watch. I wanted him to burn for me the same way I still burned for him.

Jax nipped my earlobe, then dragged his hot mouth down my neck and across my shoulder, one hand sliding up to cup my breast, the other gliding down over the front of my panties.

I leaned my head back as he tugged my nipple, my eyes opening just a fraction, my body relaxing into the pleasure of his touch. Through a heavy, half-lidded haze, I watched Elian's vicious gaze rove down my body, heat rising in its wake.

A quiet moan escaped my lips, and Jax slid his hand lower between my thighs, cupping me and rubbing the lace. It scraped against my clit, making me gasp.

"You're so wet, angel," he breathed, increasing the pressure. "Do you like it when he watches me touch you?"

"I'm... I don't know. It's... I'm just..."

Oh, God...

My entire body tingled, my skin hot, nerves buzzing with anticipation. But...

Was I even *allowed* to like this? Elian was my ex—one I still had intense, complicated feelings for. Jax was his friend—sort of. One I was also developing feelings for, and they didn't exactly get along. What Jax and I did behind closed doors was one thing, but this? Letting Jax drive me wild while Elian stood by and watched? Knowingly tormenting the man I'd once promised my heart?

It *had* to be wrong.

Didn't it?

"He's a vampire," Jax whispered, teasing my nipple to a hard point, his fingers moving harder and faster over the panties. "He already knows your answer. He can hear your heartbeat. Feel the rush of blood through your veins." He bit my neck, then kissed a searing hot path back up to my ear. In a low, hot murmur, he said, "The scent of your sweet pussy is making him drunker than all the little black pills in the realm."

"Jax," I breathed, though I couldn't tell whether my soft sigh was a warning to stop... or a plea to keep going.

He released my breast and grabbed my hair, fisting it so tight it made my eyes water.

Fuck, yes...

"Look at him, angel. Look at what you're doing to him." His mouth was still close to my ear, breath hot on my skin. "Now, I'm going to fuck you. Right here. And unless you say otherwise, he's going to stand there and watch while I make you come all over your demon's cock. Isn't that right, Saint Elian?"

I almost came right there. His dirty mouth, his hot breath, the sudden heat rising in Elian's eyes...

Holy fuck, I'd never been so turned on in my life.

I met Elian's gaze again, the fire in his eyes a reflection of the same fire burning in me, white-hot and all-consuming. Destructive. Chaotic.

Unstoppable.

Elian didn't say a word. Just clenched his fists at his sides, his jaw so tight he was nearly trembling.

He could've left, I reminded myself. Could've turned around, opened that door, and walked right out.

But he didn't.

"Yes," I finally whispered, answering for both of us.

Jax tore my panties off so fast, the lace burned my hips. He brought them to his face and inhaled, then stuffed them into Elian's pants pocket.

Still, the vampire-fae didn't move.

Gripping my thighs, Jax lifted me right off the ground, wrapping my legs around his hips from behind. I tipped forward, catching myself on Elian's shoulders as Jax slid into me with a hard thrust.

"Jax!" I cried out with a gasp, the new angle of my body giving him even deeper access. He rocked his hips, hitting me just... just right.

Elian grabbed my wrists, my hands still clamped on his shoulders, his back firm against the door. I waited for him to shrug me off, to let me fall, to do *something* other than drill into me with those penetrating silver eyes, but he didn't move. Didn't speak. Barely even breathed.

"Elian," I whispered, my eyes blurring with tears. The pain and longing in my heart intensified, mixing with the tremors of pleasure coursing through my body at Jax's every touch.

More than anything, I wanted Elian to kiss me. To claim me right along with Jax, even if it was just for tonight. Even if it was destined to become nothing more than another memory haunting my dreams, slicing me up like a razor blade every time I touched it.

I whispered his name once more, and a new fire blazed in his eyes. He released one of my wrists and trailed his fingers up my arm, goosebumps rising in his path.

Then he wrapped his hand around my throat, squeezing just tight enough to make it hurt.

Just tight enough to let me know he remembered *exactly* how I liked it.

Oh, fuck...

A fresh bolt of desire rocketed between my thighs, and Jax slowed his movements behind me, the subtle tease of his cock making me ache. He tugged on my hair again, his other hand firm around my hip, fingers digging into my flesh.

My thighs clenched tighter, and I crossed my ankles behind him, drawing him in deeper. I strained to get closer to Elian, but between Jax pulling my hair and Elian's tight grip around my throat, the kiss I so desperately wanted remained just out of reach.

This was... this was fucking crazy. I was pinned between them, the demon whose every touch made me feel like I needed to go to church and beg for absolution and the vampire-fae whose smoldering gaze still had the power to make me weak.

I hadn't seen that look in five years—not like this, close and raw. For all the shit he'd put me through, for all the nights I'd spent curled up on the kitchen floor, for all the hours I'd spent cursing his very name...

God, I'd fucking *missed* him. I *still* missed him—maybe even more now, having him so close but never close enough.

I was his captive—heart, body, and soul.

Why hadn't he turned around and walked out of here? Did he want me as badly as I still wanted him? Was this all just a game to him?

And was Jax truly okay with this? No, the demon and I weren't in a relationship. Hadn't really talked about anything other than enjoying each other's company in Midnight. But most guys weren't into sharing, no matter how much they might've joked about it, no matter how casual the hookups.

Was it crazy to think he didn't care that I so obviously wanted Elian? Wanted them both?

I was confused and angry and completely overwhelmed, but *damn*, I'd never felt anything so intense—so hot—in my life.

I didn't want it to end.

"Elian," I whispered, my breath shallow beneath the press of his fingers. Tiny pinpricks of light danced across my vision. "Jax. You... you're so... Both of you..."

"We're so *what*, angel?" Jax whispered.

"Yes, little sparrow," Elian finally managed, his breath ghosting over my lips. Heat pulsed from his fingers, radiating through my skin. "Do tell."

Jax thrust in deeper once more. I closed my eyes and melted into him, a bead of sweat trickling down my spine, his name on my lips like a curse.

When I finally opened my eyes and met Elian's gaze again, he smirked. Crooked. Cocky.

Jealous.

"Demon got your tongue?" he asked, his smirk turning cruel. "Maybe we should let your insatiable little cunt do the talking instead."

Elian might've thought his words would cut deep, but all they did was turn me on.

Keeping a hand wrapped around my throat, he released my wrist and slid his other hand down my abdomen, palm flat against my skin, fingers whispering closer...

"Please," I whispered. Begged. "Touch me, Elian."

His fingers trembled against my skin as if it burned him, but he didn't pull away.

"Touch me," I begged again.

"*Damn it*, Haley," Elian ground out. "Don't—"

"Don't what?" I whispered. "Admit that I want you? *Both* of you? It doesn't have to mean anything more than—"

"It will *always* mean more," he hissed.

Anger flashed in his eyes, his private war waging endlessly behind them. He clenched his jaw, grip tightening on my throat as Jax railed me from behind, every thrust making me hot and dizzy.

A roar exploded from Elian's chest. Fangs descended, and in a flash he brought his mouth to the spot between my neck and shoulder, his lips and breath caressing my skin, a soft contrast to his rage.

It *wasn't* a caress, though. It was a warning.

I felt the graze of his fangs, the sharp points scraping across my flesh, his hand still trembling against my abdomen, fingers inching closer but not close enough, my breath ragged, my body wound tight as my monsters pushed me down deeper into that dark well of pleasure.

If this was how I was going to die, well…

Fucking bring it.

Jax slid a hand around my hip, fingers dipping low between my thighs where Elian had refused to venture, teasing and stroking, pushing me closer and closer to the edge of white-hot bliss as I awaited the exquisite pain of Elian's bite.

"You're close, angel," Jax murmured. "I can feel it."

A shudder wracked my body, heat building in my core as he circled my clit, his pace quickening, his cock hitting me deeper, harder, my thighs tightening around him, the wave of intense pleasure rising, cresting, and then... *oh, God...*

Elian released my throat, and the air rushed back into my lungs just as the wave broke, crashing over me with a force that nearly blinded me.

Jax slammed into me with a desperate growl, shuddering against my backside as he came hot and hard, my pussy clenching around him, my body drowning in ecstasy.

I cried out for my demon, and Elian grabbed my face and sealed his lips around mine, inhaling my moans of pleasure like a drug as I rode out the intense orgasm, the wet heat of his mouth radiating across my tongue, the bastard fae stealing the very breath he'd only just allowed me to claim.

I ached for his real kiss, the slide of his tongue, the slice of his fangs, but I knew he wouldn't give it to me. Not like this. He was too proud, too wounded, too fucked up to go back on whatever promises he'd made himself all those years ago—whatever he'd done to cut me loose and burn the cords that'd once so tightly bound us.

He nipped my lip as he pulled back, finally drawing blood.

It wasn't enough, though. With Elian, it would never be enough. Not unless he decided to let me back into his heart.

A warm, wet trickle ran down my chin.

"If you were singing for *me*, beautiful sparrow," Elian breathed, his eyes blazing once more, "I wouldn't allow an audience."

His tongue darted out to trace the path of the blood from my chin to my lower lip, but that's as far as he went.

All too soon, he turned away, severing the last of our momentary connection.

Jax pulled out and gently set me back on my feet, wrapping his arms around my middle. His release slid down my thighs.

I leaned back into his embrace, anchoring myself.

Elian sighed. Held my gaze for a thousand years, a thousand mysteries burning in his.

Only one thing was clear.

Between the three of us, everything had just changed.

No one spoke.

And when Elian finally turned and stalked out that door without so much as a backward glance, it felt like I'd lost him all over again.

"Tell me something, angel," I said. "Why him?"

We were standing in the shower after that crazy shit with Saint, my hands gliding up and down Haley's soaped-up curves as she slathered conditioner through her hair.

She twisted it into a loose knot on top of her head, then stepped close, sliding her hands up over my shoulders. Her nipples hardened against my chest, and when I palmed her perfect backside, she grinned.

She looked sad, though, and I didn't know whose ass I wanted to beat harder—Saint's, for breaking her heart all those years ago, or mine, for asking about it now.

It was none of my business. But before I could tell her to forget it, she sighed and said, "it may be hard to believe now, but the Elian I knew back then was kind and sweet and funny. I mean, yeah, he's always walked on the dark side. But he was... I don't know. Different before. Not so jaded and selfish."

Selfish wasn't a word I'd use to describe Saint, but I wasn't sure what to call him, either. In the time I'd known him, he'd shown a strong sense of self-preservation, coupled with a razor-sharp ingenuity that was just this side of dangerous. That combination often spelled disaster for anyone crazy enough to get caught up in his bullshit, but it could just as easily save someone's life as wreck it.

I'd been on both sides of it. Still was.

Like most of the dark, damaged, and depraved of Midnight, Saint was a complicated fuck.

"Sometimes he'd just sit in the dark with me," Haley said, "breathing with me, letting me listen to his heartbeat. It always brought me back from the edge."

Her eyes flooded with tears, and my heart squeezed.

"The edge of what, angel?"

Despite the hot shower, a shiver rolled through her body, and she drew closer to me. "Have you ever felt completely broken? Like you weren't even a whole person, but a collection of jagged pieces, some of them missing, some of them smashed beyond repair?"

I didn't know what the fuck to say to that, so I tightened my hold on her.

"There have been times in my life..." she said. "I mean, it's never totally gone, but it's not as bad now as... Anyway, back then, a lot of times I'd slip into these dark moods where I was convinced I was just this broken, unfixable thing. But Elian... He never made me feel that way. Never treated me like I was a burden just for having feelings or expressing shitty thoughts. Never told me to look at the bright side or be more positive or any of that bullshit people throw at you under the guise of helping when all they're really doing is trying to make themselves more comfortable with your pain. He didn't try to glue me back together—and it wasn't because he agreed I couldn't be fixed. He just never believed I needed fixing at all. 'Falling apart doesn't mean you're broken,' he used to tell me." She sighed. "Sometimes that was all I needed. That one little reminder, and I knew it would be okay, even when it hurt."

"Why the *fuck* did he leave?" I hadn't meant to say it out loud, but loud it was.

"I don't know, Jax." She blew out a breath, hot mist across my chest, then pulled back. When she looked up into my eyes again, I thought she might say something else about it, but then she just shook her head and lowered her gaze. It landed on the tattoo over my heart—a skull weeping blood, mouth full of roses.

"Hudson has the same one," she said softly, reaching up to trace the outline.

I could hear the question in her words, and I nodded. "Saint too."

"From your time together here in Midnight?"

"We took an oath," I said. "After one of Keradoc's victory parades."

"Victory parades? But he hasn't even won the war."

"And if he ever does, and the fighting actually stops and the monsters of Midnight unite in peace, the whole place will crumble. Midnight runs on corruption, greed, and violence. It doesn't work otherwise." I closed my eye and dipped my face into the spray of water, eye patch and all. I never took it off around her, and I never would. Haley didn't need any more nightmares.

"After the battles," I continued, "his soldiers would bring the wounded back to the city and parade them through the streets until they either bled to death or passed out and got crushed in the procession. Not just his enemies, which would've been horrifying enough, but his own fighters too. Anyone who got themselves injured was weak, he'd reasoned, and needed to be culled from the herd."

"Holy fuck."

"The worst part was seeing the family and friends of the wounded. They'd throw themselves in front of the procession, begging for the soldiers to free their people, but most of the time they got crushed, too."

My gut twisted at the thought. Saint didn't think Keradoc was doing the parades anymore, but every time I stepped out into the street now, I looked over my shoulder, half expecting to see the half-dead armies marching through a river of blood.

"This one night," I continued, "the parade got out of hand. The injured weren't dying fast enough, so the Midnight soldiers starting killing them—just picking them off. Knives, arrows, immolation. People—not the ones unlucky enough to have someone marching in that mess, but the others—watched the procession from their windows and balconies. They cheered for the violence, egging on the attackers. They dropped roses down on the bloody streets, chanting for Keradoc. The bastard himself never bothered attending, though. He'd tell his generals he didn't think it was prudent for a leader to sully himself by publicly supporting such barbaric traditions, even though they'd all been carried out on his orders."

"And the soldiers called this a *victory*?"

"All they had to do was murder their own men, and they were champions." I pressed the heel of my hand to my good eye, wishing I could stamp out the memories. "Later on, the three of us headed outside. The streets were littered with roses and blood and death. So we stood, right out in the middle of the city, and made our oath. Sliced our palms, clasped hands, and swore that no matter *what* happened to us in Midnight, we'd never turn on each other like that. We'd protect each other. Before glory, victory, or love, the three of us would come first. Even before honor. Didn't matter that we weren't born as brothers, or that we weren't even the same species. That night, we became blood."

"Blood before roses," she whispered, and I nodded.

"That old saying, 'blood is thicker than water?' Most people assume it's talking about your blood family—parents, siblings, whatever—and telling you they're the most important people in your life. No matter what abuses or atrocities they commit, it doesn't matter, because they're your blood."

Haley nodded, her eyes darkening. "I've always hated that saying. Family—a bond like that—should be *chosen*. Sometimes you choose your blood relatives, but that's not always a given."

"No, it isn't. Which is why some people believe the saying is actually a bastardization of the original, which is, 'the blood of the battle is thicker than the water of the womb.' The people who fight side-by-side, the people who spill blood for you... That bond is stronger than a connection forged by the chance pairing of two people creating biological offspring. I always took it that way, anyway. So when I say Hudson and Saint were my blood... I *chose* them that night, Haley."

She took my hand. Ran her finger along my palm, right across the spot where I'd sliced it open for the oath.

"And now?" she asked. "Are you still choosing them?"

"Now it's... complicated. You know, sometimes things happen and you just... I don't know, Haley. Bonds break."

"*Elian* breaks them, you mean."

"No, it's… It wasn't all his fault. Not this time. We all played our parts. We're *still* playing them. But Saint… He certainly doesn't make it easy to keep choosing him."

She reached up and traced the arch of my eyebrow. "He makes you sad."

"Not just him," I said, forcing a smile. "Saint may be a grade-A dickhead, but he can't take credit for *every* fucked-up thing that's ever befallen me. Believe it or not, angel, I haven't always been such a charming gentleman."

That got a smile, but it wasn't enough to chase the new worry from her eyes.

"Sometimes when you look at me," she said, "I feel like… like you're seeing someone else. A ghost."

"Sometimes I feel like I might be."

She blinked up at me, water dripping from her long lashes, waiting for an explanation I wasn't sure I wanted to give her. Wasn't sure I even could.

But then my lips were moving, bringing the past into the present, words tumbling out before I could stop myself.

"Oona," I whispered, as if she really was a ghost. "She was a dark fae—one of the pureblood Midnighters. Keradoc's daughter, actually, though I didn't learn that until after. When his people found out we'd been together, they killed her. Saint thought they were trying to send me a message."

"Oh my God," she gasped.

"He was there—said he tried to help her, but it was too late. Too much blood. Oona died in his arms, and there wasn't a damn thing to be done. It all happened so fast, and I... The guards were after us. We had to run, and..." I squeezed my eye shut, just barely keeping the worst of the memories at bay. "An hour later, we were in New Orleans, Midnight firmly in the rearview."

"Jax, I'm so... Fuck. I don't even know what to say."

"It was a million years ago, Haley. It's done."

"But you—"

"Look, we don't need to do this," I said, already kicking myself for opening up a damn vein. "Really."

"Jax, look at me. Please."

Biting back a curse, I opened my eye. Looked down at her soft, creamy skin. The rivulets of water running over her dark nipples.

Fuck, this was not how I saw this night going. I was standing in the shower with the hot, naked, insatiable witch who'd given me the most intense fucking orgasms of my life, and we were wasting time talking about dead soldiers and blood oaths and murdered exes?

"Jax—"

"I told you, it was a long time ago. I shouldn't have mentioned her."

"Did you love her?" she whispered, her face so earnest, so sweet, it threatened to carve me right open all over again.

"I *don't* love, Haley. Period."

"Because you were hurt?"

"Because I know where loving someone leads."

"To... being in love?" She tried to laugh, but it fizzled out quickly.

Inside, I felt the old devils clawing at my heart. Burning it. Slicing me open only to heal me and do it all over again.

"Do you know the first thing you learn when they turn you into a fear demon?" I leaned in close. Gripped her jaw and forced her to meet my gaze. Then, in a dark whisper that left her trembling, "Behind every fear, every horror, every blood-soaked nightmare that leaves its victims screaming into the darkness lies but a single root, and no, it's not cancer or spiders or the monsters lurking under the bed. It's something *much* more dangerous."

"Y ou asked me once if I was born like this," I whispered, my mouth so close to hers I could taste her every ragged breath. "No, I wasn't born a demon, my sweet angel. I was human once—centuries ago—dragged to hell for my irredeemable sins and forged into the monster standing before you now."

"I... I'm sorry. I didn't know."

"From my first day in those fiery pits, they beat me. Tortured me. Stripped me bare of everything I ever knew and loved as a man. Then, certain I was sufficiently weak and malleable, they rebuilt me to their exact specifications, force-feeding me every single fear imaginable—dying alone, suffering, getting devoured by snakes, waking up during surgery, drowning, burning alive, losing loved ones, facing war, falling from a great height, getting diagnosed with incurable diseases, and yes, even facing those monsters under the bed. I lived through every single night-mare as though it was real—as though it was mine. And then, I did it again. Again and again, every day for a hundred years in a place where an hour feels like a life-time. And do you know why they subjected me to such tortures?"

"No," she whispered, eyes wide, her body still trembling in my hands, warm and wet.

"Because a fear demon needs to learn how to look into someone's soul and recognize his worst terrors without succumbing to them, all so we can turn them into weapons against him." I released her jaw and slid my hand down to her breast, the other gripping her hip. Drawing slow circles around her nipple, I said, "So when I tell you I don't love? No, it's not because I was hurt. It's because I've lived through every man's worst nightmares, and I can tell you with utter certainty the only *true* fear—the seed that blooms into all the others—is love."

She searched my face. Gripped my hand to stop my incessant circling. "You're wrong."

"I wish I was, angel. But I'm not."

"But... love? That's ridiculous. What about fear of abandonment?"

"You mean fear of being abandoned by the people you love?"

"Fear of death?"

"Fear of losing your loved ones, losing time with

them, or leaving them behind to face life without you, because they love you and you know it will devastate them?"

"Loneliness?"

"Longing for someone to love and to love you back—partner, family member, community, friend, or otherwise?"

"Pain?"

"Haley, it's still about love. Ultimately, suffering is—at its heart—a separation from or betrayal by the love we're promised, explicitly or otherwise. When pain is inflicted by someone who's supposed to care for us, it feels like a deep betrayal. If it's our bodies, then *we're* the betrayer, or maybe it's our gods—after all, aren't they supposed to love us? If a stranger hurts us, it's a violation of a sacred social contract—an implicit agreement to look out for one another, to love thy neighbor. When someone breaks that contract? We feel it on a soul level."

"Then what about the monsters under the bed? Surely that's just—"

"A perceived loss of safety and security, which is another form of love, and the failure of a loved one who should've protected us."

Her brow furrowed, and I could tell she was searching her mind for the loophole, but there wasn't one. Not for this.

"People are made to love," I said. "Humans and supernaturals alike. Anything that prevents or breaks that bond?

Give it all the trappings you want, but that's still the *ultimate* fear."

"Humans and supernaturals are made to love?" She gave me the saddest fucking look in the world. "But not you?"

I shook my head.

"Jax, come on. It *has* to be more complicated than that."

"Does it?"

"Look, I don't know the first thing about being a demon, so I'm not trying to, like, witchsplain you or anything. But—"

"Tell me your worst fear," I said. "Dig deep."

"I don't have to dig—it's easy. Screwing up this quest and losing my sisters to the Dark Goddess. If I don't get Keradoc's blood, she'll... And I'll... Oh, shit." Haley blew out a breath, then rolled her eyes. "Okay, point made. I love my sisters. Ergo, love is the root of my fear of losing them. Let the gloating commence."

"No gloating necessary. However, I will make *one* small point of clarification..." I slipped a finger under her chin, tilting her face toward me once more. Her hair slipped loose from the knot, falling down her back and unleashing the scent of coconuts. "I know what *truly* frightens you, angel, and it isn't the thought of losing your sisters to Melantha."

"It... isn't?"

I brought my hand back to her breast, palming it, then

squeezing, making her moan. Her eyelids fluttered closed as she leaned into my touch.

"You've been hiding it," I said softly, her nipple hardening at my touch, "ever since we set foot in this realm."

She shook her head, but didn't deny it outright. Didn't back away from me.

"You've been doing a damn good job keeping it under wraps from everyone else," I said, "but you can't hide it from me. One look into your eyes, and I see *everything* that haunts you."

I slid my hand down past her abdomen, slowly parting her thighs and dipping between them.

She clutched my arms and sighed. When she spoke again, her voice was breathy and faint. "Don't, Jax. Please don't."

"Don't what? Touch you?" I pressed my palm to her clit, gliding over her hot flesh, teasing her entrance. "Don't kiss you?" I brought my mouth to her ear, licking the edge, making her shudder. "Don't make you shatter for me?" At that, I slid two fingers inside, pumping her slow and deep.

A soft whimper escaped her lips.

In a dark whisper, I breathed, "Or are you telling me to look into those gorgeous green eyes and pretend I don't see the darkness lurking behind them?"

"Jax..." She tightened her grip on my arms, her mouth parted, cheeks darkening as I fucked her faster and deeper with my fingers.

"I'm telling you, angel. Inside you is an abyss so black it could turn even the most fearsome monsters into smoke if you let it. But way down at the bottom of the well, a little voice is shouting at you to lock up all that darkness and throw away the key."

"I... can't. I'm... oh, fuck. You're—"

"Yes, angel, I know *exactly* what I am. And I know what you are, too." I palmed her clit again, pulsing my fingers inside her wet heat. "That little voice telling you to run and hide? To pretend you don't feel the things you feel about me, about Saint, about this fucking place? To put on a smile and go back to being the sweet little sunshine girl that never admits how dark things truly get for her?"

"That's not... No. I'm..." With another soft moan, Haley rocked her hips, taking me in deeper, riding me, even as she tried to deny herself the pleasure. The truth.

"You're not afraid of Melantha's wrath," I said. "You're afraid if your sisters knew the truth about you—if they saw the same darkness *I* see in your eyes—they'd abandon you." I slid my fingers in deeper, faster, her body already starting to quiver around me. "And you're afraid they'd be right to, because deep down you're a bad girl, and bad girls don't deserve love."

"Don't... don't say that," she panted, squeezing her eyes shut even tighter, as if that alone could make it all go away. "Please don't say that."

"I'm only saying it to tell you it's a fucking *lie*. That voice inside you? It wants to keep you small and afraid because it thinks that's the best way to keep you safe. But that's a lie too—nothing can keep you safe from that kind of darkness, and every day you believe that lie and allow yourself to shrink is another day some part of you fucking *dies*."

Another whimper. Fingernails digging into my arms. She was about to come, but I wouldn't let her. Not yet.

I jerked my fingers out, spun her around, and pushed her face-first against the tiles, pinning her with a hand between her shoulder blades.

"Jax," she breathed. "I need... I'm so close... I just need..."

"Tell me," I growled. "What does my angel need?"

"Hard... Make it... hurt. Everything inside me is just... I need it to hurt. I need to fucking *scream*."

"You will, angel. Because no matter what you believe, I'm not afraid of what's inside you. I'm fucking *drowning* in it." I fisted my cock. Slid it between her curves, teasing her even as my balls ached to unload. "When you show someone who you really are? When you trust someone enough to give them even a glimpse? That's living, not shrinking. That's courage. And anyone who turns their back on you after that never deserved your love in the first place."

I slammed into her pussy, making her cry out in a

fierce roar that ricocheted off the tiles, echoing through my very bones.

I grabbed her hands. Pinned them to the tiles above her head.

Fucked her harder, deeper. She pushed back to meet every thrust, her whole body jerking, already so close to the edge she was barely holding on.

"I made you come once already tonight," I said. "But that was for Saint. Now I need you to come for *me*."

I clamped a hand hard over her mouth, not wanting to share this with anyone. Her body was mine. Her pain. Her pleasure. Her screams.

One more deep, hard thrust, and that was it. She fucking shattered, frantic and desperate, biting my hand hard enough to draw blood as her pussy clenched around me and she rode out the intense wave, trembling and bucking until she had nothing left.

I gave her a minute to come back to her body, then slid out from between her thighs, spun her around to face me, and pushed her onto her knees beneath the water spray. I fisted her hair, still thick and slippery with conditioner, every lock like spun silk in my hand.

"Okay?" I asked, running a thumb along her lower lip.

In response, she took my thumb into her mouth and sucked. Hard.

Then she started humming a new tune, all for me.

I almost came right there.

Still humming, she moved her lips from my thumb to my cock, her tongue darting out to tease the tip as she fisted me. Water slid down her face like rain, and she blinked up at me with those devious green eyes.

I stared down into them, watching the darkness swirl.

My cock pulsed in her hand, and she grinned, wicked and powerful. Fucking beautiful.

She needed this as badly as I did. Craved it. The roughness. The realness of it all.

In a place where blood rained from the sky and ghouls begged for bones outside the city walls, sometimes it was easy to forget that even immortal beings could still ache and bleed and die.

Not tonight. Right now, right here, we both remembered.

She parted her lips and took me in deep, her sweet music vibrating across my flesh, my hands buried in her hair as I fucked her hot little mouth until she gagged.

"Right there, angel," I growled. "Right fucking there."

She looked up at me then, another flash of pure wickedness, then sucked me in deep and raked her nails down my abs, blood mixing with the water, and I hit the back of her throat and came so fucking hard I thought I might actually disappear.

I waited until she sucked down the last drop, then pulled out and slumped back against the tiles, my whole body spent and shaking.

Haley was still on her knees. And when I looked down at her again, she smiled.

A little bit devious. A little bit sweet. All angel.

And suddenly I remembered the day of our arrival when we fought off the raven gryphons. I remembered the blood in her hair. Remembered the fae nearly ambushing us in the woods after the first time we'd been together.

Remembered the image of Saint's worst fear in full technicolor detail—Keradoc, his violet eyes alight with pleasure as he swung a sword and chopped off her head.

And right there, out of fucking nowhere, I felt it.

A flicker in my heart that had absolutely *no* business showing up again.

Fear.

Without another word, I stepped out of the shower and toweled off. I left her there on her knees, still panting, her eyes dark and dreamy as the water slid down her sexy-as-hell curves.

She flashed me a smile, her cheeks dark with a blush that threatened to make me hard all over again. "Feel free to invade my shower anytime, sinner. My door is always open for you."

I forced a smile. "Good to know. Anyone else on that list?"

She rolled her eyes and got to her feet, then turned her back on me, granting me a view of her fine, perfect ass before yanking the shower curtain closed and cutting me off.

I debated sticking around, waiting for her in bed for another round.

But then the sword flashed in my mind, and my heart stuttered again.

No, I couldn't stay. What I *really* needed to do was hunt down a bottle of something strong enough to chase away that flicker, right along with the rest of the damn ghosts trapped in my head.

I grabbed my clothes off the floor. Headed out into the hall, pulling her door shut behind me.

Saint was *right* fucking there, standing across from me in the dark, leaning back against the wall with his arms folded over his chest.

He'd probably been there the whole time, the sick fae fuck. Probably still hard from what I'd done to his woman earlier. From what he'd witnessed and heard just now, undoubtedly imagining his own cock in her mouth every time I slammed into her with a grunt.

Not like she hadn't given him the opportunity.

"Enjoy the show, asshole?" I asked.

He glared at me in the darkness, his silver eyes flashing. It took him a minute to find the words, which was unusual for Saint.

But then, finally, he leaned in close and said, "You hurt her, demon, and I'll take the other eye, too."

A sharp ache tore through my skull, the memory of a hot blade in my flesh. *His* blade.

"I'll let you in on a little secret, Saint." I grinned, lowering my voice to a whisper. "That little witch *loves* when I make it hurt."

He punched me so hard in the face my head snapped back, but I just kept smiling, even as my head throbbed so badly it felt like my skull was caving in. Even as the blood gushed hot and salty from my nose.

I dragged my hand through the mess. Smeared it across his mouth and clutched his face, making sure he tasted it.

The tattoo on my chest blazed.

"Blood before roses, Saint," I said. "*Choke* on it."

34

Long after I'd washed the demon stink from my mouth, I could still taste Haley on my tongue— her breath, her blood, the intoxicating scent of her desire.

It wasn't desire for you, *asshole. It's Jax she wants now.*

My fist crashed into the bathroom mirror, spiderwebbing it.

I stared into a dozen jagged shards of glass. And a dozen broken versions of the same man stared right back.

I never should've come to Midnight.

I wasn't talking about this time—no way would I have let Haley face this hell on her own.

I was talking about the last time. The *first* time.

If I'd ignored my instincts then, would she still be with me now? Would we be happy and warm and safe in Blackmoon Bay? Or maybe living the life we'd so often talked about in New Orleans, her with her bookstore and café, me with my club?

How many more nights, weeks, *years* would I spend playing this game?

I'd almost told her the truth tonight. The story she so desperately wanted to know but didn't have the heart to ask. She had a right to it. It was her story as much as mine.

But seeing her in bed with Jax...

I clenched my fists. My hand fucking throbbed, slower to heal than it should've been.

Good.

I slipped a pill from the bottle and pressed it to my tongue. Held my breath, waited for the familiar tingle to set in.

It didn't.

I popped another one. Stuck out my tongue and watched the Dream's black whorls dance across it.

It took a few minutes, but eventually, I felt something. The whorls grew blacker, and the dark fae magick buzzed in my mouth, sliding down my throat and slowly working its way into my bloodstream.

Shutting my eyes tight, I yanked her panties from my pocket. Pressed them to my mouth. Inhaled. Tried like hell to ignore the agony tearing through my heart, but of course I couldn't.

I'd never quite mastered that fucking trick.

Tears brimmed behind my eyelids, then spilled, my entire chest cavity about go supernova.

Sometimes it felt as if leaving her had hollowed me out inside. Carved the beating heart right from my body.

And other times, like tonight, I knew that heart still existed, because every time it fucking beat, a bright burst of pain reverberated throughout my entire being.

How the fuck was I even breathing?

"Touch me, Elian. Please..."

Her desperate whispers floated through my mind, unleashing a thousand memories just like it. A thousand other breathy moans, a thousand other nights when she belonged only to me. When I still had a right to touch her at all. To call her mine.

"Haley," I ground out. Her name felt like razor blades in my mouth, but I couldn't stop. "Haley," I whispered. "Haley."

I unzipped my pants and fisted my cock with the panties, stroking once, twice. I moved slowly at first, dragging the lace across my sensitive skin, imagining the scrape of her fingernails. Her teeth.

I was rock hard in an instant, my cock throbbing for her. Aching.

I tightened my grip and stroked again. Again. A little harder this time. Harder still. Faster, faster, the sweet memory of her moans crashing through my head, her fists tight on my shoulders, the taste of her breath in my mouth, the scent of her drenched pussy overwhelming me as the demon fucked her so hard she shattered...

"*Fuck...*" I shuddered into that black lace, coming in a fast, red-hot rush that left me trembling, my head falling against the broken mirror, breath fogging the glass.

Jerking off into her panties after I'd watched another man fuck her into oblivion was beyond pathetic.

But it was all I had.

There was a time when I enjoyed fantasizing about my little sparrow, even when it hurt.

Now, it did more than hurt. It carved the Haley-shaped hole in my chest deeper, bigger.

It fucking gutted me.

I tossed the spent panties in the trash and showered off the rest of my release, but until they made a soap to get rid of guilt and self-loathing, I was stuck with that shit. It burned through me like fire.

But for now, I needed to lock it all down.

The Feast of the Beast was in three days. We'd planned to attend together, but that was no longer an option. I needed to do some recon on the castle, see if I could identify all the possible points of failure ahead of time—before the only people in the world I gave a fuck about risked their lives walking into a death trap.

And I still had to figure out how the fuck I was going to kill Keradoc. For all our arguing about plans and timing and wardrobe choices, the assassination was a detail I still hadn't been able to wrap my head around. It would have to wait until after Haley got the blood she needed but before anyone figured out who we were, and that wouldn't give me much time to maneuver if things went sideways.

I needed to think. And I couldn't fucking do it with Jax banging my woman into a wall every night, the sounds of her pleasure floating on the air like all the ghosts I was still trying to outrun.

Gem's place was the only safe haven now. No fucking demons. No exes. No ghosts. Besides, she'd been on a need-to-know basis since our arrival in Midnight, and the time was finally here. She needed to know.

Showered and dressed, I scrawled out a hasty note, telling Jax I had some things to wrap up and would meet them inside the castle in three days.

Then I drew my hood low over my eyes, shouldered my pack, and headed out into the perpetually dark streets of the Hollow, half hoping someone would leap out of the shadows and stake me before I reached my destination.

35

HALEY

t's okay, babygirl. I got you.

Though Hudson hadn't uttered another word since the night I'd fallen apart in his arms, those were the words that gave me strength now, as Jax and I stepped through the polished obsidian doors of Keradoc's castle.

Our gargoyle was covering the exterior in his winged warrior form, keeping watch from the stone turrets. Jax would have my back on the inside in case anything went south.

But Elian?

None of us had seen him since that intense night in my bedroom.

Jax told me he'd left a note—that he was working closely with Gem to ensure everything was set up for us tonight, leaving nothing to chance. That I shouldn't fret.

That Elian would show up, no matter what had happened —or *hadn't* happened—between us.

But a fissure of worry had opened up in my chest all the same.

"Haley." Jax tightened his grip on my elbow and leaned in close, brushing a kiss to my temple. "He'll be here, angel."

I nodded and smiled because I wanted to believe him. Also, because he was wearing a fitted tux that made him even more drool-worthy than usual, even though he'd outright refused to let me bedazzle his eye patch.

But as we made our way into the castle's main parlor, a deep dread settled into my stomach. Not necessarily about Elian, though his absence certainly didn't help; I hated how we'd left things that night—how he'd turned his back and walked out.

Still. Personal issues aside, tonight was the most important night of my life. Of my sisters' lives, though they had no idea any of this was even happening. I tried to imagine them at home now, practicing their magick and keeping one another company. Getting together for dinner or drinks or just to chat.

Living their lives—lives I would do everything in my power to protect.

Even if it killed me.

The parlor was a mass of sweaty, filthy bodies—fae,

demon, vampire, human, witch—all of them crushed together, elbows and punches flying as they jockeyed for a closer spot at the buffet tables and open bars. They were dancing, too; whoops of laughter and catcalls rang out above a cacophony of discordant music—some kind of dark techno that thumped through my bones. The whole thing reminded me of a frat party, completely off the rails, and if someone busted out a beer pong table or announced a wet T-shirt contest, it wouldn't have surprised me in the slightest.

But once we got through the public party and over to the sleek winding staircase that would take us up to the exclusive level, everything changed.

Getting through security took a good twenty minutes. Two different soldiers frisked us, then wanded us with some kind of magickal device that supposedly identified hidden spells and potions. Our tickets were scrutinized so closely, I started to fear we'd already blown our cover— that at any minute, the guards would haul us down to the dungeons.

But eventually, they cleared us, and we made our way up the winding staircase to the fourth-floor ballroom, my heartbeat steadying a little more with every step as I borrowed some strength from my fearless, superhot demon.

As if he could sense my thoughts, Jax slid his arm around my shoulders and drew me a little closer, whispering into my hair for the hundredth time in an hour, "You're fucking *stunning*, Haley Barnes."

Heat rose in my cheeks. I was pretty sure I'd never get tired of hearing it.

The truth was, I *did* look pretty damn fine tonight. The dress Gem had picked out for me was black, of course—a strapless silk gown with a long sleeve on one side. The fitted bodice was hand-embroidered with tiny red roses that trailed down along the skirt, which flared out to my ankles in a series of layered petals—easy access to my thigh holsters, assuming I could reunite with them soon.

All part of the plan.

I'd left my hair down, curled in loose waves that Jax couldn't stop touching.

Jax...

I'd meant it when I told Elian I was still in love with him. I probably always would be. But I couldn't deny the feelings simmering for my demon, either. Even Hudson had found a place in my heart—a place that was quickly expanding to allow for the possibility that he could be more than a friend, too.

Something about these men—these monsters—belonged to me. And I belonged to them. Whatever happened in Midnight, whichever paths we walked when all was said and done, they'd never leave my heart.

The ballroom was as massive and ostentatious as I expected, like something straight out of a Regency romance novel. There were a few hundred people gathered there, some dancing, some drinking—a more refined version of the party exploding downstairs.

We didn't spot Keradoc, though.

"Remember," Jax said. "Long black hair. Violet eyes. He'll be the best-dressed fae here. And he's *extremely* compelling, so you're gonna need to watch yourself at all times."

I grinned. "I don't know if you know this about me? But I'm pretty good at fending off unwanted advances from creepy supernatural men."

Jax cupped my face and brought his lips to my ear. In a dark whisper, he said, "And that sounds like a fun game for us to play later, angel."

Laughing, I slipped away from him and headed into the bathroom located beside a tapestry of a fiery lake—the place Gem was supposed to leave my package.

Lifting the top of the toilet tank, I choked back a sob of pure relief. There, taped inside, was the promised leather pouch.

Gem had come through for us. She'd fucking come through.

I removed the pouch and retrieved my weapons—my favorite hawthorn stake that'd somehow managed to survive the long trek from New Orleans to Midnight. The dagger Jax had given me. My thigh holsters. And there, last but certainly not least, a tiny glass vial no larger than my pinky finger, fitted with a needle so short and thin I could only see it when I held it beneath the torchlight.

It was attached to a leather bracelet that fit snugly against my wrist, just inside my sleeve.

When I was ready to do the blood extraction, a quick flex would release the needle.

A magickal numbing agent would ensure Keradoc didn't feel a thing.

Then, assuming his blood responded to the call of my magick, I'd be able to guide it straight into the vial without it losing any of its potency.

The Goddess didn't require much—even a few drops of his blood would be enough to break the moonglass spell—but I wasn't taking any chances.

Locked and loaded, I searched my face in the bathroom mirror, trying to find the woman that Jax had seen the other night in the shower when he'd whispered all my secrets.

Inside you is an abyss so black, it could turn even the most fearsome monsters into smoke...

You're afraid if your sisters saw the same darkness I see in your eyes, they'd abandon you...

Nothing can keep you safe from that kind of darkness, and every day you believe that lie is another day some part of you fucking dies...

I'm not afraid of what's inside you. I'm fucking drowning in it...

Jax was right. I *was* dark.

And I was magick.

And here in Midnight, in the place I should've feared more than any other, I'd never felt more at home.

As soon as I emerged from the bathroom, a pair of strong arms encircled me, dragging me into a nearby closet full of musty old cloaks and a long-forgotten suit of armor.

The scent of campfire and lemons was a dead giveaway, even before his fingers started sneaking past the petals of my dress.

"Jax!" I breathed. "What the hell are you *doing*?"

His reply came low and raspy in my ear, making me shiver. "You thought you could parade around looking like this and expect me to keep my hands off you tonight?"

"I figured the whole risking-our-lives, one-man-short, dangerous-blood-heist-in-a-castle-full-of-armed-soldiers thing would put your dick on ice—at least for a *few* hours."

"Not happening, angel," he murmured, his kisses growing as urgent as his touch. "I'll *die* if I don't taste you."

He finally found his way between my thighs, fingers gliding over my exposed clit.

"Jax, I... Oh, *fuck*," I breathed, clutching his arm. "Why are you so good at... at being the *worst*?"

"Because you *love* the worst. The more important question is… Why the fuck aren't you wearing panties?"

"You kept ruining mine, so I solved the problem by removing the temptation."

"You've merely created a *new* problem, angel."

He slid two fingers inside me, a slow, delicious thrust that left me trembling, but just when it started to feel *really* fucking amazing, he pulled out, then reached for the stake strapped to my thigh, freeing it. Beneath the silky fabric, he ran the tip up along my thigh to my hipbone, then slid it across to the other one before dipping lower. Lower.

Lower still.

He grazed my clit, then dropped to his knees and pushed open the panels of silk, baring me.

I was powerless to do anything but sigh as he worked his sinful brand of magick, one touch, one kiss at a time.

With the very stake I'd used to paralyze the bloodsuckers who'd attacked me at Saints and Sinners the first night I'd met him, the demon traced delicate patterns on my skin, then followed with his tongue, each stroke burning like a magick rune.

"Do you trust me?" he whispered.

"Are you serious? Fuck no!"

"Good girl."

"Jax, wait. I don't think we should be… I'm… Oh, well that's just… *so* not fair."

He licked my clit, then sucked it between his teeth,

giving it a teasing nibble before pulling back and drawing another soft circle with the stake.

"I'm going to make you come," he said. "But there's a catch."

"I don't... care..." I panted, fisting his hair. "Whatever it is. Just... don't stop."

"You can't sing for me tonight, angel. You can't make a sound or we'll be discovered, and our whole plan will be shot to hell."

"Maybe you should've thought of that before you dragged me into the closet and—"

He tapped my clit with a light slap, then descended, his mouth and breath and tongue licking and teasing, pushing me closer, then pulling back to draw more maddening strokes with the stake until I was so wound up I worried I might actually explode, nothing left but a pile of black silk petals to mark my passing.

"Jax," I breathed, and he slid his tongue across my clit once more, then thrust his fingers inside, fucking me right into oblivion as I held my breath and shuddered against his face, not making a sound.

When I finally stopped shaking, he slid the stake back into the holster and got to his feet.

Then, cupping my face and lowering his mouth to mine, he whispered, "Every time you feel that stake rub against your thighs, I want you to think of my mouth. I want you to remember how hard I made you come on my tongue. And I want you to know I'll be waiting for you to return to me, so I can do it all over again later."

His eye blazed, but no, these weren't just the dirty words of a hot demon looking to get laid later.

The look in that eye was fierce. Protective.

And if I didn't know better...

Don't be ridiculous, girl. Jax is incapable of love. Fear demon, remember? You're seeing stars because you want to, and that's a dangerous game you can't afford to play right now.

"I knew it," I said with a wink. "You totally like me."

He grinned and swatted my ass, and then he was off, ready for us to go our separate ways and carry out the plan.

I waited a full minute before making my exit. And when I did, a new kind of magick sang through my veins. I felt strong and powerful, confident.

I can do this. I can totally fucking do this.

I slipped into the ballroom. Grabbed a flute of champagne from a passing butler. Cataloged all the exits. Located Jax across the room. Scoped out the magickal chandeliers, the gorgeous crown molding. The Midnight elite in all their finery.

And then, suddenly, there he was.

Our mark.

Keradoc.

Flanked by two heavily armed fae guards, he began a long, slow walk from the back of the ballroom to the center, the crowd parting for him as he passed. A small platform had been set up for him, and when he reached it and stepped up to the podium, the entire ballroom erupted in applause.

I was too far back to clearly make out his features, but even at that distance, I could still feel his magnetic charm. He hadn't even said a word yet, and already I felt myself leaning closer, eager to hear it.

He waited forever before finally lifting his hands and settling the crowd, then—after a brief welcome—launched into a doozy of a patriotic speech that could've given every evil dictator back home a run for their money.

To hear him tell it, Midnight was and would always be theirs. He rambled on about a major show of force, the arrival of a new weapon the enemy would never be able to defeat... I mean, honestly. Had this guy even looked out a window lately? Did he not see his entire realm burning at the hands of the Darkwinter fae?

As he *finally* wrapped up the monologue that sent the crowd into a full-on rapture, I made my way to the other side of the ballroom, still scanning for signs of Elian. I spotted Gem, but just as I was about to head over and grill her on Elian's whereabouts, the air shifted behind me, and a dark wave of magick whispered across my skin.

"Normally, I execute party-crashers," came a smooth voice, low and dangerous in my ear. "But I might be willing to make an exception for you."

Tensing for a fight, I slid my hand to my side, fingers

brushing the hilt of the dagger holstered just beneath the silk petals.

Then, I turned around to face the man who'd made the mistake of threatening me, coming face-to-face with the most entrancing violet eyes I'd ever seen.

It was hard not to stare.

The warlord of Midnight was damned intimidating.

Unlike Elian, who'd incorporated enough modern touches into his personal style to help him blend in back home, this guy was pure, O.G. fae.

His long black hair shimmered with strands of silver, woven in a mix of intricate braids and loose locks. His fingernails were as black as his hair, each one filed to a sharp point. Even his clothing was black—embossed silks tailored perfectly to his lean body and an open, collarless jacket made of some kind of leather, the edges trimmed with delicate silver and violet swirls that danced in the light.

It brought out his eyes, which now had me pinned in place, completely mesmerized.

Also, if more guys wanted to start wearing black eyeliner back home? I'd fully support that endeavor.

"Would you grant me the honor of a dance?" He held out his arm and smiled once more, a warning hidden in the depths of that violet gaze.

I couldn't help but test his boundaries, just a little.

Folding my arms across my chest, I gave him a once-over. Then, in my most sultry voice, I said, "Do I have a choice?"

"No. Not unless you want me to reconsider my exception."

"Right. The one where you *don't* toss me to the ghouls?"

"That would be the one, yes. Though I feel compelled to tell you that tossing you to the ghouls is just one of the myriad ways in which I might decide to... deal with you. A dance would be much more pleasant. For you, at least."

He flashed a devastating grin, and I flashed one right back, and the next thing I knew, I was allowing him to sweep me out onto the dance floor.

His scent was overpowering up close, like wild roses encased in ice, mixed with a hint of deep, dark earthiness I could only describe as... forbidden. For all the power locked away in his lean muscles, he held my hand with a delicate touch, his other hand warm and gentle on the small of my back, holding me just a little closer than what might be considered proper for polite company.

Across the ballroom, I caught sight of Jax, who watched

me with a mix of concern, lust, and jealousy. I wasn't sure which of those feelings dominated, but my demon was definitely spring-loaded and ready to pounce, should the need arise.

But I didn't feel threatened by Keradoc. Not even with all his subtle taunts about executions and the current of dark power crackling just beneath the surface of his touch. In fact, now that I was in his arms, breathing in his heady scent and gazing into those captivating violet eyes, I felt an inexplicable connection to him. Even my magick responded to his presence, a soft hum buzzing through my veins, warm and electric.

Keradoc twirled me, then captured me in his embrace again, pulling me even closer.

"I didn't realize you'd be so beautiful," he murmured in my ear. "So... enchanting."

Fighting off a shiver of pleasure, I said, "Didn't realize? What do you mean?"

"I... I simply meant..." He faltered, then smiled once again, dazzling as ever. "When I saw you earlier this evening. I'm embarrassed to confess... I was watching you speak with another. A demon, if I'm not mistaken? With an injury to his eye?"

"Oh, *that* guy?" I forced a laugh. "Some rando looking for a little company. I never even caught his name."

He lifted his brows, amusement glinting in his eyes. "You didn't?"

"Not everyone is worth learning something about, your... your Highness? Grace? I'm sorry. I don't know what to call you."

"Keradoc will do just fine. Midnight is not a monarchy, Haley."

My name was like melted chocolate on his lips, the smoothness in his voice making me swoon. He spun me out again, then drew me back, fingers tracing slow, almost imperceptible circles on my bare back.

There was something almost... familiar about him, though I was sure we'd never met. I'd never even laid eyes on the man until he gave that speech.

Now, as one song bled into the next and Keradoc continued to waltz and twirl me across the ballroom, I felt myself falling under his spell.

Whether it was his natural charm or just another trick of the dark fae, I couldn't say.

But one thing was certain: I needed to pull my head out of the clouds, refocus on the mission, and get this thing over with before I lost my opportunity.

Listening to the cadence of the song, I waited until I knew he was going to dip me, then I slipped my hand along my thigh, making a tiny slice with the perfectly positioned dagger just before he brought me upright.

Blood welled in the cut, just enough to coat my bloodstone ring. Under the guise of wanting to hold him closer, I rested my head on his shoulder and muttered my spell, so softly not even a vampire would've been able to hear it.

> *Blood of the realm, blood of the night*
> *Follow the magick, follow the light*
> *Midnight fae, I summon thee*
> *With these words, so shall it be*

By the time I glanced into those violet eyes again, my hand was already sliding into his hair. With a slight flick of my wrist, the needle pierced his skin.

Keradoc didn't flinch, and I tried not to sigh in relief.

Then, bringing his lips to my ear again, he said, "Tell me something, Haley. How does someone as beautiful and... refined... as yourself end up in a place as treacherous as Midnight?"

I forced a laugh as his blood continued to fill the vial, warm and tingling against my wrist, the magick inside me heating in its presence.

"Oh, you know how it is. One minute you're doing a little unsanctioned magick, dabbling a bit too deeply in the dark arts, messing with the wrong people... And all of a sudden you're being hurtled through a portal to a prison realm full of creeps and monsters and—I mean, not that it's *all* creeps and monsters, of course. It's actually quite lovely once you get used to it."

He laughed, rich and buttery, and the soft snick against my wrist told me the contraption had done its job.

Adrenaline flooded my insides, making my heart gallop in my chest.

The song was winding down, but it seemed Keradoc wasn't ready to let me go just yet. I tried to gently extract myself from his hold, but he only tightened the embrace.

"One more song, if I may? I'm sorry, but it's not often I have the pleasure of dancing with such a lovely companion."

Seeing no way out of it, I smiled. "Last song, buddy. I've got my eye on some appetizers at the buffet table I don't want to miss out on."

"As you wish." He dipped me low, then drew me up again, his footsteps quickening to keep pace with the new song, faster and livelier than the others. With each new dip and turn, he danced us further away from the crowds, deeper into the shadows at the edges of the ballroom, my stomach full of butterflies as the room spun into a blur of colors and his scent washed over me and his strong, firm embrace held me close and then, like a bucket of ice water straight to the face, I realized...

I'd never told him my name.

He'd called me Haley, all smooth and melted-chocolatey, but I was sure of it—I'd never actually shared it.

So how the fuck does he know who I am?

"Keradoc, how did—"

Before the words were out, he spun me away once more, then released me.

Straight into the arms of one of his guards.

"Take her to the throne room and wait for me there," Keradoc ordered, then reached out to touch my face, a cold finger trailing down my cheek. "Thank you for the dance and the enlightening conversation, Haley. We'll pick up where we left off very soon."

Wait... was that silver flickering in his eyes?

It was my last conscious thought before the guard blew a handful of sparkly gold dust into my face and threw a bag over my head, and it was lights out, Haley Barnes.

came back to consciousness slowly, my head heavy, my vision blurry. The ringing in my ears made me so dizzy I wanted to puke.

Where the fuck was I? How long had I been here? Did Gem or the guys even know I'd been taken?

Sucking in a deep breath, I tried to get a feel for my surroundings.

I was on my knees, wrists and ankles bound with rope, hands tied behind my back. Someone had stripped off my weapons.

The vial was gone too.

Fuck.

Fear surged in my chest, but I tamped it down. I couldn't afford to freak out. Not yet.

I took another deep breath. Did a quick scan of my body. Other than a spinning head and a little chaffing from the rope, it didn't feel like they'd roughed me up too badly. I wasn't bleeding. Still had my clothes on, aside from the underwear I hadn't bothered with. I could still feel the buzz of magick in my veins. And…

Yes. The ring. They'd ignored the bloodstone ring.

Another bolt shot through my chest. Not fear this time, but adrenaline. My vision started to clear.

Dais. I was on my knees in front of a black dais in a massive throne room, all black—the walls, the polished marble floor, the velvet drapes hanging over the windows. Magick torches lined the walls, and at the top of the platform, a shadowed figure sat on an imposing throne made of skulls, bones, and polished obsidian.

Keradoc.

Fancy yourself a king now, do you?

Violet eyes blazed through the darkness, glaring down at me.

"Enter," he called out gruffly, and a heavy door clanged open a few dozen feet behind me, chains rattling.

Footsteps echoed across the floor, along with the clink of swords slapping against armor and the sound of something being dragged.

I swallowed hard. Refused to look. Because if Keradoc's guards had taken any of my men…

The stench of wet fur and blood plowed into me. Seconds later, two beasts were deposited unceremoniously at my side.

Certain they weren't mine, I darted a quick glance.

Shifters, though it was hard to tell what type. Wolves, most likely. The poor beasts were caught mid-shift, with the heads and torsos of men, the arms and legs of... something else. Both were emaciated, with bruised faces and ribs poking through open wounds on their skin.

Tears glazed my eyes. Poor fucking creatures. I didn't care what they'd done to end up in Midnight. They didn't deserve what'd happened to them. Didn't deserve whatever punishment Keradoc was about to dish out now.

I twisted my wrists, trying not to draw too much attention. If I could just get the rope to cut deep enough to spill some of my blood, I might be able to conjure a spell...

"Anything to say for yourselves, filth?" Keradoc asked, finally tearing his gaze away from me to look at the other prisoners. The gruffness had faded, replaced with the smooth, hypnotic tone he'd used on me in the ballroom. Its liquid warmth washed over me in a soothing wave.

The logical part of me insisted it was fae magick. That he was trying to entrance me.

It didn't feel like fae trickery, though. No more than it had in the ballroom.

Yes, and look how well that *worked out for you, dumbass.*

Next to me, one of the shifters spit on the dais. The other said nothing.

Keradoc rose from the throne, taking his sweet time, his steps silent and graceful as he descended the platform. One of the guards stepped forward and handed him a gleaming sword that looked as if it'd just been forged.

Either that, or it'd never seen battle.

Keradoc approached the shifter farthest from me, who lifted his chin defiantly. Touching the tip of the sword to the prisoner's throat, Keradoc said, "You have been charged with treason, sedition, and conspiracy against the realm. How do you plead?"

The shifter lifted his chin higher. Opened his mouth to speak.

But Keradoc had already raised the blade.

It happened so fast, I didn't even have time to duck.

I heard the zing of the metal cutting through the air, felt the bite of a sharp point grazing my neck.

A lock of my hair fell soundlessly to the floor, and beside me, two heads dropped. Their bodies slumped forward, blood spilling like wine tipped from a glass.

It pooled beside me, inching closer, finally soaking through my dress.

The acrid tang of it tickled the back of my throat. Magick rushed up my spine, but that was just an instinctive response to the presence of so much blood. I couldn't actually cast a spell unless I used my *own* blood.

"Is there a problem, witch?" Keradoc asked. "Seems you've got something to say."

"You didn't even wait for their plea," I blurted out. "You

just beheaded two shifters—residents of your own realm —and you didn't even hear their plea."

"Treason carries the punishment of death," he said, his voice eerily calm. "They're lucky I made it a quick one."

"Oh? Was that for my benefit? Trying to frighten the fragile, helpless witch into confessing her secrets by showing her what a big, scary fairy you are?"

Behind me, one of the guards cleared his throat, but said nothing.

"I never pegged you as fragile or helpless, little thief," Keradoc said. "Only presumptuous." He walked around me in a slow circle, examining me as if I were a prized steer at an auction, then finally stopped to stand behind me. I could feel him looming, the air heavy with his cloying scent, but I wouldn't give him the satisfaction of tipping my head up to look at him.

"How the fuck do you even know those shifters were guilty?" I snapped, past the point of caring whether I pissed him off. He was either going to behead me or keep screwing with me, and if he chose the former? Fine. I'd make *damn* sure I was still cursing him out when my head rolled. "Who appointed *you* judge, jury, and executioner? Last I heard, you were just a self-appointed, washed-up warlord moving pieces around a chessboard with one hand and jerking off with the other. And who made that throne, anyway? Are those even real bones? Because I'm pretty sure I saw a DIY kit just like it on Amazon."

A shadow shifted over me, the scent of roses receding.

A chill crept across my shoulders, making me shiver.

And once again, Keradoc of Midnight swung his sword.

I gasped, but the pain never came.

The ropes fell away from my wrists and ankles. I was pretty sure he'd slashed a few stitches on my dress too. But...

Holy *fuck*. Had I not been so busy trying not to pee myself, I might've taken a moment to be impressed with his swordsmanship.

Turning back to his guards, Keradoc said, "Leave us."

They did as he asked. When the door finally slammed shut, he sighed and tossed the sword to the floor, like he couldn't even stand to hold it. The metallic clang echoed across the cavernous room, making my teeth clench.

"On your feet, witch."

I stood up slowly and rubbed my wrists, trying to figure out my next move. Try to go for the sword? It was mere feet away from me, but... No. He'd almost certainly beat me to it. Hell, he'd probably set the whole thing up as a test, just to see how far I'd push him.

I got the distinct feeling the guy was bored and looking for a challenge.

Why keep me alive otherwise?

So the sword was a no-go. I had no weapons, no jewelry but the ring, and my fingernails weren't long or sharp enough to cut my skin and draw blood. If I acted quickly, though, a hard bite to the fleshy part of my hand could do the trick...

I feigned a cough, lifting my hand to my mouth, and—

Keradoc grabbed my wrists and hauled me against his chest—another dance, but this one was much rougher than the last. Much more intense.

And Keradoc, the fucking creep, was hard as hell.

An answering pulse of desire throbbed in my core.

That *had* to be a fae trick. Keradoc was a fucking murderous asshole. A sociopath. We were standing in a pool of shifter blood, for fuck's sake, all because he'd felt like playing with his big sword.

"Tell me something, witch," he said. His cold-roses scent washed over me again, mixing with that forbidden earthiness that'd called to me earlier, all of it conspiring with his smooth voice and warm body to shatter my resolve.

None of this made sense. Why the fuck did he sound— did he *feel*—so familiar?

"If treason is punishable by death," he murmured, his gaze sweeping my face, "what is the appropriate sentence for a thief who attempts to steal the blood of the... what was it now? Ah, yes. The self-appointed, washed-up warlord of Midnight?"

He released me and retrieved a vial from his pocket, holding it before my eyes. *My* vial. His blood swirled inside, flickering with magick.

He dropped it. Stomped on it.

Fuck. Me.

I swallowed the tightness in my throat, refusing to shed so much as a single tear. This was far from over. There *had* to be another way. As long as I was still breathing, there was another way, and I'd fucking find it.

"How about a duel?" I asked, biding my time. "Fight to the death. Witch versus warlord, no holds barred."

His eyes flashed with mischief. "Do you honestly think you'd stand a chance?"

"Give me a sword and let's find out."

He bent down and scooped up the discarded sword, turning it over in his hands as if he were actually considering it. Torchlight flickered along the blood-stained blade. "As entertaining as a deathmatch sounds... No, little thief. I'm not sure that would be prudent. You seem quite... determined."

"Don't tell me the big, scary fairy is afraid of a little witch."

"Something tells me I *should* be." He lowered the sword to his side, and a smile finally cracked the stone-hard face. Not the smooth, charming grin of a fae spell-weaver entrancing his prey, but the smile of a real man. A fae who was as much human on the inside as I was.

And in that moment, his entire face changed.

Literally.

The sharp angles smoothed out just a bit, the nose

widening. And those violet eyes, so cold and deadly, turned... silver.

I sucked in a sharp breath.

It was all just a fae glamour, and in that brief instant, I saw right through it to the real man beneath.

Elian.

A wave of relief swept me up and propelled me right back into him like a boat tossed against the rocks. I threw my arms around his neck, tears hot on my cheeks.

"I was so worried about you," I breathed, burying my face in the crook of his neck. "You have no idea."

Then I pulled back, looked once more into those familiar silver eyes, and slapped him across the face.

"*That* was for scaring the hell out of me," I snapped, then whacked him again. "And for making me worry about you for three fucking days." I lifted my hand once more, this time making a fist. "And *this*—"

He grabbed my wrist, those silver eyes boring straight into my soul. They were clear tonight, no trace of Devil's Dream. No trace of anything but white-hot fury.

His vise grip tightened, crushing the bones of my wrist.

"I thought you were dead, dickhead!" I shouted, the agony in my wrist intensifying. "And all night you're just... what? Fucking with me? Where's Keradoc? Is this even his castle? Or was this all just another one of your bullshit schemes?"

His brow furrowed, a look of genuine confusion

settling into his features. His eyes flickered between silver and violet.

I had a million more questions, and they all rushed through my mind at once. *Where the hell have you been? Why didn't you get in touch with us? What kind of glamour is this? Why did you kill those shifters? Why did you act like you didn't recognize me when we danced?*

But none of that mattered. Something else was welling up inside me too, chasing away all the questions—the new as well as the old.

I no longer cared where he'd been.

No longer cared why he'd left me all those years ago.

No longer cared why he'd gotten exiled to this terrible realm in the first place.

Suddenly, I just wanted to kiss him. I *needed* to kiss him.

"I hate you," I whispered.

Then crashed into his mouth.

He resisted for a second, then dropped the pretense, releasing my wrist and kissing me back.

The sword clattered to the ground, and he lifted me up, claiming me with his brutal mouth as my legs wrapped tight around his hips. Without breaking for air, he turned and lowered me to the dais, kneeling between my thighs, pushing me down against the steps as he devoured me, his hands winding into my hair, his breath hot, tongue sweeping into my mouth, cock grinding against my center, every touch sending spasms of pleasure straight to my core.

And in that moment, here's what I knew:

The kiss was epic. The kind they wrote songs about. The kind that would, if things progressed, have *me* singing.

It turned me inside out and left me reeling.

It made the stars scatter behind my eyes.

It filled me with a fire unmatched by any I'd imagined from such an explosive reunion with the man I'd loved for most of my life.

But here's what else I knew:

The man kissing me senseless right now? It *wasn't* Elian.

Not even a glamoured version of Elian.

Didn't matter that we hadn't kissed in years. Didn't matter that so much had changed between us, we were practically strangers.

Some things you just knew. You just fucking *knew*.

I shoved hard against his chest, and the imposter pulled back, just as breathless as I was.

Hands still in my hair, rock-hard cock straining against his silken finery, he stared down at me with heavy-lidded eyes, violet once again. "It seems our realms have rather different interpretations of dueling. Admittedly, I like your version better."

"You... You're not..." I sucked in a sharp breath and

pressed my fingers to my tingling lips, mind reeling. "Who the *hell* are you?"

A slow, devouring grin slid across his mouth, his face flickering back to the version I'd seen earlier. Menace flashed in his eyes.

"Kiss me like that again, Daughter of Darkwinter," he whispered, "and I'll be whoever you need me to be."

Daughter of Darkwinter?

No. There was no way he knew about that. Not even Elian knew about that. Only my sisters, who I hadn't spoken with since I left Blackmoon Bay and had no idea I was even here, and...

Oh, fuck.

The goddess Melantha.

"The question remains," Keradoc said, "Are *you* going to be what *I* need?"

At that, he smiled and lowered his mouth to mine once more, then pursed his lips and blew out a sweet, gentle breath, so soft it tickled my lips. Golden smoke swirled up before my eyes, and all at once, the room spun.

For the second time in an hour, my world turned black.

"Where the fuck have you *been*?" Jax fisted my lapels and hauled me close, his fury barely contained. "Tell me you've got Haley. Tell me you didn't fucking blow this and risk her fucking life, you piece of shit, or I swear I will throw you over the wall and feed your useless ass to the fucking ghouls."

Fuck.

Adrenaline spiked. I tried to swallow down my fear, school my features, but it was no use. Jax could sense it a mile away.

No, it wasn't his bullshit threats that had me tied up in knots.

It was fucking Haley.

Despite Jax's accusations, I'd been here the whole fucking time. Gem and I had been keeping watch all night, taking turns checking on Haley while we cased out the best opportunity for me to get my shot at Keradoc. I knew Haley had gotten her weapons. Knew she'd fucked Jax in that damn closet, too.

And I knew my girl had sealed the deal, accomplishing what she'd set out to do—get that Midnight bastard's blood.

But now, Jax and I were alone in a little-used parlor adjacent to the ballroom, and Haley was nowhere to be found.

"Last I saw her," I said, "she was dancing with Keradoc. She already got the blood, Jax. I saw it happen—figured she'd make her way back to you so you could take her home."

"I can't fucking find her!" he roared. "I saw her with him, too. Twirling around the ballroom like a fucking ballerina. The next thing I knew, she was gone."

Gone?

No. It wasn't happening. It wasn't *fucking* happening.

"Get Hudson," I ordered. "If someone grabbed her, they can't have gotten far. We need to do a full sweep outside. Make sure no one—"

"Saint!" Gem burst into the room in a blur of red dress and purple hair, her cheeks streaked with mascara-stained tears. "Thank the devil. I've been looking everywhere for you guys. They've taken Haley!"

"Where?" Jax asked. "Who? Gem, what the *fuck* did you see?"

Fresh tears glazed her eyes. "This is all my fault. I should've left her more weapons. I should've stayed by her side. But they were dancing right out in the open! I never thought he'd—"

"Gem." I put my hands on her shoulders, trying to calm her the fuck down. "Breathe. You need to fucking breathe and tell us exactly what you saw."

"I don't know... I mean, one minute she was dancing with Keradoc, and then he just... handed her off. I almost didn't see it, it happened so fast. But then I caught a flash of their uniforms."

"Whose uniforms?" Jax asked.

"His guards. They were waiting in the wings, Saint. Fucking guards, like he'd positioned them right there the whole time. So either he knew what Haley was planning, or he wanted her for... for something else. Either way, they nabbed her."

"Fuck." It took everything I had not to smash my fist through the fucking wall, but that wouldn't help anyone, least of all Haley. "Any ideas where they would've taken her? Holding cell? Private chambers?"

"Throne room," Gem said. "That's where he... I mean, if she's... if she's still alive, that's where she'll be."

"She's still alive," I insisted, refusing to allow for the possibility of anything else.

"Keradoc took her just so he could force her to bend

the knee and kiss the ring?" Jax let out a bitter laugh. "I don't think so. What the hell is going on, Gem?"

"No, he..." Gem swallowed hard. When she spoke again, her voice was a brittle whisper. "Some prisoners he kills right away. But others, he... He toys with them first. Torments them. And then, once he's bored of his sick little games..." She closed her eyes and shook her head, tears falling.

"What happens then?" I whispered, my heart lodged so far into my throat, I nearly choked on it.

She opened her eyes, nothing but two pits of hopelessness. "He chops off their heads and adds the skulls to his throne."

I'd never fallen into a meat grinder before, or been set on fire, or had my skin flayed off and my ass dropped into a salt bath.

But in that moment? I was pretty sure any of those options would've felt better than the agony ripping through me.

"If we've got any chance of saving her," Gem said, rubbing the tears from her eyes and straightening her spine, "we need to move. Now."

"We can't just go storming in there," I said. "The castle is crawling with soldiers. We won't get anywhere *near* that room. If they even *suspect* we're on to them—"

"There's a back way," she said. "But if we don't go now... Look, it's not just her life at stake. If Haley breaks and tells them she wasn't working alone, they'll lock this place down faster than the ghouls in the moat can eat a corpse."

Jax nodded. Straightened his jacket. Cracked his neck. When he met my gaze again, his blue eye blazed, his whole body trembling with a rage I hadn't seen since I carved out his other eye.

He looked like a fucking omen of death.

"Lead the way," he ground out.

We followed Gem back down to the main level, fighting our way through the throng of drunk and filthy masses and out the main entrance. More revelers spilled out onto the grounds, which slowed us down, but made it easier not to draw attention. After what felt like a fucking lifetime, she finally got us to a servants' entrance at the rear of the castle, unguarded but for a cook on a smoke break.

He pointed at us as we approached, then exploded in a hearty laugh.

Devil's Dream colored his tongue and clouded his eyes, the poor fucking idiot.

Jax grabbed his head and grinned. "Goodnight, asshole."

He snapped the guy's neck and dragged him inside, stashing the corpse in a meat locker, and on we went, following Gem through a maze of servant passages until we finally ended up one level above the ballroom. Music and revelry hummed below our feet.

"It's here," she finally said, stopping at a set of wooden double doors, plain and unguarded. "It leads into a small sanctuary behind the dais. We open these doors, we'll have maybe ten seconds before anyone spots us. I'll get Haley. You two take down the soldiers and Keradoc."

"Let's fucking do it," Jax said, and I nodded, fangs descending, adrenaline coursing through my blood. My mouth was already watering for a taste of Midnight blood.

Keradoc's, if I got lucky and he didn't.

Gem drew her short sword and pushed open the doors.

We followed her in, and in the span of a single breath, a few things became readily fucking apparent.

This wasn't some sanctuary behind the dais. Just an ordinary fucking room currently occupied by a firing squad of a dozen Midnight guards with crossbows, all pointed at me and Jax.

Gem had fucking betrayed us.

Half the crossbows were loaded with hawthorn stakes for me, the other with good old-fashioned bolts for Jax.

I didn't need a closeup to know they'd be carved with devil's trap sigils—a demon's worst nightmare. As soon as one of those fuckers nailed him, he'd drop, completely immobilized.

Gem lowered her sword and stepped behind us, pushing us forward. "On your knees, tough guys."

Outnumbered and outgunned, we did as she asked. My heart fucking liquified.

"I trusted you," I breathed. "I thought you were one of us."

"I'm sorry," she said coldly. Flat. Nothing like the Gem I knew. The Gem I thought I'd always known. "But it's like I always say, *Elian*... Nothing in Midnight is ever what it should be."

She crossed over to join the firing squad. Then, her gaze locked firmly on mine, she stepped behind them and said, "Fire at will."

Seriously? This is your A-game, Keradoc? Fairy-dust roofies and some light bondage?" I struggled against the ropes binding me to his throne, but it was no use. Unlike the last rope, this stuff had been spelled.

I had no idea how long I'd been unconscious this time, but judging from the numb ass, it'd been a while.

Where were Jax and Hudson? Gem? Elian? Did they still not realize I was missing?

Or had they been captured, too?

Had Elian even shown up tonight?

"Let me go," I gritted out, "and I promise I won't throw your corpse to the ghouls after I kill you."

Standing in front of his precious skull throne, Keradoc glared down at me, unimpressed. "I don't know the guise under which you were sent here, Daughter of Darkwinter, but your purpose is neither to kill me nor to steal my blood. You're here to help me win this war."

"Don't call me that. I'm not Darkwinter."

He set his hands on the arms of the throne and leaned in close, his scent nearly suffocating me. "I can *smell* it on your blood, witch. The darkness in you."

I fought back a shiver. "How can you smell *anything* with all that cheap cologne you're drowning in?"

"Taunt me all you wish. Melantha assured me your ancestry can be traced and verified."

Melantha.

So it was true, then. The bitch betrayed me.

Fury boiled up inside.

But... Why had she gone to all the trouble of sending me on this doomed blood-heist mission if her intent was to turn me over to Keradoc? It made no sense.

Still, my gut told me he wasn't lying. Not about this.

"Melantha?" I sneered. "The same one who ordered me to steal your blood for a spell to free her son? Yes, she's certainly a reliable narrator. Good call trusting her."

"Her son?" He let out a dark chuckle. "It seems Melantha was hedging her bets. I regret to inform you she has no children—only tricks."

"Says the master illusionist himself. Nice glamour, by the way. Might want to touch it up a bit—it's starting to show your age. And those eyes... Are they violet? Silver? Who can tell?"

He hesitated, just for a moment. Just long enough to let me know my arrow had hit the mark.

So it was a glamour. And he didn't realize it was faltering.

"Why did she want your blood?" I asked, taking advantage of his momentary distraction. I needed to get him talking. Ranting. Ranting villains always increased your chances of mounting a successful escape.

"She's trying to blackmail me into reversing her permanent banishment from Midnight. With my blood in her possession, she could've crafted all sorts of curses to harm or manipulate me." He sighed, as if the topic bored him. "You're a blood witch, Haley. You know how this works."

"But it sounds like you guys already made a deal, no? She gift-wraps me in a nice little bow and delivers me to Midnight, and you let her back in. Right?"

"That was the agreement, but I never had any intentions of honoring it. I suppose that's why she made a backup plan."

"She wanted a win-win," I said, the pieces finally clicking into place.

Melantha must've figured it would go one of two ways —either I'd get the blood and make it back to the Temple, granting her the powers she needed to blackmail him, or I'd fail and Keradoc would get to keep his so-called present, granting her that shiny new passport to Midnight as a thanks.

"Well, fuck her," I said. "She's officially on my shit-list.

Hey! Here's a thought." I flashed my most award-winning smile. "Maybe we should team up and kick her ass? The enemy's enemy is my friend?"

"Oh, but we *are* teaming up." A cruel smirk twisted his otherwise handsome face, and a chill skittered down my spine. "To make a weapon."

His earlier words echoed, the speech he'd given the crowd. Something about... a weapon the enemy could never defeat?

And if he needed Darkwinter blood to make it...

"It's me," I whispered, more to myself than to him. "I'm the weapon."

"Did you not wonder why it was so easy for you to traverse this treacherous realm?" Keradoc asked. "To breach my wall without the guards raising the alarm? To slip into my castle with a forged invitation?"

His words crashed over me in a dark wave. I'd thought we'd just gotten lucky with our escape from the raven gryphons and the relatively unimpeded trek to the wall. With the starshowers that'd distracted the guards. With securing Gem's help.

But no—luck had nothing to do with it. Keradoc had been expecting me all along, and he'd rolled out Midnight's version of the red carpet, luring me right into his trap.

He must've seen the realization dawning on my face, because when he spoke again, his tone dripped with smug satisfaction. "You will use your blood magick to summon your Darkwinter ancestors. Our necromancers will take care of the rest."

I closed my eyes, trying to recall everything I knew about my Darkwinter heritage. I'd only just found out about it recently—it all came out during the attacks on Blackmoon Bay, and since then, I'd been doing my best to ignore it. We fought against Darkwinter in the Bay too, just like Keradoc was doing in Midnight. They were evil assholes. I didn't want to believe I'd come from them— who would?

But now, I could no longer deny the truth.

My sisters and I were descendants of one of the very first witches and… wait for it… her Darkwinter lovers.

Yes, lovers. Plural. Apparently, it runs in the family.

My sister Gray had said something about a spell with the ancestors. If I remembered it right, there was a way you could summon them and resurrect them into new vessels. *Living* vessels.

Is that what Keradoc intended?

To resurrect Darkwinter ancestors into the bodies of Midnight soldiers?

Holy shit. The existing Darkwinter soldiers—Keradoc's invaders—would have no choice but to surrender. Not unless they wanted to dishonor their entire bloodline and slaughter their own family members.

Sort of.

I opened my eyes again, my head spinning. This was insane. All of it. *They* were insane. Melantha, Keradoc, the Darkwinter fae... Why didn't they just fuck off to their own private island and kill each other there? Leave everyone else out of it?

"You *will* help me, Haley," Keradoc said.

I lifted my chin, just like the wolf shifters had done earlier. "And if I refuse? You can take my blood, but you can't force me to do a summoning spell. The magick won't work if my heart isn't in it."

He retrieved a dagger from inside his jacket—my dagger. Fresh blood had only just begun to dry on the blade.

I shuddered to think whose it might be.

Keradoc grinned, then dragged his tongue along the blade, his eyes wicked and cold.

How could I *ever* have mistaken Keradoc for Elian?

Yet... he wasn't the real Keradoc either, was he? Just someone wearing the *illusion* of Keradoc.

How many layers deep did the glamour magick go?

And who the hell *was* the guy behind all the masks?

"If you refuse to aid me in defeating my enemies," he said, "your friends will suffer the same fate as the wolf shifters you so ardently defended earlier."

Alarm shot through my chest.

"What friends?" I forced a laugh. "If I had friends, don't you think they would've rescued me by now? I came alone at the behest of Melantha. If you don't like how this little blind date of ours is turning out, take it up with *that* bitch."

"Tsk tsk," he said. "Lying, on top of all the crimes you've already committed? Unwise."

Before I could say anything else, he snapped his fingers, and the door at the rear of the room creaked open.

Four guards entered, once again dragging prisoners.

Only this time, they weren't treasonous wolf shifters.

They were my men.

My monsters.

My fucking heart.

Hudson wasn't with them—the only glimmer of hope.

But Jax and Elian were. It was the first I'd seen my vampire-fae in days.

The guards dropped them on their knees at the bottom of the dais, barely conscious, both bleeding from multiple wounds—hawthorn stakes for Elian, metal bolts for Jax, likely cursed to trap demons. It was the only thing that would've rendered him so weak.

They both looked up at me, agony twisting their faces when they saw me tied to the throne.

I couldn't help the pained gasp that escaped, the tears that leaked from my eyes.

I could hardly breathe.

Blood soaked their shirts. Their faces had been severely beaten, eyes swollen and blackened, teeth missing. Jax's eye patch was gone, revealing a crater of old scar tissue and fresh gashes.

Thanks to the hawthorn poisoning his system, Elian wouldn't be able to heal. I couldn't even imagine his suffering.

And yet, when he finally turned away from me to look at our captor, it seemed as if he was suddenly gazing upon the face of a god.

Elian's breath caught, and for a moment, he stopped breathing altogether. Tears streamed down his face, but the pain in his eyes was gone, replaced with relief. With joy.

I glanced at Keradoc.

The glamour was fading again, and now he looked more like Elian than he ever had earlier. Same silver eyes. Same face.

Still on his knees in a rapidly spreading pool of his own blood, the real Elian smiled, his lips curving into that sexy, crooked grin I loved so much.

And when he finally spoke through that broken, bloodied smile, he whispered a name I'd only ever heard him say in the throes of his most fearsome nightmares, thrashing so hard he'd torn off the sheets, bolting upright in a cold sweat and clinging to me in the darkness as if the devil himself was on his way to personally drag him to hell.

"*Evander?*"

It's not over yet! This story continues in book 2, Blood and Malice!

A gut-wrenching betrayal leads to a mysterious and unexpected reunion, but with enemies closing in fast, will Haley and her monsters survive the vicious warlord's cruel games? And what about the battles of their own hearts?

Haley, Hudson, Jax, and Elian are waiting for you in **Blood and Malice, book two of The Witch's Monsters series!**

Are you a member of our private Facebook group, <u>Sarah Piper's Sassy Witches</u>? Pop in for sneak peeks, cover reveals, exclusive giveaways, book chats, group therapy to deal with these killer cliffhangers, and plenty of complete randomness from your fellow fans! We'd love to see you there.

XOXO
Sarah

MORE BOOKS FROM SARAH PIPER!

THE WITCH'S REBELS is a supernatural reverse harem series featuring five smoldering-hot guys and the kickass witch they'd kill to protect. If you're wondering about Haley's sisters, the spooky Silversbane prophecy, and the Battle for Blackmoon Bay, this steamy series where it all begins!

TAROT ACADEMY is a paranormal, university-aged reverse harem academy romance starring four seriously hot mages and one badass witch. Dark prophecies, unique mythology, steamy romance, and plenty of supernatural thrills make this series a must-read!

ABOUT SARAH PIPER

Sarah Piper is a witchy, Tarot-card-slinging paranormal romance and urban fantasy author. Through her signature brew of dark magic, heart-pounding suspense, and steamy romance, Sarah promises a sexy, supernatural escape into a world where the magic is real, the monsters are sinfully hot, and the witches always get their magically-ever-afters.

Readers have dubbed her work "super sexy," "imaginative and original," "off-the-walls good," and "delightfully wicked in the best ways," a quote Sarah hopes will appear on her tombstone.

Originally from New York, Sarah now makes her home in northern Colorado with her husband (though that changes frequently) (the location, not the husband), where she spends her days sleeping like a vampire and her nights writing books, casting spells, gazing at the moon, playing with her ever-expanding collection of Tarot cards, binge-watching Supernatural (Team Dean!), and obsessing over the best way to brew a cup of tea.

You can find her online at SarahPiperBooks.com, on TikTok at @sarahpiperbooks, and in her Facebook readers group at Sarah Piper's Sassy Witches! If you're sassy, or if you need a little *more* sass in your life, or if you need more Dean Winchester gifs in your life (who doesn't?), come hang out!